THE
MACHINE

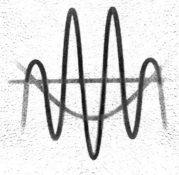

THE MACHINE

ARTHUR DUNOON

REDEMPTION
PRESS

Published by Redemption Press, PO Box 427, Enumclaw, WA 98022.

Toll-Free (844) 2REDEEM (273-3336)

Redemption Press is honored to present this title in partnership with the author. The views expressed or implied in this work are those of the author. Redemption Press provides our imprint seal representing design excellence, creative content, and high-quality production.

ISBN: 978-1-68314-863-0 (Paperback)
978-1-68314-864-7 (ePub)
978-1-68314-865-4 (Mobi)

Library of Congress Catalog Card Number: 2020900390

1

The idyllic life in the idyllic town in an idyllic world, and Joshua hated it. He'd never heard anyone argue, and people seemed to know everyone else's thoughts about everything. Strangers talked to each other like long-lost friends. Family treated every member like brothers and sisters—except for those who hadn't been through the Machine.

When his parents came home from Town Hall and talked about the arguments so-and-so had, Joshua listened for the salacious details about savage insults and fiery testimony. Instead, he heard about well-reasoned discussions and polite civil discourse. There was no excitement, no violence, no bizarre acts of self-destruction to awe a crowd. Compared to the history he was taught, life seemed dull with no hope for anything different.

Even their diet was predictable and measured—no excess, waste, or variety to tantalize the senses and unmask the mysteries of the greater empire. Joshua often wondered how different things might be on one of the other planets or moons, whether they ate exotic foods and had wild parties and violence like the stories he'd read about the time before the Machine. He imagined that his town must be the dullest in the universe. Did other young men feel this unfulfilled—alive in a world of hollow husks? He knew there must be somewhere, maybe just over the horizon, where the adventure his soul yearned for could be found, where he would feel alive and be allowed to live.

His cousin had proven this was not the case. He was as wild as Joshua, even more so. Yet his town was just as boring, just as oppressively kind. His existence meant there were people left in the world who found this perfect life offensive to their idea of truly living. He was the one who introduced Joshua to the idea of wild meat and hunting. His cousin had snuck into his father's library and read about feral people who caught and ate other animals. His cousin had become intrigued by this idea. When he arrived in Joshua's town to spend his final few months in preparation for the Machine, he drew Joshua into the fantasy with him.

They captured a squirrel in the yard by luring it with nuts from Joshua's father's grove. When it trustingly came to his hand, Joshua grabbed it by the neck and hit it against a decorative stone in his mother's garden. They snuck away into the forest with their prey and lit a tiny fire. His cousin cooked it on a stick shoved through its mouth and out through its anus. He didn't know how to clean it, but old stories about the violence of their past were enough to educate him in its basic preparation. When it came time to eat it, the squirrel's hair was singed, and the guts had been shoved out by the stick. After taking the first bite into its back, Joshua had no idea why anyone ever considered this wild meat worth craving.

The experience with the squirrel did not go unnoticed. Their small fire caught some leaves and scorched the forest floor. Smoke could be seen from Joshua's house, and a general alarm called every able-bodied person to put it out. When townspeople arrived on the scene, there was no question what or who had started the blaze. Joshua and his cousin didn't get in trouble; people merely murmured and shook their heads.

He heard one of his neighbors, a man his father helped with building a new barn last spring, say, "We'll have to keep an eye on him till he's old enough to go through the Machine. The other one will have a hard time in a couple months."

At the time, Joshua didn't know what the man meant; he was just glad he didn't get punished. His mother and father no longer allowed him to play alone with his cousin though.

"He isn't good for you," they said.

Joshua's cousin went through the Machine soon after the squirrel incident. His parents came into town the week before, along with his older sister and grandparents. They all went to the Machine together and all played their role. Just before sunset the family finally emerged, weary and exhausted. They hailed a carriage and rode back to their hometown together. His cousin stopped by to thank Joshua's parents for their hospitality. He apologized for a broken chair and all the trouble with the fire, then he walked back to his hometown ten miles away.

It was raining that evening, and Joshua could not figure out why his cousin insisted on bearing that misery instead of waiting for a carriage. Joshua's father just looked down and said, "He had a harder time than most, but he'll be all right."

Shortly after that, Joshua was enrolled in school full time to learn the necessary skills and knowledge before his turn in the Machine.

—⁂—

The years passed and the world never seemed to change. The routines remained and life became even more agonizingly dull. The older Joshua got the greater his longing for adventure grew. The more he learned in school, the more he learned of the alternatives to the life he lived. The restlessness grew in him, and were it not for the oppressive watchfulness of the community around him, he might have left long before to find the life-affirming misery and suffering he dreamed about.

His best friend, Isaac, a boy who could have been mistaken for Joshua's twin, lived up the road. Kim, the neighbor girl, lived just a little farther. They all wore the same muted colors of country life, bleached by the daylight and worn by the dirt that proved their days were well spent.

The three were all in the same age group and had grown up together. Their first days walking to school were the beginning of their friendship. They were the only people alive in their world, the only ones who felt the fears and frailties of youth, and the only people they could count on to understand. They were inseparable.

Isaac spoke of his own brother's transformation as they walked to school at the start of their final year as the living. "It was like he had seen the universe die. There was no life or joy left in him after that. He stayed at home for the next few weeks to earn some money packing carts for the neighbors. Then he gathered up his possessions and arranged for transportation to the spaceport so he could get some land of his own on the frontier. There was no fear or anxiety in him while he packed and planned. He put things in order as if he'd done it a million times. He told my parents he would write and let them know where he was. Just before he turned to leave, he looked at me with those emotionless eyes and said, 'I'll be seeing you soon. Study hard.' *Study hard?* For *what?* So I can become a zombie like him? I don't know what this Machine does, but it seems horrible. I'm thinking that life as a wild one would be better."

Kim chimed in. "My father's youngest sister was the same way. She came to stay with us and spent the first couple weeks after the Machine helping plant crops before she went to work at the spaceport. She didn't even acknowledge me when she left. Before the Machine, she played dolls with me and told me the old stories about dancing. I can't imagine her dancing anymore. She has no heart to feel the music. It was so sad."

All the kids in the class had similar stories of the Machine. The class was a mix of all ages, the youngest hearing the lectures for the first time while the oldest absorbed the familiar lessons as much as they could for their impending exams and trial with the Machine. Joshua wondered who would be the first of them to go through and whether they, too, would lose their souls in the process, along with their joy, emotions, and hope for the future. The transformation was so great that most returned unrecognizable. They said very little other than to warn their friends and siblings, "Learn your lessons well or it will be much harder to bear." After the Machine, they went into town to find gainful employment and started talking to older people as if they bore the wisdom of a life fully lived and the sorrows fully felt and were now equals. While their cherubic faces and soft bodies reflected the sixteen years they had lived, their minds seemed suddenly ancient.

The class bell rang. The teacher stood at the head of the class waiting silently for the gossip to break up and the students' attention to turn to her. She was balding, but not as much as her parents. According to what Joshua had learned so far, she was not quite fully adapted yet, though ten years had gone by since she had emerged from the Machine. Though the psychological transformation was instant, the physiological process was slow and continued for the rest of a person's life. She encouraged the gossip, considering it healthy to be skeptical and fearful of the Machine to keep the students attentive. Though she knew the truth, her place was to teach these students the lessons they needed to succeed. It was better if they were worried about the Machine so they would learn their lessons more diligently. So she let the gossip continue.

When the class finally turned to their teacher, she began the class the same way as always: "Class, there is nothing more important than the lesson we will be learning today. The world we live in is a result of our ability to understand these principles. History is our tragic failure to practice this. These lessons are laws of the natural order, and when you go into the Machine, you will suffer or thrive by these lessons. This is your warning."

The hint of a smirk curled at the corner of her mouth, though undetectable by the pre-Machine students. The class was suitably attentive and alert, except Joshua, as usual.

"Joshua, what is the purpose of these lessons?" she asked pointedly.

He was looking out the window at the wind in the bushes and how they seemed to dance, reflecting first the charcoal-colored top and then the frosted-green underside. He spotted a bird hopping in the sheltered branches and imagined himself as that bird, free from this prison.

"Joshua," she stated loudly.

Startled, he sat up straight in his chair. He knew roughly what the question was. This was their regular routine. He took a guess. "The patterns of history reveal the principles of nature and our failure to understand them will make us doomed to repeat them."

His fellow students laughed. He cringed. He'd given the same answer the day before.

Isaac double over with forced laughter.

The teacher waited for the noise to die down, then told Joshua, "You learned yesterday's lesson well enough at least." She turned to Isaac. "What is the correct answer?"

Recovering from the bout of laughter, he answered, "To show the principles of nature so our time in the Machine is easier."

"Good," she said curtly. "Let's start with history and politics."

With that she began the lessons of bloodier times and what caused them. Joshua only half-listened as he dreamed of the way the world used to be and how exciting that must have been. The day passed in this way. The lessons of history segued into anthropology, then to psychology and sociology, then to statistics, then to calculus and physics, then to geology and geography, and finally back to the introductory topic to tie them all together. The lessons were the same. Though the people and their place in time differed, the lesson was always that events are largely predetermined, that everything is part of the natural process. History is a result of laws and cultures. Events are caused by mass or individual psychologies. Those events occur when statistical social triggers are identified. Those events are bound by the physical laws of nature. And the environment that hosts and shapes those cultures and events are created by those laws of nature. Those events transpire, those cultures grow, and those people become the heroes of legend simply by the accident of their situation. By the end of the lecture, every student knew how the universe had conspired to make every event happen, that all of history was predestined by circumstance, and that only a supreme being was capable of making anything deviate from its predetermined course.

Joshua rolled his eyes at this point. He was offended by the notion that his life was not special, that he was not in control, that the thoughts he harbored were merely a manifestation of his particular personality in his particular environment within the confines of his particular place in time and space. He was special, and he knew it.

Joshua was content with his mediocrity in school. They discussed nothing but inconsequential topics. He wanted nothing more than to just get out and be free from this life. But his one obligation was school, and with the looming threat of the Machine, he went.

The lessons that interested him were of the wars fought long ago, before the Machine. Vast armies marched to defeat the ideology of the other. The teacher never gave the reason for the wars or the details about who was victorious or what that victory meant, only that it happened.

She said in an even monotonous voice, without contempt or remorse, "War is meaningless but illustrative of nature."

Joshua perked up. "Who won?"

"No one did. Millions died but no minds were changed. Nations were extinguished but their ideologies still persisted. Resources were wasted, and everyone cheered for their team. That is all that is ever accomplished. But this is not the point. *Who* is not what's important. Two nations at war is no different than two species vying for dominance in an ecosystem."

"Well if it's the same and it's natural, why don't we fight wars like this anymore?" Joshua spread his hands with the question submissively, hoping he'd caught her in a logical error.

"The Machine has cured those inclinations." She put down the stylus she used to write lecture notes on the screen. "It forces you to endure all the consequences of shortsighted beliefs. There is nothing I can teach you that you won't know intimately in the Machine."

Isaac chimed in. "Well doesn't being right matter? Aren't there always two sides of an issue? Only one side is right. Doesn't that mean we should still see this sort of conflict in our society?"

"There is only one right way to live in harmony, but unlimited ways to live in chaos. Our society is built on the Machine. There is no person in our society who has not experienced it. All actions have consequences, all inaction has consequences, all consequences have consequences. And all people who have faced that reality understand implicitly that there is nothing that can be done to change a determined mind. But that is often the cancerous cell that metastasizes and poisons society. It is the weed that must be plucked before it stifles the productive garden. We don't live in a society where people decide to become that cancer. They can't. It takes too much energy and defiance of the universal truth."

Someone in the back asked, "What is that universal truth?"

Joshua and his friends were all poised on the edges of their seats. Finally they were hearing some insider knowledge about the Machine. Something valuable.

"There is nothing new under the sun. No one is so clever that they can surprise society. No one is so self-destructive that they can know this and defy that logic. Cancer is to be destroyed. There is no alternative. The Machine teaches you that."

As she finished that statement, the final bell rang, seeming to add punctuation to her sentence.

Joshua walked home with his friends. Kim and Isaac were acting like fools. It was obvious to everyone that they were sweet on each other. For whatever reason, Joshua didn't have any special feelings for anyone in his class. He was, in that regard, an outsider. But he saw the way they joked and smiled. How Isaac played harmless jokes on her and the way she chased him playfully, feigning anger, so she could have an excuse to touch him.

Isaac often purchased a ripe fruit or a bag of roasted nuts from one of the outgoing carts and shared with Kim, but he seldom asked anyone else if they wanted some.

Joshua was okay with this though. The dirt road to their homes was a long one, and though they all were friends because of proximity, those two were friends because of something deeper. A real bond. But how would that survive the Machine?

The road was shady and the sun still out. The green fields of the young grains danced in the breeze as Joshua and his friends approached his home.

"What do you guys think? Is the Machine a good thing or a bad thing?" Joshua asked for the thousandth time in as many walks on this same well-worn path.

"I think it's good," Kim responded. "The result is the important thing. It's really scary what it does to people, but it is appalling what society used to be. Of course, like the adults always say . . ."

"You'll just have to see for yourself!" they all said in unison, then burst out laughing. This didn't relieve Joshua's questions or his fear. But at least he and his friends were together in their fear.

Joshua said goodnight and watched his friends walk off down the road. Isaac stepped on Kim's heel playfully, and she reacted the way he hoped—by pushing him and then chasing after him. Joshua smiled, then turned toward the front door of his house and back to the dull lifelessness of the world he despised.

He didn't have any chores to do after school or family conflicts to worry about. Joshua and his friends never talked about chores or their parents' anger or any of the things they'd read about in the fairy tales of old. Not because they were avoiding the trauma in their reality, but because they didn't have any. Children who had not undergone the Machine did not have any obligations other than school. There were no domestic disputes, no dark tragedies secretly tormenting anyone's lives in the solitude of their homes. Children played, explored, and experimented not because their parents told them to but as a result of the adults' apathy. They received no guidance other than pointing out examples of failure in the Machine.

"The Machine will make you see. There is little I can teach you that you won't know after the Machine, so run along and play while life is still an adventure."

They did have one concern: the wild ones.

Joshua had heard his neighbors talking with his father along the fence line one afternoon about a raiding party of wild ones in a nearby town. Their assault was deadly for one family. But they were quickly repelled, and several of them were captured and put into the Machine. One of them didn't come out—he had not survived. The rest either went back to their hideouts or stayed in the town to take on work.

A homesteader happened upon a small cave near where some wild ones were last seen and found bones and decayed flesh with what appeared to be bite marks from people. The fact that there were no defensive wounds suggested the victim just accepted their fate. It was speculated that this was one of the converts of the Machine who had gone back to their old home. Joshua had watched his father and the neighbor shake their heads and sigh.

No shock or emotion.

Even funerals for the dead were largely emotionless affairs. There were no priests or deacons, no churches like those Joshua had read about. The remains were typically buried on their families' land in an equally unceremonious way. The family usually planted a fruit or nut tree with the body to mark the grave so the person could live on through the tree, the produce nourishing their heirs. Someone said a few words, but there were rarely tears. Nobody argued over their possessions. The children simply took what they needed and gave the rest to newly minted products of the Machine. And then life would move on.

Joshua felt affronted by this. His own great-great-great-grandmother had died suddenly while working her gardens. The coroner found a number of bug bites that contributed to the cardiac arrest. She was Joshua's favorite relative because she would sneak him interesting treats and tell him secrets about the rest of the family, who they were, and what they had done before they went into the Machine. Her mother had come from another town to pay her last respects and to comfort the pre-Machine children who were confused about this irregular event in their lives. Yet there was no sadness, even from her own mother. Joshua found this odd when he saw her. And though he had a special relationship with her, even he didn't cry at her passing. Her death was simply a consequence of life.

A difficult life for someone with the desire to live.

2

In one week, Joshua would turn sixteen, and he was cramming for his final examination. He had avoided studying or paying attention in class all year, fearful that he would be scheduled for the Machine if he passed. Then Isaac told him that his cousin had said their teacher said the final exam informed the Machine's Technician how long the session would likely take, and ready or not, you were scheduled soon after. There was no avoiding it. This news made him study harder than he had ever studied in his life.

His teacher told him, "Joshua, you need to focus on your social systems. There is a lot value in the nuances. It is an effective tool for separating a population. I want you to spend less time worrying about the details of how they formed and by whom and instead focus on how they divide a population. Religion is a force of nature, just as government and economic institutions are. Together they are a magnet that allows us to weed out those who practice out of habit from those who practice out of understanding. Those who obey laws out of obedience from those who obey out of understanding. And those who produce out of obligation from those who are naturally productive." Her tone was soothing but a bit exaggerated.

Joshua's hands clutched his thick black hair, ready to tear it out. "I don't understand the difference. I can't relate to this. I don't know what a temple or church *is*, let alone what it means to be a part of some religion. What can I gain from reading about them? How do people come to believe in one weird thing over another?"

"We have a religion. It is one of family and community and living with nature. We create altars to our God in the peace we create around us. There is no altar to God that is molded by our hands, only those molded by God's hands. That is our religion." She said soothingly.

"I have never practiced it," he mocked.

She chuckled before saying, "You have to know peace before you can practice it."

Joshua was not amused by this obvious dig at his pre-Machine understanding. "So am I to believe the Machine was the cause of all these religions ending? None of them had any truth—they were all lies, and the Machine simply *poof* . . ." He splayed his fingers and pulled his hands apart to simulate an explosion. "They disappeared overnight?"

She looked at him, seeming somewhat bemused by the question and the gesture, and simply said, "In essence, yes. Though all had *some* merit, which simply became our common wisdom."

"So why would it be helpful to understand something that has no more bearing on our lives?" His frustration came out more forcefully.

"Because it will be a major part of *your* life in the very near future. Because as a society we are inoculated against charlatans selling salvation through a collection plate. Because we all know how they form and why, but we also understand the truth. There is no true religion. Everyone has a piece of the truth, some more than others, but the truest religion is the relationship between a person and God with nothing in between. We don't need a shrine to remind us of that anymore, and we don't need an interpreter for the word of God. We know God because we know ourselves. More than you can possibly understand at this point, but what religion represents is a tool. A tool for *you* to use. That is why it is important."

He stared at her, confusion and anger and surprise all fighting for control of his features. It wasn't the answer that shocked him. It was how candid she was about it. Religion was a tool. He didn't understand how or why, but evidently he was destined to be some kind of religious leader. Maybe she saw in him someone who would break this droning world and give it purpose once again. Maybe there was a silent craving within his society for something new, and he was the only one who saw the decay of the spirit and could bring change.

Did she see all that? In *him*?

As he thought this, his frustration subsided, and he finally asked the question that seemed to please her, "So what is truly important about these religions if not the truth of their guiding principles?"

Looking pleased, she leaned back into a relaxed position. "The nuance of their differences. How does an adherent live? Where does their inspiration for that way of life come from? How is their religion organized? How does it spread? How does it ultimately die? What do their enemies believe? The who, the what, the where, and the when are irrelevant except as a way to organize your thoughts. The why and the how are critical to understanding the principles, however."

"Any hints you can give me before I walk blindly through the forest?" he asked with just a hint of sarcasm.

"Just this." She leaned forward, putting her elbows on the table. "Most people are drawn to what is popular and convenient in their environment, or at least what's *perceived* to be popular. People are also stubborn. So there is no changing their beliefs without destroying their faith in those beliefs first."

Joshua crossed his arms. "I don't think that's always true. Everyone is unique. If something is popular, it is because most others have determined on their own that it is valuable." He said this defiantly as if this victory of logic would make the exam proctors and this Technician forgo their scrutiny of him. He already understood everything they had to teach. He was unique. He was certain of it.

The teacher looked at Joshua with sadness. "You will have a much more difficult time than others, I think." Her statement cut through the hero's parade in Joshua's mind. He sat quietly and barely looked up from his notes and books as his teacher rose and walked to the next student.

It was impossible for him to decipher on his own what was important and what was not. He memorized dates and numbers of casualties in famous battles, and when he proudly recited the names of generals and heroes of the battles, the teacher told him "Don't worry about such trivialities. Focus on the strategies." Dejected, Joshua focused on the victorious nations and their achievements and again was rebuffed. "They were nothing special. Focus on what policies and ideologies caused the war to begin with." When he identified a treaty or policy that was the catalyst for the conflict, again he was shamed. "A treaty does not demand action. Focus on the type of people who chose to act the way they did, and what form of government they had to attract such people."

There was never a correct answer, no fact worth knowing, only the principles and natural laws that governed the outcomes. All options existed at once and all could be exercised; experience and luck often dictated the victor. The outcomes were predictable, though, and the suffering was magnified frequently by the confluence of multiple deleterious ideologies. Joshua had an impossible time of understanding these underlying principles, and his frustration led him to apathy.

In these moments, Joshua's father would sit with him and tell him a story about a great warrior he'd never heard of or a country that he'd never studied. His father knew these stories by heart, retelling them as if he had seen the events with his own eyes. He told Joshua about the pitfalls of arrogance, the collapse of mighty empires, devastation caused by nature, and the resilience of life, the story always tailored to whatever seemed to be frustrating Joshua at that moment. Afterward, Joshua would reengage his studies with that new insight. The eerie resemblance to real life and his studies made its lesson more powerful still.

Joshua's father came into his room on the second floor, still dressed from his work in the fields, his hair all but completely gone now, barefaced, bald-headed, with just the faint trace that remained of his eyebrows. His overalls were sun-bleached and faded. His black coat perfectly accented his personality: stern and stoic but warm and wise. He checked in on Joshua every night.

"How are things today?" he asked, leaning on the door jamb.

"Same as they have been. Frustrating and pointless." Joshua dropped his pen in the crease of his notebook and leaned back in the ancient chair his family had received when Joshua was born.

His father nodded. "It's always difficult to understand the purpose of the lessons. Why learn history at all if none of it is important, right? But it does teach us the principles. Not just of the large systems, but of the failures of individuals as well. To me, that is what makes the facts important."

"I wish my teacher saw it that way," Joshua said dejectedly. "No matter what I study, I am studying it wrong."

His father straightened up. He let out a heavy sigh and shook his head slowly. "Did I ever tell you about the king and the fisherman?"

Hoping this related somehow to his current crisis and eager to take a break from his studies, Joshua said, "No. Is it the same king from the lesson about religious persecution?"

His father smiled, and then sadness overshadowed him. "No, it's a different king from a happier time."

Joshua got up from the chair and gestured to it for his father to sit. He moved to the bed and stretched out, getting ready to be enthralled.

"It all happened at the dawn of the second kingdom in the realm of Valenta. The king was much closer to his subjects then, though further than when they helped him secure his throne. He surrounded himself with the greatest warriors, strategists, and organizers in the land so he could create a government that would help his kingdom thrive." He reached for the chairback and sat down.

"Each day, these wise men thought of all the ways to organize the world—labeling, categorizing, and analyzing everything from birds to mountains. The warriors needed to know where the enemies of the realm might come from, and the strategists needed to know how difficult the terrain would be for supply and commerce. The organizers wanted to predict population growth and try to design a forward-thinking system. Everything was recorded in a multitude of books and shelved in libraries. The children of the wealthiest found comfortable work analyzing data. They took field trips to gather samples and then spent months testing those samples and preparing long documents about their properties and speculations about their origins." He looked upward as he drew the story from deep inside his memory. "They were, more often than not, wrong about everything." He smiled, the creases at his eyes scrunched slightly, and his normally weary face gentled.

"They spent years in closed environments weaving intricate tales about how species were related and how all of nature was controllable and the world could be theirs if they simply understood what lever would move the mountains. Every time they were proven wrong, they doubled down and proposed an even more complex idea that illustrated that they were really right."

He went on, explaining that the king was a more practical man. He knew laws of nature would be tested and the laws of society had consequences, while theory and descriptive facts meant very little. War was seldom about precision. He recalled how many plans he had executed as precisely as they were planned. Not a single one. He understood that there were natural leaders and natural followers. Winning a battle didn't require killing every man, just those who inspired others to move forward.

Joshua leaned in to listen more closely when his father explained why the times of peace became the most difficult. "Peace was an opportunity to prepare for the next battle. But the longer peace sustained itself, the more restless the king became. His advisers sowed distrust for his people and wrote more laws to hamper their lives. 'Thou shalt not cut the pinnae tree, for it houses the symbol of our realm. Thou shalt not fish after the summer solstice. Thou shalt not live thy life according to thine own best interests.'" He emphasized the last rule with a flippant air and a disdainful look on his face.

Joshua sat up straighter in his bed and beat a pillow into a tighter wad to prop himself up, not wanting to interrupt the story but unsure how it related to his current issues. His father seemed to understand exactly what Joshua was thinking. "Trust me, I'm getting to how this relates to your troubles." He raised his hand in a placating gesture and then continued the story.

"One day the king held court to hear the case of one of these lawbreakers who stood before the king for execution. The evidence was clear and the trial was all but over; his crimes were capital and violent. Yet a question took shape in the king's mind.

"He asked the villain, 'What brought you to this end?'

"The villain replied, 'My father was executed by your soldiers for cutting down a tree. He cut it down to keep us warm through the winter. My sister died that winter from the chills. From then on, I determined that no law was just if it caused one person to suffer. I am a product of your unjust laws. My failure as a citizen is on your hands.'

"Those words weighed heavily in the king's heart. The consequences justice demanded were born of his own signature on a trifling law that held no weight in his own life. The king put down his scepter and told the villain, 'Your crime warrants that you die. However, your life may have been entirely different were it not for events beyond your control. It is the failure of my government which led you to this fate. Though it was your decision to take it as far as you did, I am still responsible for you. Your punishment is to be branded and banished from the realm. If you return, you will be executed as an enemy.'

"He turned to the court and announced, 'Furthermore, my decision is this: There shall be no law whose punishment exceeds the nature of the crime. No tree is worth more than a person's life. We cannot survive as a kingdom where laws create criminals from the desperate.'

"From that day forward he walked each day through the villages and along the roads and through the forests and along the river's edge looking for the ill effects of the laws he had written. Wanting to appear common, he dressed accordingly.

"One day, he came upon a fisherman. The king watched as the man pulled his net in and unloaded his catch into a bucket at his feet. His young son grabbed the full bucket, replaced it with an empty one, and carried the full one to a nearby wagon.

"He called to the fisherman, 'You there! What are you fishing for today?'

"The fisherman cocked an eyebrow. 'Why, fish, of course!'

"'Which species?' There were laws and seasons for certain species.

"'All of them,' the fisherman replied.

"'Are you not aware that there are laws?'

"The fisherman retorted, 'The yellow ones only swim upstream this time of year, following the laws of reproduction. The slimy green fish eat the yellow ones according to the laws of hunger. And these pink-bellied ones follow the laws of nature and eat the insects that land on the water's surface.'

"The king was amused by this but not entirely satisfied with the conversation. 'No, I mean the king's laws.'

"The fisherman cast his net in the water again. 'Of course, I know. The green ones are never to be caught. The pink-bellied ones are only in season in the summer, and the yellow ones can only be caught after they spawn in the first month of spring.'

"The king then raised his hands palm up and then asked, 'So what are you doing with them all in the same bucket in the early fall?'

"'Well, sir, if you must know, it's because the yellow ones travel upstream *only* in the fall, and they die after they spawn. I catch them to sell to the king's men, who insist on serving them at *every* party The green ones need to be caught so they don't overpopulate the river and eat *all* the yellow ones, and the pink-bellied fish are better left alone in the summer unless you want the biting insect to leave red welts all over your ass. The laws were written in isolation. God's laws are practical. Does the king know the hypocrisy of his laws or the foolishness of their application?'

"'I suspect he might be able to understand someday if he can be guided by simple wisdom from folks such as yourself.' The king began to withdraw.

"'The more laws the king creates, the more lawbreakers there are. The king would be wise to know this truth.' The fisherman stopped his casting and looked at the king, peering into his soul. 'I expect the king will find advisers that understand the world they intend to regulate. Or he will watch his realm decay.'

"The king was visibly shaken by the intense look in the fisherman's eyes. He waved a hand in his direction, then stepped over the loose stones next to the roadway. 'I suppose that's a problem for the king to resolve.'

"'I suppose it is . . . your highness.' The fisherman turned and cast his net once more in the same elegant motion."

Joshua sat quietly and thought about the story. *The king was wise. But what was the purpose of this story?* He voiced his concern to his father. "What does that have to do with me?"

His father exaggerated his surprise. "How can you not know? The king was wise in the ways of war but a failure as a governor. The consequences of his decisions destroyed the lives of otherwise productive and happy citizens. Governments are fallible, people are fallible, and laws are fallible, and the best intended ones frequently fail just as the most malevolent do. All the facts of the world, all the knowledge they could obtain did not overcome that. You need to know the principles that make a system function, not the details. Just as the facts didn't help the king govern, they will not help you to understand the principles of these systems." His father was dramatic in his defense of the story. He had raised his hands and shook them pleadingly as he asked for Joshua's understanding. He felt it was a good act.

"Why do you insist on telling me these fairy tales, Father?" Joshua mumbled. "There's no Valenta, just like there was no Cumber and no Schodderia. I've looked. They are made-up places, and the morals are nonsense."

His father turned to him and wore all the sadness he could muster. "I'm sorry you feel that way. It was very real for me." He turned away and reflected on that day with the king. He had always hated the taste of that green fish. "Better get some more studying done."

He turned and walked out, proud of his performance but a little disappointed in himself for his rambling. The story wasn't quite as succinct as he would have liked it. *But what can you do? A memory doesn't always have nice neat storylines with morals clearly packaged for delivery.* He went downstairs to get some tea and enjoy the stars with his wife.

Joshua watched his father walk out.

Sometimes Joshua would ask his mother about those stories, and she would nod her head and then tell the same story with a different country, hero, era, and everything. The details were never the same, but the lesson was, at least, similar. Joshua wondered how those adults, who never seemed to talk about anything, could know so many stories and have such colorful detail that made those events come vividly to life.

Joshua was still worried about the exam and knowing the right lessons. *How much time has been wasted with the stories?*

3

The exam would be comprehensive. The teacher had been steadily building upon lessons from the past few years, using math to explain science, statistics to explain psychology, science to explain history, history to hypothesize about psychology, and then science to explain math. On and on the subjects intertwined to make a complex network. More capable students understood the connection and purposes of everything much quicker, and now even Joshua was beginning to understand. He still daydreamed, but the daydreams took on a curiosity about the natural engineering of birds and how a particular tree had come to be.

This curiosity distracted from the more important lessons, and he knew he would spend more time alone secretly struggling and too embarrassed over how far behind the class he was getting to ask for help. But the exam didn't care how ready you were. It came based on your age and measured you against all the other sixteen-year-olds throughout the empire.

It was rumored that this would affect what he could do as a career, and the worst jobs were reserved for those who scored the lowest on the test. The empress herself was chosen because of her score.

<hr>

When the day arrived, Joshua awoke early and turned on his bedside lamp to go over his disjointed notes. He'd memorized useless facts, despite being advised against it, and skimmed over the concepts that formed governments, unified peoples, and divided them. He looked at the margins of his notes, at the doodles and bullet points that highlighted the most important lessons, which he had not paid attention to. The pit of his stomach was in knots. The restless sleep he had only seemed to emphasize his sense of despair.

He began to sob softly. The tears dotted his notes as he accepted his defeat. He knew his life was over, his options were few, and he was going to be little more than a farmer like his father.

Joshua dragged himself downstairs to breakfast, his eyes puffy from crying and dark from lack of sleep. His skin was pale and clammy. He hadn't bothered with a shower or even straightened his hair or brushed his teeth. Mother and Father were already at the table with their tea and breakfast.

"The township will vote on the expansion of the market tonight," his mother said as he shuffled in like a wrung rag. "It will bring in more merchants from nearby areas. But the road use will increase, so there will probably be a levy for that, which will reduce the number of merchants. My guess is they will underestimate the costs and overestimate the benefits like always, and we will have to vote no."

His father nodded and opened his mouth to speak but turned to Joshua instead. "Are you not going to clean yourself up?"

Joshua paused at the threshold of the kitchen and looked down at his tousled shirt, mismatched socks, and wrinkled pants. He felt grimy, but he wanted the whole world to see and take pity on his misery.

"Joshua," his mother said soothingly, "we don't wear our burdens for attention." She gestured meaningfully at his outfit. "Your dignity is what inspires others to help. This looks like you have given up, and no one wants to carry both your burdens and their own. Go get cleaned up. I will get your breakfast ready."

When he came back down, he still wore the shabbiest clothes he had, but at least they were fresh. His socks matched and he was clean.

"Now this is the sort of wretch I can pity," his mother commented wryly before placing his plate on the table and pouring some tea.

Her golden hair was tied in a bun. Though rapidly thinning, it still accented her soft features and pouting mouth. She wore a demure dress of dark maroon over a conservative white-collared black blouse. This image of her failed to capture her warmth. Joshua always thought of her as the only adult who seemed to have genuine emotions. While she was much less expressive than Father, she was more natural in her expressions, and that made her seem more alive.

Joshua quietly ate his egg and toast. Thoughts of what awaited him made his heart heavy. He forced himself to overcome each tiny morsel on his plate as he contemplated his doom.

His parents seemed amused by this display.

"It seems you haven't adequately prepared for your exam." His father hid the flicker of laughter in the corner of his mouth with his teacup.

"We'll just have to hope you can even become a farmer. Even living by your own produce requires a minimum score. It will be such a disappointment if we can't pass all this on to you someday." Mother gestured at the grayed walls and warped cupboards and out the window at the patchy lawn and weather-beaten garden.

The revelation of what he would be worth made Joshua break down again. He buried his face in his hands and unleashed a fresh batch of heavy sobs. There was just so much at stake today. He felt like he had already failed. Without the first question answered, he had failed.

His father cleared his throat loudly, in a way that let Joshua know he was uncomfortable with the display.

His mother reached over and patted his arm. The downslope of her eyebrows showed all the real emotions of a mother watching her child suffering, but she knew it was always this way, and necessarily so. Humility is a great way to relieve performance stress, and it would make their recoveries much quicker when they realized how little it really mattered.

The test was arduous and long. It seemed to touch on everything Joshua failed to study and none of the things he did. He knew he had failed miserably.

Then he got the test back.

It didn't even have a score on it. The proctor merely said, "You'll be the judge of how well you did when you return from the Machine."

Joshua was furious. He took the exam home and threw it on the kitchen table.

His mother came in upon hearing the clamor. "He's right, you know. It's unimportant what the results are. What matters is how prepared you are to face the Machine. You're scheduled for a week from now. I'll hang on to this; it'll be your gift once you come out."

Joshua seethed and marched up the stairs to his room. He needed to be noisily alone.

Joshua saw Isaac and Kim a few times in their last days of innocence. They didn't laugh anymore. The evidence of freshly dried tears became a permanent feature on their faces.

"When are you scheduled to go in?" Joshua asked Kim while they all walked down the road to the pond. The summer heat was just beginning to make a daily visit. Cicadas chirped in the reeds along the roadside ditch.

"Two more days, first thing in the morning," she said flatly. Her eyes began to water, and she glanced over at the boy she loved, who had his chin tucked into his chest. Joshua had asked the same of his best friend that morning. He was scheduled a few days after her, and Joshua was the day after him.

Joshua wondered who had it worst.

Haunted by the memories of those who preceded her, the husks that emerged, Kim was the first of their group to face that . . . that *lobotomy*. Isaac would see his girlfriend go through, knowing she might not have the same feelings for him afterward. Joshua would have to watch his two closest friends face the trial and become the husks that everyone seemed to turn into. Then it would be his turn.

Their having to face the Machine was all he could think about as they sat quietly the rest of the day, watching the reeds sway in the breeze and listening to the cicadas sing along the shore.

———⁂———

Two days later, Kim walked down the road toward Town Hall. Her parents and both her grandmothers plodded ahead of her. Joshua stood out by the front gate and watched his teary-eyed best friend run to catch up to her. Though he was out of earshot, Joshua could read the desperation on his friend's face. He was telling her everything he wanted her to know. He took her hands and she let him. She leaned in and they kissed. She leaned into him and wrapped her arms around him, holding him in an embrace that seemed so final.

Her mother walked back after a few moments and put her hand on her shoulder.

Joshua looked on as Isaac stood there watching them walk away, the girl he loved bawling into her hands as her mother ushered her down the road. She took one last glance back at him and smiled meekly through her tears.

As she passed Joshua's house, she looked at him sadly and waved, her eyes silently pleading for him to remember her as one of the living. Her loose blue-and-white dress was one she had worn a hundred times, and her hair was tied back in a ponytail. Everything in her demeanor suggested she hadn't slept at all. Hadn't eaten. Hadn't stopped crying since the night before.

Isaac slowly walked to Joshua's house, where they both stood at the gate watching the family walk away until they were at the edge of Market Square.

Without a word between them, they walked toward Town Hall. His friend was pale. They got there just in time to watch her step through the lobby doors and disappear as they closed heavily behind her.

———————

All day they sat waiting. Nervous and pacing, Isaac kept asking questions Joshua couldn't answer.

"Do you think she'll be at all the same?"

"Does any part of who we are now make a difference?"

"Do you think she'll still love me?"

"I don't know," Joshua said honestly. "Why have the Machine if it erases every part of who we are? I can't believe we are all destined to lose our individuality. But the results speak for themselves."

He knew this was not a comfort to his friend. He wanted to be placated. He wanted the lie. To believe there was still hope that what she said she felt would remain.

At that moment, the doors opened slowly. The girl who held

the door seemed to be feeling every grain and observing every detail of the world around her, but there was no emotion in her face. As she walked past the statue in the courtyard of Town Hall, she placed her hand gently on its well-worn foot and gazed up at it. Its ears were large and rounded. The eyes were beady and offset. The long snout was wrinkled in a permanent snarl. And though there was only a hint of hair in patches on its upright body, it was very definitely a rodent.

Joshua realized that Kim had never shown the statue the slightest bit of reverence until now. In fact, she had always been disgusted by it and asked why their little town would have such an ugly thing at all.

Today, though, she was reverent.

Isaac sprinted up to her, Joshua trailing behind. As they approached, she looked at them indifferently, if slightly puzzled.

Isaac was visibly startled by the change. There was none of her warmth, none of her kindness and sociability. He seemed afraid to even reach out to her and withdrew his hand when he did try.

Kim watched him passively.

Joshua and Isaac couldn't find the words to ask the questions they had been forming all day. But they were answered with one look in her eyes. Devastated, Isaac turned and started to walk away. His mouth hung open in disbelief, and his eyes seemed to be counting the thousands of pieces his heart had shattered into. Without a word he walked back toward his home. Joshua watched him as he went.

She finally spoke as calmly and coolly as an owl tearing apart its prey. "You will know everything." With this, she began to walk back home with her family. Alone, though surrounded by her entourage. She was a husk like the others.

For the next few days, Isaac was missing. He did not go home. He wasn't at the pond. He was found at the edge of a farmer's field in a lean-to hut he'd built from fallen branches. He had run out of provisions and started drinking from the drainage ditch and had become violently ill because of it. The farmer found him covered in his own vomit and stinking of other bodily functions, weakly begging for death.

The farmer brought him directly to Town Hall where the clinic was set up. After running an IV, they sent a messenger to fetch his parents, who were overly calm for what they had just endured and knew their son had experienced. He received medicine and food and, after a couple hours of observation, was released into his parents' care. Joshua had only heard the rumor of it all and never got the chance to see Isaac again before he went into the Machine the next morning. Sick or not, he was scheduled.

Joshua knew what would happen to his friend. Isaac was heartbroken and ill, and it was rumored that he would probably die. Most adults shrugged it off as a sort of necessary sacrifice. But this was Joshua's best friend. He was sick with fear.

It was the longest session the town had seen in a hundred years. His friend went in during the morning and didn't emerge until after dark. He looked even hollower than before. He wore his continued sadness though it was much more contained than the previous day. Though he held himself tall with dignity and patted the foot of the statue reverently like Kim had done, he was visibly weak and tired. Even when he passed Joshua in the courtyard, he had no kind words or helpful clues to offer. Instead, he looked through Joshua as he walked away.

Joshua overheard his friend's parents say flatly and quietly, "He was very close for a while. It's a lucky thing she came when she did. The Technician was ready to let him go."

At that moment, Kim walked through the doors of Town Hall and headed down the road after him.

The relief over his friend's ordeal did not make Joshua feel any better about it. His friend had tried to run away. He would have become a wild one if not for becoming ill from drinking the ditch water. If Kim hadn't gone in and helped him, he would have died in the Machine.

They didn't leave together, and they didn't say anything to each other, so what could she possibly have done to help him? But that didn't matter at this moment. Joshua was scheduled for tomorrow morning, and he had more reason than anyone to fear what was going to happen.

Dinner was the same old balanced plate Joshua had always seen waiting for him after school. Some form of protein, cheese, leafy greens, cold tea, and a medley of seasonal fruits. His mother's parents were both seated at the table when he came in. They would obviously be going with them the next day. Joshua wasn't very interested in eating tonight though, and despite not having seen his grandparents for some time, he excused himself and went to get cleaned up before going to bed.

He'd hardly slept all night. He kept envisioning the horrors this Machine produced, the soulless wretches that emerged, the near death of his best friend, and he was sick with anxiety. He didn't know what the Machine was or why he had learned such useless knowledge that the adults didn't seem to even care about. His room was too hot, then it was too cold. His blankets were too itchy, and then the air around him was too. He was frustrated and finally, when he reached the limit of exhaustion, was able to get to sleep despite his concerns.

He saw a shadow smothering him and laughing in the most sinister way he had ever heard. He saw from horizon to horizon outside his window a fire burning and leaping higher and higher, creeping ever closer to his home. The fields around his village were engulfed in flames, then the houses, then the people themselves.

Everyone he knew passively watched it without concern. He saw Isaac standing beside him, and then he started walking toward the flame. As he was engulfed he turned to Joshua, and with that blank face melting away like wax, he asked Joshua, "What is left of ourselves when we are finished?" Joshua wanted to run, but the shadow held him. He then heard it say, "You will know everything." The shadow's voice was too familiar, and he tried searching the dark abysmal shroud in front of him for a face, but the shadow swallowed him and he found himself falling through a void.

He awoke on the floor before dawn in the tangled net of his own blankets and lay there contemplating his imminent doom.

4

It was a thankless job. There was never a time when he was proud about what he had to do. It was simply necessary.

The Technician observed his aged appearance as he brushed his teeth. The long hair of his youth had long since receded and disappeared. Once he took his own turn in the Machine, his body found it an unnecessary waste of energy and resources, and it quickly fell out to reveal the sleek, soft skin he stared at in the fog of the mirror.

His hands moved the ancient toothbrush back and forth as he thought about how he ended up in this position. How he came to be the Technician. It was a cruel irony that so much of his early life took place behind bars—while he still enjoyed freedom of the mind and heart—only to find himself imprisoning the minds of so many others. Every few days a new candidate. Every few days a new torture. He stole the souls of youths and turned them into adults.

The trauma he caused and endured changed him a little more each time.

What was this one's name again? Joshua?

A dull and uninteresting name, but it was no better than anyone else's. The vanity of names had long gone. A name was simply a device to identify a person in a crowd. There was at least one Joshua every town, along with at least one Michael, Maria, Kate, Kim, Sarah, Isaac, Matthew, Mark, Luke, and John. They were easy to recycle and easy to forget.

Joshua was once a name of kings. But history meant nothing these days. There were no great battles or heroes. There were no more nations and no longer any real government. An empire was ostensibly what they lived in, but all real decisions were caucused at the local level. Roads and infrastructure were planned at the district level. Only the opening of new territories and the terraforming of new planets fell to the imperial government. How those people obtained those postings was a matter of performance. Performance in the Machine. The empress herself was once his naïve candidate. How miserably she performed.

The government was a perfect place for her.

He spit the foam from his mouth and inspected his teeth before turning off the light and going to find his robe. His naked skin was dry and gray, his long limbs slender and sinewy. The Machine made a body efficient. No excess energy was wasted on sweat or hair, and even once-daily urination and defecation became uncommon.

As every morning, he prepared a breakfast of seasonal fruit and yogurt, a cup of tea, and a handful of homemade biscuits with butter. Some people might have called this excessive, but they lived lives without the stress of destroying innocence. He could be as indulgent as he wanted.

Besides, this will be my last one.

He had served his time. More than that. This would be his fifty thousandth candidate. The billions of years he spent with each was time enough to understand why he was there. Time enough to be rehabilitated. Every time.

———∞∞———

Joshua's mother was already downstairs waiting for him when Joshua walked down to the kitchen.

"Good morning," She said. "I heard you stirring and already have your breakfast ready."

Joshua saw his father in his favorite chair, snoring softly, and wondered whether they had been up all night themselves. His mother set a glass of milk down and cooked an egg with some toast. This was standard fare for his morning meal, but the mood was slightly different.

Mother sat quietly across from him as he ate, then finally said, "Some kids run away before their appointments. Some of them are never recovered and become the wild ones, but most are found. We wanted to make sure you didn't have thoughts of running."

Joshua forced himself to swallow a bite of toast. "What made you think I was going to run?"

She smiled warmly, reminiscing. "Because I did." She chuckled.

Joshua choked on his toast.

His father woke up suddenly, hearing the commotion, and asked, "Was he considering it then?"

She replied, "No, I don't think so. It's fine, you can go back to sleep or come get some breakfast."

Father stretched and got up to get some tea. After fixing his cup, he turned to Joshua. "This is a big day, son. You will not be the same, but don't ever regret the experience. Everyone is reluctant before going in. Your mother and I will be there to make sure that everything goes well."

Goes well? I've seen what "going well" means.

They left their house with plenty of time to spare. The morning was crisp but getting warmer. The dew on the grasses made the place mystical, and the light fog of the morning was hovering low across the fields. Joshua's parents walked beside him. His grandparents trailed behind, bantering idly over the season and its commonplace marvels. To Joshua, they seemed overtly protective today. But that thought couldn't protect his mind from the task ahead.

He found his steps toward Town Hall, each one more forced than the previous. The years of mystery surrounding this day and the Machine were nothing short of terrifying when compounded into this final march of the condemned. He had visions of probes and spikes penetrating his entire body, violating his identity until he capitulated to the will of this Technician.

Joshua's father put his hand on his shoulder and reassured him once again that it would be all right. That it was a rite of passage.

They walked past the statue of the town's mascot to the doors leading into Town Hall, Joshua's parents reverently patting the stone foot as they passed. They entered the familiar building, the one Joshua had seen every day when going to and from school, but this time his family took a different hallway than the one leading to the classroom. This one was well lit and had no other corridors or offices attached save for a restroom. A middle-aged-looking man sat behind a desk. He wore a loosely fitting white jacket and a badge which read *Technician*. He smiled warmly in a well-practiced way.

"You must be Joshua. Please come in and have a seat in the Examination Room there." He pointed to a door to his left.

As Joshua entered the room, he looked around. There were two comfortable-looking chairs facing each other and a door which read *Generated Alternate Universe Device*.

The name was blunt in its purpose. It generated an alternate universe, but how did he fit into the mix? What universe would it generate, and what was the purpose? How did it change people so dramatically over the course of a single day? These were the questions rolling through his mind when the Technician came in and took a seat in one of the chairs.

"Please have a seat right here, and I'll answer any questions you have. Then I'll ask you a few of my own before we go into the Machine. I know you've heard a lot of rumors. Most are true, but once you're inside, you'll understand."

Joshua halted briefly midstride at that. *Most are true.* That alone meant that everything he speculated would happen. He would come out lobotomized by the experience like everyone else.

Seeing this hesitation and Joshua's face blanch with fear, the Technician reassured him. "You will still be you when you leave here. Despite what you've seen, you will be you."

Though this didn't dissuade him of the countless husks he had seen emerge from Town Hall after their ordeal in the Machine, Joshua took a seat across from the Technician and tried to find the most comfortable position allowable in the chair. It had a familiar sense about it, like his father's chair when he'd curl up with his textbooks and daydream about the way life was before.

The Technician waited patiently until Joshua stopped fidgeting, then asked, "Is there anything you would like to know before we get started?"

A flood of questions entered Joshua's mind that moment, but he couldn't decide which one was the most important. Maybe one would answer all the other questions and elicit the most information possible. His voice tight with hesitation, he finally asked, "What does the Machine do?"

Smiling gently, the Technician replied, "It creates a universe in which you will play god and determine which of the many people and creatures lives or dies. Everything and everyone in your domain will be elements of your personality. In the same way light is refracted through a crystal to create bands of many different colors, we will refract your conscious and unconscious mind through a sort of digital crystal to split your personality into the many aspects of yourself. You will make decisions based on how strong each element is."

Shocked by his candor Joshua asked, "Will it hurt?"

"Only emotionally. There is no physical pain in this process, but there may be some neurological damage that can impact your physical being. Most people suffer some minor nerve damage. Yet some people have made profoundly self-destructive decisions in the Machine, leading to total mental collapse, and they died."

"Is that what happened to the wild one they say died in the Machine? Is that what almost happened to my best friend?"

The Technician stated matter-of-factly, "That is what happened." He put down his clipboard and steepled his hands in his lap as he spoke. "He was grief-stricken by losing the girl he loved to the Machine, so he refused to avoid catastrophes and sculpt his world to the level he needed to for them to advance on their own. It was a struggle for my colleague and his family to keep him afloat through it all, and it wasn't until his love interest noticed the length of his session and plugged herself in that he was able to recover enough to face the trials he needed to and finish the simulation in a satisfactory way.

"As far as the wild one goes, he refused to be a part of our society and chose not to understand, even with his Technician's constant guidance. He still chose death over life among us, and his body shut down. His Technician was traumatized by the experience. Our duty is to observe and advise and test when necessary to ensure the highest quality possible. We've been doing this a long time, but it is very rare that anyone makes decisions against their own well-being, and it can be very painful to watch someone destroy themselves in this way."

He was quiet for a moment and then added, "We will be making some procedural changes because of the young lady's interference. It was highly unusual behavior. By all rights, your friend should have been allowed to die. But her actions were, by all accounts, heroic."

The fact that this Technician was so willing to let people die in the Machine made him every bit as ugly and terrifying as Joshua had expected him to be. But the casual admission that his friend was a hero made him wonder just how heartless this Technician could truly be. He was being honest at least, and Joshua had seldom experienced this level of conversation with an adult, so he clung bitterly to the conversation about the task at hand to delay the experience as long as possible.

"Will I be aware of myself in there?" He picked at the lint on his pants leg.

"More than you ever thought possible. You will be aware of every person, creature, and plant in your system, but they will only be vaguely aware of you. Each one is a part of you, and each one understands only their own perspective of their role in that system. They will all be you, but they will also be themselves." He crooked a half smile and cocked his eyebrow up slightly. "And you will have to decide which ones are corrupt and cancerous, and which are constructive."

Terror gripped Joshua as he recalled the hollow husks that had been his friends emerging from Town Hall.

Joshua finally asked the question that had been on his mind every day since he first became aware of the Machine. "Why do people come out of the Machine the way they do? Why does everyone come out . . . *hollow?*"

The Technician's eyebrows narrowed a bit, and his gaze withdrew to a distant memory. He remembered his first time and those who came out before him. And though every candidate asked this question, he never failed to respond the same way. "Because you will see everything that is possible, and you can never unsee it and never *unknow* it. Life will never again be as mysterious to you as it is right now. You can never get that back. That is why people come out like that. They aren't hollow, they are too *full.*"

This answer sent a chill down Joshua's spine. Avoiding the answer and too afraid to probe any deeper, he persisted with his unnecessary questions. "How can they not know me if I am completely aware of them?"

"They are each like a grain of sand on a beach. They don't know that they are part of the beach, only how they fit in with other grains of sand. Only the beach knows that each grain makes up the whole beach." The Technician probed Joshua with his eyes. "Does this make sense?"

The confusion was plain on Joshua's face, but he pressed on. "If I have to decide which ones I kill and which ones I don't, but they are all part of me, isn't it all self-destructive?" Joshua smirked, proud of his clever question. Poking holes in the logic of the Machine might help him overcome it, or maybe despite all the candidates tested by this Technician, this youth might prove to be his undoing, somehow making him question his own purpose and freeing Joshua of his burden.

The Technician didn't seem surprised by the question. "Yes, but some elements in a person are more destructive than others. Those need to be eliminated so that the less damaging parts can be allowed to grow. You will see many generations of your people. It is the process of evolution. You are selectively breeding yourself. I will be in the Machine to guide you and answer any questions you may have. I will also be there as a safeguard against your early decisions, which are typically very clumsy. You may find that you will have to start from scratch several times, but whatever you do cannot be reversed. It is a very steep learning curve, full of difficult choices and many mistakes. You will think you have finished and created perfect harmony, and then I will test you. I will make sure that you have been exposed to every potential trauma and every joy. Then I will shock the system and see how it reacts. I am your adversary in this regard. It is your duty to ensure that you have truly found harmony. Only then, when I have no power over you and your creation, will you be finished and the simulation completed."

"How long will that take?" Joshua shifted in the seat.

"As long as it needs to. In our time, six or seven hours, but inside the Machine it will seem to last billions of years. When you emerge, you will have truly lived those billions of years and will not be the same. No one ever is. But you'll be grateful for it."

Trying to think of another question, Joshua asked, "How old are you?"

With a burst of forced laughter, the Technician replied, "I have not been asked that in a long time. You must really be stalling. I am seven hundred and forty-three years old next month."

Joshua's jaw dropped open and tried to form words.

The Technician spread his hands and replied, "It's the Machine. You go through the process when you're young and mature very quickly within it. When you have reached that state of harmony in your own mind, your body and mind stop taking actions that are detrimental to your well-being. The neuroplastic effect of this purely mental transformation is that your body develops the ability to repair itself as your nervous system responds harmoniously with exactly what your body needs and demands only what it needs. A perfect equilibrium is established, allowing the body to require only a minimal sustenance. Eventually, you refine your external lifestyle to match only what you need. Ambition, especially the destructive elements of it, is destroyed."

Joshua was dumfounded. There was nothing else to say. He had reached the limit of his ability to delay.

"Do you have any other questions before I ask mine?"

Joshua shook his head.

"Let's begin then."

The Technician began hooking up a number of suction cups with wires that measured biorhythms, along with heart-rate monitors and a heavy helmet, all connected to a portable device that seemed to be a recorder of some type. He placed the helmet on Joshua's head, then started a series of questions. The first few were mundane: "What is your father's father's name? Where were you born? What is the nearest town to your own?" They required little thought.

Then he asked more embarrassing, probing questions.

"When was your last bowel movement?"

Joshua was taken aback. Why was it important to know this? His face flushed as he mumbled, "This morning."

"Which girls from the town do you fantasize about?"

Joshua shifted nervously under the weight of the helmet. The Technician was insinuating a lot.

"No one. I'm not interested in any of them."

What does this have to do with the Machine?

The Technician nodded. "Why did you burn down the forest?"

Joshua flushed again, this time with anger. "It was my cousin's idea. I didn't have anything to do with the fire."

"That's interesting. Your cousin said the same thing about you. So who is lying?"

How could his cousin betray him like that? "He's a liar! He burned down the forest, and he's the one who suggested we kill the squirrel."

"It seems you forgot your part in all that. Did he force you to participate?"

"It wasn't my fault, and it wasn't my idea." Joshua growled as he crossed his arms and slouched in the chair.

The Technician suddenly changed his tone. "When your great-great-great-grandmother died, you didn't cry. Why?"

"I don't know my family very well. She was nice to me, but I barely knew her. I'm sorry if I didn't cry!"

"Do you have so many nice people in your life that one more dying was so inconsequential?"

Joshua was silent. Of course not. The death of his great-great-great-grandmother was too far removed from his life. She was too unrelatable for him to feel any more for her than he did for the stories of the wild ones. That didn't mean he wasn't sympathetic or didn't care.

Joshua felt the swelling of fear and embarrassment, and before long he completely clammed up and would no longer respond to the pointed questions that made him feel naked in the presence of this person. He had only just met the Technician that day but felt like he had been watched since birth. How did the man find out all this information about him? How did he know his deep, dark secrets?

The Technician put down his pen and looked at Joshua. "Everyone goes through this. These questions are designed to trigger your emotions. We gathered the questions from your parents, your teacher, and other townsfolk that know of certain situations you were involved in. We are not really interested in the answer, but we need to measure your stress response for the Machine to calibrate properly."

Joshua felt relief for the first time that day. He let out a heavy sigh and slumped in the chair.

The Technician reached over and turned off the recorder. "We also needed to measure your sense of relief. It'll tell us when it's time to test you. When you're too comfortable. Too complacent." He pulled the disc out of the recorder and put it in a case he pulled from the breast pocket of his lab coat. Then he set down the clipboard full of unanswered questions, a catalog of betrayal from those who knew him, and led Joshua into the room.

5

The Machine filled the majority of the room. Though it was all one contiguous piece, it looked like it had been updated and upgraded through the years. Slabs of off-color paneling and random juts and jags looked out of place against the sleek and smooth chassis. The Machine reached to the ceiling, with a few built-in terminals as well as several stations that had been added for multiple users. It had chairs around it with wired helmets and straps to hold the subjects in place during their session. Two of the seats had labels that indicated where the Technician and the subject would be seated. A bundle of cables traced the base of the wall and picked up additional wires from each station, then fed back through a conduit that led to another room hidden from view. The Technician directed Joshua to his place and strapped him in, then lowered the helmet and adjusted the fittings until it was snug but not uncomfortable.

Then the Technician said, "Your parents and grandparents will come in shortly and will be here to observe and monitor your progress, but they will not be able to communicate with you while you are in the Machine. They will, however, be able to interact with your creation if necessary. Think of them as your guardian angels. I will be able to hear them, and they will be able to pause the simulation if they have any concerns, but you won't notice any change. I will bring them in from the waiting room shortly and get them set up in their stations while you get started.

"Keep focus on your objective. The only passing grade is a perfect score. I will begin the tutorial session for you as I get your parents and myself strapped in. Don't be alarmed at what you see. It is automated to give you the general idea of its physics, your abilities within the universe, and how to use the tools at your disposal. Once you have the hang of it, you will begin the test. Are you ready?"

"I think so," Joshua said over the strap keeping his jaw closed.

"All right then, here you go."

"Wait!" Joshua's voice was muffled by the chin strap, but he managed to halt the Technician. "How will I not be able to see them or know they are there?"

The Technician's hand hovered over the button. The question obviously annoyed him. "You will see them by their impact on the world around them—through dreams, through visions, through active interaction. They will not be bored, and you will have too much to do yourself to ever notice them."

The Technician then looked intensely into Joshua's eyes and pointedly asked, "Any more questions?"

Before Joshua could reply, the Technician pressed the big green button to the left of Joshua's seat.

Joshua ceased to be aware of the outside world and saw tiny little one-dimensional strings, as he understood them to be—the binary code that generated the atomic and subatomic devices that made up the fundamental pieces of the universe in the Machine. As the code took shape, it formed a vast expanse of blackness. He felt like he was being pulled helplessly toward some great energy. As it pulled, he became disoriented. He could feel his whole self being crushed and broken; he shrieked as he shattered and fell into the impenetrable blackness.

The dark's depth was imperceptible, its width infinite. A single point of light appeared out of the void. It grew and grew until it filled Joshua's field of vision. His whole being was thrown with the force, and though he was vaguely aware of his own complete self, he felt like he was now scattered and incomplete though conscious.

He could see the nebulous body shoot out at enormous speed to fill the whole of the blackness. Brilliant reds and blues and greens, light and dark, and the colors of heat and cold twisted and turned and continued to expand. He could see infrared and ultraviolet and spectrums he couldn't articulate. The nebula began to dissipate, but in its place colorful swirls emerged with vast emptiness between them. Then the swirls took on more definite shapes, and individual points of light emerged in the swirls. Like water circling a drain, the loose matter flowed toward the vortexes and crashed into larger and looser orbs and vortexes. The points of light had a variety of bodies floating around them, which smashed together in a spectacular display to form larger bodies, and then again to form even larger ones. This process repeated until all the blackness had found a natural rhythm and the chaos had largely ceased.

All was calm for a single atomic moment, and then Joshua felt the tearing of his body once more. He watched again as the bodies collapsed back into their points of light, and the lights pulled back into swirls, and then the swirls converged with one another until all were again a single point of light.

Joshua felt the push and pull over and over as the universe expanded and contracted multiple times, causing nausea and vertigo. When he looked closely at a particle, he could feel the pull of every other particle that was part of this existence. He saw the magnetic pull, like strings, attaching every piece to the others. No matter how far apart two particles were, no matter how infinitesimally small the connection between the two, they were permanently linked.

All atoms were linked. All electrons pushed away from every other electron. All protons repelled every other proton. All electrons were attracted to every proton. The cluster of protons were separated at the nucleus by the neutrons that filled the void between the phase lines of the protons. The electrons formed a tight shell around the nucleus, as tight as they could get without crossing each other's magnetic fields. This kept the system in equilibrium and the infinite cycle repeating into infinity. There was no escape, no loss of energy or electrons or particles of any kind. Everything was indelibly linked to everything else.

Joshua understood the basis of string theory. He knew that it was real, but he hadn't realized it was such a simple idea. It took the Machine to show him that the backdrop of all existence was a digital binary matrix called strings. The theorems were long complex calculations prone to errors that Joshua had little interest in solving in school. But here, he could *see* it. Here he knew it was true, but the formulas were too complex to be analyzed.

Joshua watched particles from the singular electron to the most massive of stars. He saw the formation of the elements. Every chemical reaction he had dabbled with in school, every chart he had studied—every chemical formed naturally or unnaturally was being formed and broken in this process. He could see the atomic orbitals crashing together and forming new elements. There were equal numbers of protons, electrons, and neutrons. All of what could be known about chemistry was occurring before him.

And he understood it. It was no longer hypothetical; he could *see* it.

As one particle crashed into a molecule of much greater mass, it redirected it only fractionally, proportional to its size, relative to the size of the larger molecule. Those molecules crashed into larger bodies and moved them, proportional to their mass and velocity and vector and relative to the mass and velocity and vector of the larger body. A head-on collision between a massive object and a tiny particle seemed to make no difference in the velocity of the massive object, but it was slowed by the exact velocity and mass of the particle. This continued until the swirling chaotic mass revealed galaxies, stars, and planets. The cloud gradually pulled into the orbiting bodies and added mass to them, increasing the pressure at the core and creating more frictional heat that fused more atoms together to create more elements.

The laws of physics played out in real time to form planets and stars and everything else that was possible. Without formulas or equations, he understood how it all worked.

The planets held their orbits by the tangential velocity of their aggregated mass and were pulled toward the star by the magnetic field produced. A north pole on the planet attracted to the south pole of the star. There was far less chaos than Joshua had previously believed, and the dance repeated itself over and over with the same effect. He saw a governing principle to the chaos.

The speed of the rotation when accelerated would increase the internal frictional energy of the planets and stars, causing stars to burn brighter and planets to warm up. The vortex pulled in more and more free molecules. Bits of dust floated through space, breaking down and recombining into other elements. The densest ones migrated to the planet's core and the lightest to the surface, where they gassed off and formed the atmosphere. The faster the rotation, the thicker the atmosphere and the more powerful the vortex pulling those particles downward, which increased the aggregated magnetic field.

Some stars accelerated too much and would pull so much mass into themselves they would prevent even light from escaping. Their formation proved that light itself had mass, detectable only by the colossal pull and the corona that surrounded them. Dark stars—black holes—accelerated faster than light and created invisible vortexes propelled by the same orbital forces that pulled all the universe toward the center. Collisions of two of these black holes slowed this rotation enough for light and matter to escape.

Seeing the universe being born, then collapsing, and being reborn again a moment later left Joshua in awe. No matter what, the universe followed those basic laws. While it had taken his civilization a thousand years to understand this outside the Machine, it took only an instant of observation within it to completely comprehend the truth of it all.

Joshua heard the Technician in his mind. "This is the foundation of the tools you will use. Your understandings of how the planets form will allow you to manipulate them. Their tilt, their rotation, their mass can all be adjusted, with severe consequences either beneficial or detrimental. You will be responsible for one solar system in this simulation, but if you are successful, your consciousness will be carried across the stars."

Joshua thought for a moment. "If the universe collapses and is reborn again over and over, what use is conquest of the stars?"

The Technician replied, a hint of amusement in his imagined voice, "No more than the conquest of any part of nature." After a brief pause, he continued. "You will find that you are benefiting from the visitation of those who came before you. Their consciousness will expand and grow and explore the stars terraforming planets to expand their growing civilizations. They will find you struggling in yours and help you in some ways and hinder you in others. But a civilization cannot reach the point of interference with another without succeeding here in the Machine, so you will have nothing to fear from them. They are as much a guide for you as I am."

6

Joshua observed a cloud that would become another star system. He watched, as before, the vortexes form.

Joshua asked no one in particular, "How do these dead orbs turn into planets? How do they fill with animals and plants and people? I see it happening, but I don't really understand what is going on."

The Technician spoke out of nowhere. He sounded bored from observing this process so many times, "The universe—the galaxies, the stars, the planets, and every molecule and atom that makes them up—is alive."

Then his explanation became more clinical. "The velocities, masses, and vectors of individual particles become larger and create a swirling vortex. A star forms at the geometric center of gravity of the nebula, and other bodies form farther out. Each is a living vortex. Each is elastic and malleable and capable of supporting life in the right conditions."

"Is this how we have terraformed the frontier planets?" Joshua asked.

"For the most part. We can change the tilt and rotational speed of planets with asteroids and by piling up matter where we want the equator to eventually be. Once the process has started, water and air begin to form on their own. The frictional energy in the planet creates the heat to allow the chemical reactions to take place, and the planet becomes habitable. But it takes a long time for planets to reach that habitable range and even longer for the violent change to cease, allowing people to inhabit the planet safely. As they say with a fig tree, 'I plant the seed for my children to enjoy the fruit.'"

Joshua watched those nascent planetary bodies move through the cloud picking up particles. While locked in a dance with the star's magnetic poles, they increased their rotation, creating a day and night cycle that allowed for rapid heating and cooling of the steadily growing atmospheres.

The Technician pointed out, "Some of these planets maintain very thin atmospheres and a slow rotation because of the proximity of other orbiting bodies. But all have the capability of becoming planets teeming with life if they have the proper rotational speed and tilt for their density."

An asteroid belt outside the fourth planet prevented many of the benefits of rotational acceleration from affecting the planet, so it remained lifeless and cold. Others had exceedingly dense atmospheres and rotational speeds that were too fast for life to properly form, or so Joshua assumed. "Is there a certain rotational speed that is ideal then?"

The Technician replied, "More or less. It is like a bell curve in statistics. At a certain speed, life finds it easiest to form and grow. But life is capable of incredible things even under extreme conditions."

Joshua saw a dense core of heavy metals inside each planet, even in the gaseous giants, as different elements and complex particles were knocked out of orbit only to be caught up in the swirling vortex of the outer planets forming.

The Technician continued. "Some planets are ideal candidates for life to emerge. They have dense but light atmospheres, rotate slow enough that they are able to heat up when facing the star, and cool off considerably when facing away from it. This creates the thermodynamic energy that allows the air to move and pulse enough to carry dust and bacteria around with it and allow enough natural chaos to stimulate evolution. Yet it still maintains a certain degree of predictable stability to allow life to emerge cautiously. These planets are naturally suited for life to emerge. Others require more nurturing."

Even as the Technician spoke, Joshua watched a planet emerge from the cloud, still steaming and gassing and spewing magma into the atmosphere. The friction at the core was high enough to keep the dense rock liquid and to allow the various elements to form into their most efficient molecular bonds and escape. Hydrogen and oxygen merged in massive quantities, forming water molecules. The heat allowed it to expand and push through the soft molten rock and escape in geysers of steam. The steam quickly condensed into droplets of water and fell back to the surface as liquid. Very rapidly this water began to pool, transferring the heat from the semi-molten rock into the air with the wind and steam and falling again as liquid water as it cooled.

Those pools turned into ponds, the ponds into lakes, and the lakes into oceans. The steam vents left gaps that allowed the liquid water to penetrate back into the crust. That water found pockets of crystalline sodium chloride, formed from the same process and displaced upward from the core by denser materials. The water dissolved the crystals and changed the composition of the water, filling it with dissolved solids, adding grit to its force. That salt reacted with other elements locked in the rock beneath the water, and that reaction changed the surface. No longer pitted and upheaved, it became smooth as the salt water carried the fractured sediment across every jut and crevice, sanding and polishing the ocean floors. Every day the water heated and the excited molecules moved faster and expanded slightly. Every night it cooled, and the molecules settled. This pulsing, breathing repetition weathered the rough surface. The atmosphere too thin to fully insulate the surface; the droplets of water froze and cracked the rock. The next day the ice would melt, and water would again cover the rock and fill the gap that had cracked open the night before.

This erosion took millions of years, but merely a blink of the eye as Joshua observed it. There was no more mystery to the formation. The gases kept escaping, the water kept falling, the salt kept dissolving, and the cracks kept growing.

He'd once heard an ancient theory that there were continental plates floating around bumping into each other, seemingly defiant of the laws of physics. It was easily debunked in the observance of this chaos. Joshua laughed. So much of what they'd been taught as fact failed the test of reality.

Joshua observed as the downward force of the water carved through lighter materials, creating tides as the water at each end simultaneous heated and cooled, dragging sediment with it. The softest materials were carved first, leaving deep ruts at the edge of the hard crust. The deeper the waters were, the farther under the shelf the waters carved as the pressure at the bottom, coupled with the thermodynamic tidal forces that moved the water, gave lateral and vertical force to the carving of the rock. These undermined shelves, heavy with dense materials trying to migrate to the core, sought to displace the less dense water that undermined the shelf and caused natural fissures to begin to appear above. Fault lines slumped and shifted with the planet's rotational forces. The tension created frictional energy, and volcanoes emerged along the line where the break would eventually occur. Gases escaped, creating violent eruptions that sent shock waves throughout the crust, causing violent earthquakes in the process.

Joshua watched islands forming in these bodies of water. The center of the oceans became a swirling vortex of their own. The sediment torn from the shelf migrated toward the center—chipping, grinding, colliding with everything it touched and creating more sediment. At the center of the vortex, islands began to form from the steady pressure and the constant motion of the water around this growing pile. Frictional heat that melted the sand and rock erupted when the bubbling internal cauldron formed gases from the reaction of complex molecules breaking apart to form stronger molecular bonds with other elements. The external pressure of the oceans constantly deposited sediment and pushed the molten rock through the path of least resistance to the surface where they gassed out. The ash and rock redeposited on the surface of the growing volcano, growing larger and larger and eventually overcoming the surface of the water, where it grew still faster and faster as the pressure of the water no longer cooled and crushed the airy charred sediment back into sand. Rainwater and algae found sanctuary in the porous rocks.

The surfaces of the larger landmasses were pocked with rocks made of varying elements. If an element was particularly resistant to change, the water and air flowed around it, affecting it less than the elements surrounding it, leaving behind veins of dense minerals and crystals.

The water transferred energy from the sea to the sky, and evaporation fell back as rain. The pockets of salt within the crust eventually dissolved completely away forming caverns. When enough calcium and other dissolved elements filled the gaps and the frictional heat from inside the planet slowly evaporated the moisture back through the microscopic pores of the rock above, the vaults sealed, and the water in the ground was trapped, only to emerge from time to time as a spring when a crack formed and created a pathway for it to spout forth.

The core grew more and more dense as the materials with highest mass migrated inward and formed new elements, some of which would never find their way to the surface.

The atmosphere, stable yet reactive, was made up of the lowest mass gases. The crust made up of the lowest mass metals and transition metals. Carbon reacted with both to create the majority of the surface and atmosphere.

Some of these planets held a glimmer of life that spread and collapsed and spread again. Over time it grew large then collapsed, spread again, encountered other life and fought, collapsed, and grew again.

Joshua cried out, pointing to the emerging civilizations, "Look, there they are. That's life; that's people!"

"Yes," the Technician replied, sounding as if he'd seen it hundreds of times. "Observe them as closely as you can to see how everything takes shape. You will be following a very similar pattern in your system. Every observation you can take in will be helpful to you."

Eventually, one species emerged and dominated. While most collapsed again and disappeared, they were soon replaced by another. This process played out over and over at astronomical speeds. Joshua was mystified by how the people achieved milestones of culture that allowed them to go from common beasts to advanced civilizations, but it occurred the same way every time. There would be vast biodiversity, and then suddenly a civilization would arise, leaving a scar across the surface, smothering everything in its reach, and then it would recede, much like a tide. What remained were tide pools of civilization. The rest of the ecosystem would recover and erase the blemish. Then the individual tide pools would swell and collapse again.

The planets were constantly in flux and evolving with these civilizations. Though the catalyst for any rise or collapse was a mystery, Joshua saw a pattern like in the ocean tides he watched. While specific users guided these civilizations, they seemed to take on a life of their own with or without interference. While some were obviously much quicker to rise and more resilient than others, the process played out the same every single time.

After so long, despite his amazement, the same miraculous process over and over became a predictable dance, and Joshua was ready to move forward.

It was as if the simulation knew this, and a new voice resonated through the ether. "Hello, user, I am DAVI. The Digital Audio-Visual Interface. I am here to assist you in familiarizing yourself with the tools available to you and your functional abilities within your sector of the universe. Each point of light you see represents a different user from around the known user universe who has created a profile. Your individual data will be stored locally until completion of your Generated Alternate Universe Device experience. Do not be concerned for your well-being while we initialize your profile and add you to our growing network of GAUD users.

"In a moment we will begin your tutorial, and you will learn the basic user interface. Upon completion of this tutorial, you will receive your very own system star in the network where you will be in control of your own destiny. Do you want to be braver, more productive, confident, or caring? Simply use the tools available to introduce new knowledge and technology into your system. But watch out! Some actions will have side effects not initially anticipated and need to be offset with other actions. May I advise a light touch to achieve these aims? The ultimate choice is yours in the Generated Alternate Universe Device!"

As this speech went on, DAVI showed Joshua multiple tools that he could use to affect the decisions and well-being of the creatures and people in his universe. Natural disaster tools, God's aspect, divine knowledge, and several other tools would allow Joshua to interact with his world. It was designed to bring levity to the soul-crushingly massive process and had clearly been introduced after the Machine was built. It seemed out of place, as if it was meant to turn the Machine into a game, but it failed to smooth out the rough edge of the introduction from what had already been witnessed.

When he had become familiar with the tools, the intuitive response algorithm ended the tutorial, and he saw a glowing nebula against the starry background of the universe. As he moved toward it, he saw that it became a star and the core began to glow as the heavier particles displaced the lighter ones. As the density grew, the area surrounding the nuclei of the substances began merging, creating new elements, which were slowly pushed out of the core toward the surface of the emerging star. Its light was a brilliant blue-white, and its radiation and heat were enormous, but as it aged, the light dimmed and the radioactivity diminished.

In the end there were nine planets, dozens of moons orbiting the larger ones, and two main asteroid belts, where they had achieved a largely stable orbit with similar mass and velocity relative to the distance from the star. The further out the planets and meteors were, the greater their mass but the lighter the elements that made them up. Even in the nebula, elements like water were common and made their way to the outer edge where they collected and formed celestial bodies. The slower their orbit, the larger they were as the inward pressure was not great enough to compact the molecules to their most efficient density.

It seemed like hundreds of millions of years had passed, but time had also gone quickly. Joshua felt paralyzed with excitement at what he had just witnessed. He had never seen anything like it. He understood completely what had happened and, most importantly, why it had happened.

The solar system wasn't yet finished stabilizing when Joshua heard the voice of the Technician from somewhere in the void. "Joshua, your family is all in here. They are going to be monitoring for the time being. Try not to make it too boring for them. Get life going as quickly as you can. How much time do you think has passed where you are?"

"I can't tell. A trillion years?"

"In the real world it has only been about fifteen minutes. In here it has been about a hundred trillion years, which is inconsequential considering how little involvement you had in it. You can slow time down when you need to simply by adjusting the clock speed."

Joshua looked around. "I don't see a clock."

"The planets in your system are the clock. The galaxy is another clock, the universe is another clock, and so on. At this point, the only one you need to be concerned with is the star system. Each planet has an independent orbit speed, and when they all line up, this is basically midnight on our analog clocks."

Joshua broke in, "What does that mean, though? Will the star explode or something?"

"When?" The simple reply dripped with disdain for such an ignorant question.

"When the clock strikes midnight." Joshua persisted.

"No. This isn't a fairy tale here. You are in control. If you want midnight to mean doom and gloom, you have to make that happen. But why you would want to do something so arbitrary and superstitious is entirely up to you to answer. Shall we continue?"

Joshua tried to nod, shamed by his question, but in the void that is a meaningless gesture and he was forced to croak out the affirmative. "Yes."

Without hesitation, as if rehearsed a thousand times, the Technician continued. "We will continue until you are able to pass all the tests. You can ignore the clock if you want to, slow it down, or speed it up during certain periods, such as during your breeding processes. Your creation won't notice anything. As I mentioned before, you will be able to sense every thought and action of every creature. They are all part of you. If you sense danger in some action, slow the clock down and pick your way through to find the best solution. As long as some life exists in the system, you can start again. I can step in and help you along if something goes wrong, but I can only get you back to the basic level. The rest is up to you.

"I have tools of my own, which I will use to test you from time to time. You will be able to sense my movements, but you won't necessarily see my actions. I merely plant seeds to grow the weeds you need to pluck. Your family will be able to protect certain aspects of your personality even though they can't interact with you. When they feel that you have reached a state of higher understanding and their selections are no longer endangered, you will be nearing the end of your trial. I apologize in advance for what I have to put you through, but you will be better off in the end. Well, it looks like there are only a few wandering bodies left, so we can begin."

Those words, so blithely stated hung in Joshua's mind. *For what I have to put you through.* The dread he felt was magnified by the casual delivery.

At that instant Joshua felt something new occur. On all the planets a stirring had been taking place. The combination of elements had been sizzling and reforming into tight structures, and the chemical process allowed certain substances to be formed, lacking electrons or containing an abundance of them. Alkaline or acidic, seeking equilibrium and neutrality, the murky pools were buzzing with static. The stealing and giving of these electrons energized these pools, and the complex chemical clusters began to generate their own motive force from the electrostatic movement. Life, in its most rudimentary form, emerged from the cauldron of creation, little more than a complex chemical compound of stable molecules lacking a single electron to make them whole.

Joshua had observed this repeatedly in the formation of the universe, but this time he felt the fizzing and cracking and melding.

The Technician's voice echoed through the ether. "You are witnessing the self-sustaining engine of creation. Once this chemical and physical process is started, it is very difficult to stop entirely, as you will find out."

"What do you mean, I'll 'find out'?" Joshua felt even more alarmed as the menacing words were thrown haphazardly in his direction.

"Testing will begin soon, but you have time. Play. Practice. Enjoy this experience as best you can."

As the Technician spoke, gases, liquids, and solids emerged from the fire in the planetary body and formed molecular structures. As they continued to interact, they formed larger and larger structures of chemically stable bonds. Some elements found a perfect harmony with other single elements; others needed a combination of elements to create a perfect balance. It was as if they were eating one another, stealing from, and destroying one another based on what they needed, with the larger molecules consuming more and more of the free elements to create a harmonious balance. But the larger the molecules grew, the weaker their bonds, and other smaller elements and molecules would tear them apart and try to fit the chemical compounds together with themselves. The simpler the chemical compound was, the more prolific it became.

Even as the spheres of gas and metal and matter and vacuum were forming, Joshua could hear the faint whisper of life emerging, a cacophony of organisms formed by the chemical process and awakened by the electrostatic friction. Then came the screams of death as they were overtaken by the tumult of a system uncertain of itself. The screams became static, a constant din over the individual planets. The process for life existed all the same. While one organism cried its last, another screamed its presence at birth. Life was there. It would remain, and it would grow and fade, and it would continue forward in halting spurts, but it would continue despite the environment's ferocity.

Each whisper filled Joshua with wonder. He felt himself in every life form—in the protozoa that swam across an acrid pool. He could hear his voice in every cry and feel the pain of every torn cilia in the microcosm of his own mind.

No amount of study had prepared him for this sudden and perfect understanding of the emergence of life. He felt naked and free of all expectation at that moment. To see the event awed him. He watched the birth of his own consciousness.

I t didn't take long for life to adapt and find a natural rhythm. Pools began teeming with single-celled organisms. Some were just blobs, absorbing nutrients and moving on. With feeler cilia poking out all sides, they moved with the current of the water, sensing its flavor to find their next meal.

Another was longer and darted to and fro, coiling up and thrusting forward with ease to attack both free nutrients and other organisms. Others were stationary and grabbed at whatever passed by.

As Joshua watched the most basic life forms swimming, the buzz in his mind told him these were the first part of his education.

The Technician spoke in his unemotional, almost bored way. "These are the very foundation of your personality. They are the autonomic nervous system—what makes up the very end, or beginning, of the signals your brain receives and processes. You can play with them if you wish."

"If this is part of my nervous system, how will this not cause permanent damage?" Joshua asked while observing this chaotic choreography.

"Everything here is merely a representation of these parts of your being, not your actual being. But any damage done in here will be felt in your real body as your real brain is rewired by these events. But as you know, you can cause such devastation through negligence that you can actually die here. Think of each orbiting body as a different organ in your real body. Stopping the machine that creates the process you see before you can be fatal, just as shutting down the organ itself is fatal. You will eventually mold these protozoa into species that will become a civilization. Civilization will always expand, so once you have succeeded in the final test, you can be assured the civilization you leave behind will optimize the rest of these planets for their benefit, which will be like optimizing the function of the organs of your body in real time. The civilization is your brain; as it develops, it is rewiring your real brain. That is what the Machine does."

"What are the tests for? Can't everyone simply be molded to the level of civilization that optimizes them?"

"Yes, and no. The tests are to ensure that our society gets a citizen that understands the concepts of life and understands the importance of vigilance and how we are all connected. Simply giving people the gift of this long life without the necessary hardships and humility that come with the struggle to create that outcome would leave only a subconscious understanding, and the foibles and failures of our nature would still dominate. The gift of the Machine would be neutralized by our own self-destruction. The Machine is a very dangerous tool in the wrong hands. Its gifts come with terrible responsibility, which is why people like me are here to ensure that no one is allowed to leave without understanding all the struggles and failures of our nature. This is not speculation; this had to be learned the hard way."

Joshua thought about that for a moment. "What would stop

someone from sneaking in and experiencing it without someone like you there?"

"Aside from the locks on the doors, the power-up sequences, the sign-in credentials, the calibration, the alignment of the sensors, and the fact that the terminals all now require a minimum of two people to run? The universe cannot be started without someone in your chair. And the user cannot leave without someone in my chair. But the final reason is that everyone who goes through this experience knows how vital it is to retain absolute purity of the product. You will never hear of it anymore, but those who use the Machine maliciously are hunted down and destroyed. No trial, no excuses. There is no exception. That is the way it is, and for the rest of our collective lifetime, that is the way it will remain."

"So everyone is doomed to this fate for—"

The Technician cut him off, "Everyone is *saved* by this fate. You will undoubtedly understand why as we progress."

Joshua focused on one pool. He found one of the organisms and watched it for a while. It seemed to prefer the static prey over the mobile ones and picked at the cilia growing from them. It was slow-moving—only fast enough to outrun its prey—and slow-consuming. In the few thousand generations, it had evolved into little more than a blob. Joshua began looking around the pool for something more aggressive. He concocted a scheme to destroy all the passive organisms, leaving only the aggressive ones and the static prey. He did this by isolating the slow, squishy "cows," as he called them, from the aggressive streamlined "lions" by chasing them to different areas of the pool and waiting for the water to evaporate from the thermal and atmospheric heat.

In their isolation the cows consumed all the available static shrubs and quickly fell into starvation. But Joshua found that a few with slightly different genetic structures were willing to consume the corpses of the now dead cows. They continued to reproduce, and while the cows and the shrubs were quickly eradicated, these omnivorous protozoa clung to life by consuming their own dead.

Joshua asked the Technician, "Is this where all omnivores start out? As cannibals?"

The Technician stated flatly, "Not always, but they almost always start out as herbivores. No dietary changes come without crises. Even ours developed from people long ago trying things in moments of starvation. Thus, this little organism you are toying with became an omnivore like the bears of our world. Slow and lethargic but opportunistic eaters. It is the most adaptable survival strategy."

These omnivore "bears" were purely accidental, but Joshua could see the sense of it. Consume whatever is available. When the water levels rose again, these omnivores became the most prolific and diverse in the pool.

Joshua noticed four successful strategies that served to feed the others. The lions ate the bears and the cows, controlling the populations of each. The bears ate the cows and the shrubs and the lions when they died. The cows ate the shrubs. And the shrubs ate everything that died, decayed, or passed through the organelles of other molecular life and processed the raw nutrients from the rock that held the pool.

Again, the Technician spoke. "These organisms can only digest so much. The rest comes out as waste or, in the case of the plants, as a form of fruit." As he said this, the plants bore their microorganic fruits, which the herbivores and omnivores feasted on. "When your herbivores can no longer obtain nutrients, they begin to starve." Again, the Technician forced the pool to act out his words—the plants died, and the herbivores clustered around the increasingly sparse plant life in that pool.

"You are changing the whole pool in real time as you talk," Joshua said in amazement.

"Lots of practice. It's all the natural process, just accelerated."

The explanation went on. It was fascinating to Joshua to finally see in action what he'd been told about in biology lessons. He shared his own explanation of what he saw.

"The bears, forced to fight with the lions for survival, have developed little arms to deflect them and thicker skins to withstand attacks. The lions became quicker, and I see a tail emerging and long, pointed mouths that could penetrate their prey and eat them from the inside out." Joshua was speaking as the teacher, but he was the student too, voicing the explanation he was building in his mind.

Joshua marveled at how quickly species could diverge and become entirely new organisms suited to their local environment. Each pool seemed to sprout visionary new concepts for the way life could emerge. The speed at which it formed was astronomical.

The shrubs consumed the excrement of the other organisms but also, and primarily, excavated the hard rock around them, exploring for various minerals in the rock itself. On finding something, the shrub would proliferate unconcerned with the pool itself, and from this the cows would flourish, feasting on the fruits borne by the shrubs. The lions abounded, and the bears thrived, all because of a small pocket of minerals the shrubs had excavated.

With different minerals came different varieties of shrubs. The epigenetic effect on the same organism consuming different minerals meant the organism changed to make optimal use of the nutrients available in its environment. A divergence occurred. The whole microecosystem changed, driven by the very composition of the environment. The lions, the bears, the cows, and the shrubs all adapted to it, so they became different from their cousins.

Joshua kept playing with this one pool, allowing certain traits to thrive while others died. There was no method to his madness, but there was almost nothing he could do to completely destroy one group or another. He tried to kill them all off at one point, but again, this only created more diversity, and the system reordered itself into a cycle of death and consumption leading to rebirth.

This was frustrating at first. There was nothing he could do to destroy the life in this tiny pool. As he gave up he was suddenly aware of the entire world and the life going through the same rhythms in every pool and ocean, and on every rock and even in the air, though to a much lesser extent. The ebb and flow of the tide pools' water spread these organisms to other more homogenous pools, where the chaos forced adaptation. He was suddenly filled with a sense of hope and pride that no matter what actions he took, he seemed incapable of destroying the life that had emerged in the mixing of elements and the heating and cooling, pressurizing and depressurizing of the local environment.

He wondered, though, what it *would* take to sterilize an environment of even the most rudimentary microbial life. He had the idea that he could change the weather pattern to make the environment inhospitable to life. Then he wondered how inhospitable it would have to be to completely destroy the life in his tiny experiment.

The star system was full of random orbiting bodies he could use to affect the planet. He had observed countless times in the billion years or so the effect that the tilt of the planet toward the star had on climate and weather. He opted to change the tilt of the planet.

As he was selecting the asteroid he suddenly thought of the squirrel—an ultimately pointless act that had yielded absolutely no satisfaction and only caused harm. Still, he hurled the asteroid at the planet, remembering the admonition to use a light touch. When the asteroid crashed into the planet in the chaotic display, he thought of the fire and the disappointment on the faces of the townsfolk. As the weather was changing, he looked around the world from beyond the pool he'd been so focused on and felt the cries of trillions of dying organisms. Many incinerated in the impact; many more were affected by the ash and debris that erupted from the wound in the molten crust of the planet. The subsequent blackness cooled the planet, leaving pools frozen solid where there should have been no ice, and the rocks on which the pools had formed began to crack from the expansion of their cargo. The entire world was changing as a result of his drastic and shortsighted decision in the interest of experimentation.

"What is the point of that?" The Technician demanded coldly.

"I wanted to see what it would take to destroy the whole pool."

"Did we not have this conversation before? I told you that the process creates the life. Changing that process destroys that life. Can you not think beyond your own limited vision? You could have achieved the same result by diverting the internal heat source from the water in the crust. Did you not see that you might bring yourself to the verge of death with such a foolish action?"

Joshua had never heard or felt such fury. "I . . . I wanted to see—"

The Technician cut him off bitterly. "You can't see—even what's right before your eyes. You act without thinking, and you think about the least important things. You are a fool. I am not here to protect you from yourself. I will allow you to die if that is the course you are going to take. You will live with this error. Just be glad you are lucky enough to have lived through it." The Technician punctuated that statement with a bitter and perpetual silence.

Joshua felt sick with guilt over his actions. He still didn't know the full consequence of them, but he was frozen with inaction even as his planet was rapidly covering with ice. The constant din of life was fading noticeably.

For eons after, the planet was a frozen wasteland, the pulse of life almost nonexistent. Yet some remained. Those on the equator were better suited for the sudden freeze as they did not encounter the worst of the icing over. Atmosphere, cold and still at the poles, was still fluid there.

Shame over his brutishness tore at Joshua. His eagerness to experiment had left much of the world void of life, and in that moment, he knew that there were ways to destroy all life. And he knew how the others had managed to kill themselves in the Machine. He could still feel the pulse of life though. He searched all over his young planet and the fabric of his very being to find the life he had so haphazardly offended. Finally, he found a tiny colony of microorganisms clinging to the underside of a sterile pool of alkaline water. This was not the only colony he knew of, but hope grew again in him that all was not lost.

As he examined the colony, he found the same basic system that he'd encountered in the first pool: a vast array of static, passive, aggressive, and passive-aggressive organisms in a thriving ecosystem. The decay of the other organisms had provided enough nourishment to the static organisms to allow the food chain to survive. He wanted to nurture this colony. Make it strong again. Restore the conditions to ensure the survival of these living parts of his being.

He first tried to slow the planet's rotation. This only seemed to exacerbate the problem. The ice covering the planet reflected the star's light back into space, and the dark side got colder. As the catastrophe continued, he sensed the faint wisp of life extinguishing all over the planet's surface, while the bitterest and hardiest of organisms still clung desperately to it.

He tried volcanoes, but there was too little movement on the planet to provide the necessary friction to create the magma chambers. Nothing seemed to work.

He begged the Technician, "Please, I need guidance. I am out of ideas."

His pleas were met with silence. The Technician seemed to be making a pointed effort to force Joshua to figure it out on his own. A test?

He fumbled with moving ice to allow the light of the day to penetrate the dark water and provide some heating. The ice moved but created a more impenetrable surface. The light the star provided was offset by the mountain of fractured ice. "Please, I need help."

Finally, the Technician responded. "You haven't tried everything. You stopped the planet's rotation with a meteor; you can restart it with one as well." His answer sounded cold and flat.

Joshua was taken aback. "Is there any other way?"

Silence.

"Please, I don't want to make a mistake again."

"You can let your planet slowly die as you fumble around, or you can make the difficult choice to do what is necessary. That is the only other option for you. It's up to you. Death is not so bad. Just inhabit the bodies of your creation as they are doing it, and you'll see." The Technician spoke even more icily. "You have created plenty of death already for you to make opportunities to comprehend it."

Joshua was silent but felt the shame of the damage he had wrought. He knew the Technician was right. It was his responsibility to repair the damage of his own naïveté.

He brought in an asteroid from the nearby belt and sent it on a collision course with his planet. It was a clunky effort, and several other asteroids were knocked out of orbit and went careening in various directions. But his appeared to be on course. It was a massive, metal-rich asteroid and seemed to be exactly what he needed.

As it entered the thin atmosphere, it barely fizzled, but its impact caused a shock wave throughout the planet's surface and a cloud of steam and ash and molten rock to spew over a third of the planet's surface. Immediately, he felt the death of his little pool colony that he was trying to protect. It was not directly in the asteroid's path, but Joshua's panic had led him to make a mistake in his calculation of its area of impact, and it struck just above the equator toward the northern pole.

The asteroid impact didn't change the tilt by much—half a degree maybe. But the impact managed to accelerate the rotation of the planet, which allowed the internal friction to expand the magma layer beneath the crust. The subsequent shortening of the day led to smaller nighttime decreases and allowed the ice to recede from the equator.

The dense metal-rich asteroid gouged a deep hole in the surface. The force and heat of the impact ejected the lightest dust out of the atmosphere into a cloud above that began forming a loosely packed moon. The ash and water vapors that remained in orbit fell to the surface again. The denser chunks of the crust orbited for many years before falling and pelting the whole surface with fiery explosions of superheated rock. Life was, for a brief moment, extinguished.

It was not well done. It was not graceful. It was a catastrophe caused by ignorance and curiosity. How foolish and irrational he was.

He felt numb.

8

Joshua knew life could be extinguished—how easy it was to break the ecosystem. He *knew*. Yet he'd persisted like a child, pushing the boundaries of patience and being surprised by the reaction. He had *killed*. He destroyed the world. He destroyed *himself*.

He felt each tormented flight of terror in the apocalypse he had unleashed. He heard each fatal scream as the tide pools boiled away in a flash of steam and vapor. He absorbed every instant as the world was scorched and blackened. This was his fault, and the effects were his to discover.

Slowly, life returned. The engine that created the mechanism for life had been restarted. A hundred million years had passed. Joshua had stopped interacting with the world, afraid to cause more harm. Ice still covered large swaths of the planet, but it was receding.

Then Joshua heard the Technician say, "You have killed your

brain's connection to your skin, but not permanently. You will not feel cold or heat as intensely as you did before, more like a light tapping against you when the rain is in its heaviest downpour. You may get frostbite and not notice it until you look at your fingers. There really is no telling what the extent will be until you are finished here. All I can say is, it is a common but necessary lesson for those who wish to survive, which is why you were allowed to learn it. You must find a lighter touch if you wish to preserve your well-being. You are responsible for your own growth. You are responsible *to* yourself for your own carelessness. You are responsible!"

The Technician's words burned like acid in Joshua's ears, but he'd already learned the truth of them.

"I'm sorry." Even Joshua's voice sounded like it was ready to burst with barely contained sorrow.

"You apologize to me, but I am not affected by your decisions. Your family just watched you attempt to kill yourself, helpless from their positions to do anything to save you. They are the ones you should be apologizing to."

For all that time, Joshua had forgotten that there were more than just him and the Technician in the Machine. His heart dropped as he felt the weight of his actions even more.

The Technician continued his vicious admonishments. "Had you *experimented* in this way with a more advanced society, you would have caused serious brain damage to yourself. You can recover from anything, but total annihilation of your higher functions is akin to lobotomy. You have no idea of the power you wield and the danger of that power in the hands of someone who doesn't take it seriously."

"I think I understand now. I'm sorry. Please tell my family how sorry I am. I'll be more responsible, I swear."

"They can hear you. But your words are meaningless unless you demonstrate your lesson with every action moving forward." With that the Technician went silent and left Joshua feeling empty and alone on a stage under a spotlight in front of a disapproving and critical audience.

"I will do better," he promised the void.

⟨⟩

Joshua felt life on the other planets as well, but they were all very slow in their development. The majority were too cold and distant to adequately spawn. Their mix of elements was off, such that the basic molecules to start the process weren't able to form in large enough quantities. They weren't fluid enough in the colder depths of space to warrant his attention. "Besides," he told himself, "I would only snuff out those organisms too."

He waited and waited, his self-pity stagnating any activity that might progress the planet beyond its current state.

It took a long time for Joshua to sort himself out emotionally. He chose to ignore the birth pains of life still emerging and adapting to the new environment. He had to consciously dismiss the admirable strength of purpose life took on. The prime directive to reproduce overcame everything else, even certain death.

Joshua spent much of this time inhabiting the bodies of his creation. He felt what it was like to be torn apart as prey, digested and dispersed as broken molecules. He knew what it was like to feel the gnawing hunger of an organism on the brink of death, and to catch and destroy another organism to quell that hunger for just a little while longer. He felt the pull of his being divided by mitosis, the pleasure of seeing a living reflection of himself, and the agony of watching that reflection face its own tragic end.

Life in every form was miserable. It was a struggle. It was tragic. And it hurt. Joshua wanted to feel that hurt, to let out his pain and anguish and show demonstrably to all those who observed him that he was sad and sorry. The self-flagellation was itself a learning experience.

Life persisted nonetheless, one more molecule broken free

from the rock, digested and defecated, consumed by something else, and providing a slight increase in the amount of life that could be supported. Life found moments of prosperity, though, and that brought contentment and peace, which became a goal of its own.

Joshua thought of a lesson from school, which taught, "Life is a tool of nature that helps to reorder the static parts of the hard, chemical spheres we call planets. It sorts the elements into component parts. Metals are clustered together; carbon, gases, all elements, and complex chemicals are exposed, released, and sorted by the various efforts of life. The loosening of the surface from digging allows the denser elements to migrate downward. Lighter elements are carried upward by living organisms and introduced into the organic life cycle at the surface. The displacement of the lighter elements allows denser ones to be sifted through the churn, to get deeper and deeper, overcoming the barricades of the planet's crust. These holes release other elements trapped in the rock and expose fissures that allow water and air to penetrate and transform the elements themselves into something new. Life produces the artificial churn that allows nature to sort itself into its aggregate parts."

It had been difficult to visualize when he learned that lesson. While the thought provided some foundation for the purpose of life, it did little to satisfy the lack of meaning for individual lives. Each species played a part, and each individual had to find meaning within that purpose. But the meaning was elusive to Joshua.

There was no reason for that thought to come to mind now, but something about it made him feel better. Even as life was slow to emerge, it had a function in the universe that made it inevitable. He could sense that he was through his slump.

As he picked through the organisms and drove each one to destruction, he found the pool forever altered by the changing balance he created. He often chose the fastest organism, or the toughest, and exhausted their abilities until death or boredom seized him. Those beneficial traits were eradicated little by little, and the species that would have benefited from it suffered for many generations to come.

Death was almost insignificant to Joshua now. Even the pain of it was a dull experience.

Without conscious effort, Joshua began to manipulate the world again. It was no longer satisfying to simply allow the pools to evolve based on the lives of individual organisms. He wanted to shape something on a larger scale.

He dipped into a pool and counted the organisms by species. Maybe he would create a plague in one just to kick-start some diversity again. He watched as the organisms grew larger and larger. Each time he saw an organism grow to become the largest in the pool, he marked its genetic patterns, compared it to others sharing those patterns, and then killed that one. Its death fed the larger food chain and allowed fewer organisms to die in the process as the whole chain feasted on the corpse and flourished because of the increased nutrients in their diets.

The colonies increased when they became more concentrated instead of scattered across the vast puddle, running into each other by chance. Yet their proximity produced more homogeneity.

A greenish film began to grow on one of the rocks in a southern pool. It was at a latitude south of the equator, so it experienced slightly more heating and cooling than the equatorial or polar pools. As the seasons changed, so did the depth of the pool. Some of this film became exposed on the barren rock without the watery ecosystem to nourish it. Some of the organisms were able to adapt to both aquatic and arid conditions. When the colony had spread beyond the covering of the pool in all seasons, the organisms adapted to life on dry land. The extremes enabled the organisms to expand to their limit, and catastrophe would ensure only the toughest survived to reproduce.

The organisms found their niche from every possible direction. Some swam on the ocean of air that surrounded the algae forests.

Others lived in the canopy of the forest, high above the predatory organisms that stalked them on the ground. The canopy dwellers snatched the flying organisms from the air while others slowly grazed on the algae itself. Some still fought for survival on the forest floor, outrunning, outbreeding, or outfighting their predators.

Still Joshua admired how, even at this level, life behaved the same, the world looked the same, and even the sky hadn't changed. While he imagined the stars in constellations, steadily morphing, twisting, and distorting as the galaxy that his star revolved around pulled those points of light to the center, he thought about the nights he had admired those little points of light as a child. He'd sung songs and traced imaginary lines between them to make shapes.

As a child, already so long ago.

9

Joshua's strategy had worked. The pools were now filled with life. The shores of the pools were growing, and larger organisms had emerged, changing the landscape around them. The cycle of consumption, defecation, and decay ensured that every organism faced peril and found pieces of paradise in the tiny oceans and islands teeming with life. Stress and satisfaction created the pendulum of extremes forcing the evolution of the organisms that filled every gap in the tiny landscape.

This process continued until the entire landscape was transformed. The creatures grew larger and larger until looming masses towered over the landscape. All the life in the world had become linked. At every level Joshua was able to affect the outcomes of the systems. He was eventually able to stop the growth and movement of individual cells that could shut down a whole being. He could stop a single cell in the heart of a giant and send it into ventricle fibrillation. Once the heart cramped up, it stopped pumping blood and the creature died. A single cell did that. But it was knowing the right cell to kill, and the right spot. Given the amount of time and the quantity of creatures wandering the vast planet, there were plenty of subjects to test his skills on.

Joshua became fascinated by the ripple effects of one action. He could feel it and even see it. While those directly influenced by the shock wave had no idea that they were part of it, Joshua could see the wave of consequence moving through the living landscape of these creatures. He could make ripples simply by killing the right creature at the right time. Then as the shock waves converged, he could see a magnified effect.

Sometimes the effect was as benign as to change the direction of a herd of animals, but other times it caused a chain reaction that collapsed an ecosystem. Over time, though, Joshua learned the lever and the fulcrum that would move all of his creation and devised complex strategies to shape the world.

He could make that same ripple occur at a molecular level. He saw into the DNA of every creature and how each amino acid was structured with a different combination of chemicals. He saw that the amino acids depended on certain nutrients from the environment to be able to reproduce. When they were deprived of those nutrients, the amino acids failed to form genetic alleles, and those traits withered away. The less critical to the survival of the cell the traits were, the more likely they were to wither when the nutrients were merely deficient rather than absent. When they were absent, the cells couldn't form, so they died. Then the creature died.

He found a way to push evolution in any direction he wished. He merely reduced or increased the availability in the environment of certain food sources. This was already the case due to changing seasons, which caused creatures of the same species born in different seasons to manifest different traits and personalities. But he was able to create the same effect simply by creating the shock waves until he had guided a more prolific resource competitor to the environment, redirected predators, or isolated environments to deprive creatures of their staple foods.

The more he practiced, the more adept he became at it. He was able to keep his attention on tens of thousands of individual lives and shape them deftly into tools to shape the greater environment. He could predict how they would evolve even as the traits that were nourished duplicated in the DNA structure. He saw it all and understood it. Most importantly, he learned that he could trigger evolutionary changes very simply and permanently.

Initially, Joshua was mostly making arbitrary choices to see how each would affect the system. He began sorting the traits into categories of good and bad according to his own desires and targeting those whose traits he thought were bad. When he introduced a plague targeting one creature, allowing its prey or competition to flourish, they strained the ecosystem by overconsuming. They squeezed out others and devastated the environment.

For all his practice, he couldn't remember everything he learned, and he failed to understand the principles. The Technician ensured that there were always new lessons, new challenges to face, and new techniques to master.

As the world changed throughout the millennia, Joshua's thoughts often wandered to himself and his society. He realized that his own evolution had reached a certain climax. His own classes suggested similar beasts had once roamed his world. The people he knew were all the result of this process. Then he realized, *We are only the most advanced so far.*

It was easy to pick phenotypes at random. Not knowing what the results would be meant he had to make predictions. He started shaping the creatures of the world in his own image. To create short-snouted creatures meant he needed to select those with shorter and shorter snouts. From hairy ones, he chose the balding or thin-haired ones. He no longer needed to use such cumbersome tools as plagues and disasters to do his work. He could merely shape the local environment, allowing the favored creatures to carve out a larger and larger niche in the ecosystem. He could target one fanged beast at a time and kill them to protect his creatures. He could perform miracles that saved his creatures just in time. But he found that it was best to sit back and be objective with them, watching their reaction and interaction with the environment to see how well they coped. Yet these creatures seldom survived.

They were made in his image, or got as close as he could make them, but those traits that were acceptable for an advanced civilization of an evolved species were detrimental to those still evolving. Hairlessness meant the creatures were more sensitive to weather. Shorter noses meant they had fewer scent receptors and were less capable of finding food or discovering predators. The phenotypes of his own species were a disadvantage to those he tried to shape in that image.

It was those he had forgotten that proved the most resilient. The ubiquitous vermin that fed on everything were the most adaptable, shaped by the environment and necessity, rather than his clumsy hand. Even as he dabbled in vanity, his whole world eventually became overrun by these rats. They reminded him of the town's mascot. The rats remained simple, feeble, and a good meal for whatever could catch them. They adapted to any condition. The beasts that were plagued dominated after they recovered, and the creature was able to fight the more common viruses that tormented them before. The creatures that fed on them similarly faced a mutated version of the same plague, and though they faced catastrophic dieback, they soon rebounded stronger for it. It was tough love—more effective than protection and isolation because it forced his creatures to adapt to the real world, not the petri dish of an isolated environment. The rats were the easiest to mold. Of all the creatures in this world, they were the most agreeable to him, and though they were ugly, they proved to be the perfect clay to mold the world.

But even the rats had competition from the bottom rung of the food chain. Little scavenger lizards emerged and went head to head with them. The Technician made himself known during this time. Whatever species Joshua favored, he modeled one to push it to near extinction. Those that were weak or slow or had specific traits that were unsuitable to this challenge were eradicated. They competed for resources or preyed on Joshua's creatures or simply drove them mad from constant noise and harassment. Very few survived the harassment, but those that did were much stronger for it.

The Technician was ruthless in these challenges, and Joshua was constantly frustrated with them. But in the end, some did survive. And the species experienced a population explosion. Though not formed from the best of their kind, they were molded by Joshua's guidance and proofed by the Technician's challenges.

The Technician made creatures that were large and savage, scaly and cold-blooded. Despite Joshua's efforts to match them, they were tyrannical in their dominance of the world. Mammals were Joshua's favorites, but the larger they were, the better the snack they proved to be, and millions of species went extinct from the melee. Only the humbler, smaller mammals managed to avoid this fate and, for the most part, did so by breeding rapidly. The rats were no exception. As a result, Joshua's affinity for them grew as the multitude of other mammals dwindled.

Despite this, Joshua wanted to know what the Technician's creatures represented.

"They are more than a mere ripple in the pond," he told the Technician. "Why did you design them to be so monstrous?"

The Technician sounded more casual than normal when he replied. "The environment shaped them more than I did. The thick atmosphere and increased temperatures are perfect for creatures of this type. Their blood runs cold, so the increased temperature allows them to remain mobile for longer periods of the day. Warm-blooded creatures are lethargic in high heat, so they become easier prey. These beasts are not thinkers in any sense, merely instinctive. But they are necessary to evolve the creatures that will come later after you destroy these."

Joshua wasn't sure how to respond. The guilt from the previous destruction still weighed heavy on his mind. "What makes you think I will destroy these creatures?"

The Technician stated flatly, "Because everyone does. These creatures are necessary only to evolve the brain stem. There is no real affinity for them other than being a curiosity."

"Destroying them won't do much harm then?"

"Oh no, it definitely will. I expect you'll be smashing the planet with another large rock to make the climate inhospitable to them."

"Wh-why would I do that if you say it's harmful?" Joshua was incensed at how casual yet accusatory his tone was now.

"It doesn't matter. The life you have evolved won't be totally destroyed. Mammals favor cold, and that is ultimately what you will replace these creatures with. Probably with those little rats you are so fond of." The flippant air in the Technician's voice goaded Joshua toward some outcome, but he couldn't quite figure out what it was.

Joshua challenged, "I guess it's all decided then, huh? I'm completely predictable?"

"Everyone and everything ultimately is."

Joshua was reluctant to change the world so dramatically again. He practiced on the rats, used them to counter the Technician, who had become so distant and cold. So adversarial.

Despite his defiance, Joshua *did* get bored. The goliaths did what every other creature had—they grew and propagated until their environment changed and they died back. The meekest of their species—those already used to suffering—proved to be the most suited to surviving the new environment. The next generations adapted even better, were smaller, and consumed less. The environment thus recovered, and the species flourished again. The ebb and flow, the constant overcompensation, catastrophe, and adaptation, was never-ending. Survival of the fittest didn't mean the strongest, but those already used to the conditions of comparable hardship. The meekest inherited the world.

He was fairly certain that, because of their ubiquity, the rats would be preserved in the event of the major catastrophe meant to kill off the majority of the giants he despised.

Joshua stated flatly to the Technician, "You were right."

"I always am," came the reply. "But you held off much longer than I anticipated. You are surprisingly stubborn—a good trait in survival."

Joshua was silent as he went through the process of choosing his projectile. He wasn't going to pick one randomly. He remembered the stoichiometry from chemistry and planned accordingly. Though he didn't make any calculations, he remembered the formation of the universe and the feel of each element and the attraction between two distinct chemicals. He looked for the highest composition of those elements.

When he found it, he carefully displaced it from the other asteroids nearby, throwing them out of their orbits only slightly. He carefully calculated the trajectory to strike the planet in the southern hemisphere using a blow that would go against the rotation of the planet, slow it down, and cool it. The cold-blooded beasts would have very little area to keep warm, and the enormous plants would wither away.

The meteor hit just south of where Joshua had aimed. It burned hot in the atmosphere as it reacted with the molecules that floated in its path. The resulting ash blackened the sky, so light couldn't penetrate. The planet's surface temperature fell dramatically, freezing the water suddenly in many places. The denser core of the meteor unsettled the gyroscope of the planet, changing the rotational center of gravity. The ash killed off plants that depended on the sunlight to photosynthesize and feed themselves on the carbon-dioxide-rich atmosphere.

The behemoths starved as the plants died. The carrion predators lived well for a time but perished as they found less prey in the dead forests and plains. The rats, however, found plenty to eat between the fallen corpses and the withered plants. The carbon dioxide was too thin for most of the plants that remained, and they were stunted and frail where they were able to grow at all. The behemoths couldn't survive off these.

The days grew longer because of the slower rotation, and though thinned by the chemical reactions from the meteor, the slower rotation made the halo of the atmosphere larger and even thinner. The thin air allowed water to evaporate more easily, and the resulting snowfall blanketed much of the planet in snow and ice. Only a tight band of temperate warmth enabled the reptiles to cling to life.

And so, effortlessly, the dominance of the reptile was usurped by that of the humble little rats.

Joshua was proud of his work. He had effectively utilized the tools to drive the evolution of his creation. The rats had developed a variety of traits to suit their local environments. Those left in the northern and southern regions of the planet suffered grievously at first, but diversity arose from their torment, and he was rewarded in time with a broad spectrum of these warm-blooded, furry creatures filling in the niches left behind by the dying giants. Some were as ugly as the beasts they replaced and exhibited traits he didn't particularly appreciate, but he was satisfied, knowing that they were on the way to his desired outcome.

In the eons that followed, Joshua molded them into every conceivable shape. He made them large. He made them small. He made them primarily carnivorous and then vegetarian. The more he played, the more he learned about how to shape creation.

He wanted to continue in this way until he had molded these rats into a creature of his own likeness. But the voice of the Technician chimed in.

"You've played around enough. You need to set the axis back. It's time to start the next phase of testing."

Joshua's view was pulled away from his little planet back into the greater star system. The Technician showed him an asteroid and without warning sent it careening out of orbit toward the third planet.

"What are you doing?" Joshua almost screamed.

"I'm accelerating your learning. You need to redirect this asteroid to hit your planet to reset the axis and allow your creatures to expand again. It's your choice where it hits, but you need to make your decision fast. It will reach your planet's orbit in one year."

"I'm not ready yet. I just got things back in order." Joshua flicked the asteroid into a different trajectory, missing his planet.

The Technician immediately flicked another one. "That other one will come back around in a few thousand years and hit your planet then, but here's another one for you to deal with. Nature isn't about designed order. It's controlled chaos and utilizes its own energy. You have spent some three hundred million years toying with this concept and haven't progressed much. It's time I took control of your learning."

Again Joshua changed its trajectory. He was getting frustrated now. "Will you stop it? Just let me change its axis a little bit manually, and I'll let them grow again. I don't want to keep smashing meteors into the planet."

"No? You've done it so much I thought you suffered from a complete lack of creative expression. You need to set your planet to be more hospitable for life. A smaller tilt will enable life to expand much further and still ensure there are seasons to pressure them."

He knocked a dozen large asteroids out of orbit on a course for the planet. Joshua successfully parried them, but two snuck through. One struck just north of the equator and sent a shock wave halfway around the planet. The giants and furry rats alike were obliterated in the area, and still the axis was tilted too far. The second struck in the southern hemisphere, flattening the landmass between two oceans and shifting the axis toward the star by three degrees.

The converging shock waves piled dust and debris miles high, and the colliding particles and rocks became molten. This molten core destabilized the debris above it and, as it settled, caused more friction, heat, and magma. The organic matter, rock, and dissolved minerals from the waters mixed together to form explosions, blasting the mountain from the inside out. The gases bubbled out and caused the mountain to cave in. Landslides stripped away the support for the mountain peak, and the ridgeline crumbled. The added friction and weight of the resettled mass of debris pushed inward toward the molten core of the mountain, and more debris liquefied, allowing more gas to escape and more landslides to occur. Over and over this process continued until it finally settled.

The landscape was barren except for a few creatures hidden in valleys, caves, or burrows. Those not immediately killed withered from starvation. Only the smallest creatures and a few plants survived.

As the crust realigned, the metals and magnetic fields that made up the slowly churning medley of surface minerals and magnetic pull heated the crust even more, and volcanoes released the pent-up fury of the planet, melting the ice and warming the planet with ash and gases that created a thicker insulating atmosphere.

The core's magnetism was aligned with that of the star, keeping it in orbit. Slowly it absorbed the shock wave and the shifting magnetic field of the crust forced the more liquid mantle and core to realign. Though it wasn't an immediate change, it was quick enough that Joshua could see it happening without fully comprehending it. The magnetic field was thrown out of balance. He watched it dancing as it fought to reestablish equilibrium. The polarity of the core reversed.

Suddenly the whole planet was in a state of chaos. Enormous magnets repelled or attracted to each other based on the alignment of their poles. More heat, more eruptions, more catastrophic shifts in the crust created more landslides and tsunamis.

The polarity of the star, however, remained unaffected, so the planet's moon was pelted with ejected ash and debris that managed to escape the atmosphere, making it bigger even as its core flipped from the opposing polar magnetism of its planet. The poles of the star repelled the planet enough for it to lose its orbit and cool the inferno of the planet's surface enough for life to hang on. The momentum of flipping of the magnetic field allowed the south pole to catch the star's north pole, flipping it again, and the attraction locked the planet back into orbit.

——— ∞ ———

Joshua felt enraged but impotent, both for the unwarranted assault on his planet and the physical assault that this act had on his actual person. Half his planet was now desolate and its life forms barely clinging to life. The other half's creatures were in such shock from the rapid climate change that they were dropping dead from the sudden wave of disease, floods, panic, or increased pressure on their environments from creatures escaping the dead lands and wanton killings for food.

The meteors had unleashed so much energy that the skies filled with steam from the ice and blocked heat from the star. The extinction of many of the various species did not surprise Joshua. He could do nothing. He knew that taking bold action to rectify the chaos could cause even more damage and would potentially lead the planet to another billion years of quiet desolation. All he could do was watch and try to pick and choose the creatures he wanted to save.

He urged as many of every variety of creature possible toward depressions in elevated areas. Birds of every color and form found this area easily, carrying seeds they had eaten in their feces. These seeds sprouted anew after their hard shells had been digested, allowing the plants to once again take root. These depressions could hold many creatures, yet they massacred each other once they arrived.

There was nothing Joshua could do. They competed for scarce resources in a region they were largely unfamiliar with, meeting direct competition for the first time and facing off against the desperate.

Predator against predator, prey against prey, there was so much confusion and fear in the creatures that they took it out on one another. The smallest of them were able to hide in the rocks and pick at the dead littering the valley floor. The birds were well off, but they too suffered from the diseases spread by the rotten dead they feasted on. Once the melee was finished, Joshua still had a wide variety of different creatures, but they were all very sickly.

All told, the variety of his creatures had been reduced by about eighty percent. He knew they would rebound again. There were only so many ways the chemicals could arrange themselves to form life, and only so many variations in which that life could efficiently develop. He didn't know what effect this would have on his actual person. If the extinction of his microorganisms made his skin less sensitive, what would the extinction of many of these larger creatures do to him?

The Technician piped in, "You need to keep track of those other asteroids. They will be coming back shortly. Your planet still needs to be hit to straighten out the axis. I recommend you calculate their trajectories to impact on or near the dead zone so you don't kill all your creatures again."

"Why did you do that? I wasn't ready for you to test them and didn't have the chance to save the ones I wanted to keep."

"If testing were up to the student, how much learning would take place? Pressure forces the emotional response of stress, and emotions create memories. You need to lock in the lessons you had so passively been learning, and you also needed a largely blank slate to limit the creatures you are working with so you can improve what you have available to you. I have limited the number of creatures you have to worry about so you can refocus on shaping them in your image."

"I was already doing that! You're acting like you did me a favor," Joshua insisted.

"No, you were toying with it. You were a child poking at an anthill. I need you to be a farmer capable of culling his beloved herd to improve his stock. When you are able to manage more than a few billion specimens, I will allow you to continue, but my tests aren't always geared toward widespread destruction. Besides, this isn't some game you can passively play. It does have a purpose, and I am here to ensure that purpose is realized."

"What's the next test then?"

"I have an idea, but I'll be more certain by watching what you do, what you need. You have about thirty years until the first asteroid returns. Use it to fix your axial tilt. You need it to be between fifteen and twenty-five degrees to get the optimal mix of seasons for your planet to develop. I'll be watching."

Joshua raged inside, but there was nothing he could do about it. He was strapped in and wouldn't get out of the Machine until he had reached the goal, whatever that was. He saw the asteroid approaching and redirected it toward the third planet. He tried to time it just right, so the southern crater was facing the asteroid when it struck. He needed it to hit precisely so as not to kill all the creatures in his little valleys.

His anger could only be expressed with a calculated and directed effort. The emotional reaction that he might normally have was stifled in the Machine. Anger turned into bitterness; the bitterness calcified and helped to focus him. The fact that the Technician was not affected by anything inside the Machine meant there was no retaliation. Reaction only affected Joshua.

He measured everything he could. He realized that the rotation of his planet would have the opposite side of the planet facing the asteroid on impact, so he tried to slow the asteroid down. But when he did, it was thrown slightly off its trajectory so that it would only cause a glancing blow. The spin of the planet continued, and finally he pushed the asteroid straight at the planet. It crashed into the southern hemisphere just north of the second asteroid, reducing the tilt of the axis another two degrees, creating another chain reaction. Because the region hadn't returned to normal, it caused minimal damage to the ecosystem but left a massive crater which quickly flooded with water. The usual shock wave and earthquakes and tsunamis wiped out whole sanctuaries that Joshua had preserved after the previous impact.

He watched helplessly as his world was changed by the impact. Desperation and death everywhere. The fate was inevitable, the tests unavoidable. And the purpose was unforeseeable. But he was trapped here, and despite the presence somewhere in the world where his family aided him in some unknown way, he felt alone.

He alone could save himself, but he also knew he was the problem, and he had no idea how to defend against himself.

10

Joshua spent more time in the bodies of his creation. He spent less time worrying about the whole global environment but looked at the world from the perspective of the herds of mammals that were emerging from their hiding in the wreckage of the world. He soared over the ocean as a bird and watched the world reshape itself subtly but violently.

Again, he thought of his teacher's lessons. Even through the fog of daydream, he managed to capture enough details to form a faded memory. Though billions of years had ostensibly passed, the evidence he witnessed made the lessons stand out.

"The oceanic currents can change dramatically in a short time. As the heat from the star accelerates the molecular motion at the equator, the molecules of salty water bulge and press toward the poles. Cooler water falls deeper and displaces other molecules warmed by the friction of the oceanic creatures and circulates toward the surface of the water, creating current. The low-pressure, high-density cold water from the polar regions generates massive amounts of force against the rock and landmasses, and the friction from the currents creates heat, which creates more currents and more friction. The molecules bump into each other constantly, and where the landmass is more resistant to erosion, microcurrents form, creating the irregular shapes and patterns we see along coastlines. The series of irrotational vortexes affects the air above them, and a jet stream carries weather to and fro across the planet surface.

"The atmosphere behaves like the oceans. At the equator the air is rich with moisture, and that moisture causes the air to swell and press against the calmer polar air, and where they meet, huge storms emerge as these air currents seek the path of least resistance and equilibrium.

"This new current creates vortexes, which carry sediment from landmass toward their center creating the foundation of islands. The heat of the friction and the pressure of the ocean allow these foundations to form magma chambers of their own, melting and churning the sediment, releasing the gases that were locked in the rocks, and making a denser, more solid foundation upon which more sediment is deposited by the ocean current."

The teacher had droned on and on uninterrupted. Students had furiously scribbled down notes, none seeming to grasp the concept of the hydrologic cycle that breaks down and creates new landmasses.

Joshua had raised his hand, hoping to slow the lecture down so he could retain some semblance of understanding. "What does this mean? That islands are formed by water?"

"Not necessarily, Joshua. They are formed by friction. Friction is caused by pressure and movement, and pressure is caused by volume and density. A column of water the width of your thumb exerts the amount of pressure you use to scratch an itch. Twelve thumb-widths will stop the flow of blood in a vein. Twelve thousand thumb-widths has enough pressure to crush stone. There are depths in our seas and oceans ten times that depth, and with the force of currents, everything is scoured clean and pulverized into its smallest possible size. The heavier the element, the lower it sinks, and the lighter materials are swept up into the currents and drift away. As the vortex turns, those elements are washed up against the shores of landmasses, and the denser metal-rich molecules and grains of sand migrate toward the center of the vortex as they roll against the ocean floor, moved by the tides."

"I can't picture this happening in real life though. Not on such a large scale. It's too theoretical for me." Joshua had attempted to drag the conversation on until the end of the school day.

"Fill a bucket with water, then take a handful of dirt, and drop it in. As you rotate the bucket, the water moves in a vortex. You can see the soil separating. The rocks and sand fall to the bottom and migrate to the middle; the organic matter floats and catches on everything that it can." As the teacher had said this, she had used the trash can at the front of the classroom to simulate the motion. "This is the same principle that creates islands in the oceans. The denser rock and metals that migrate to the middle pile up thick enough that magnetism, the friction of the moving currents, the pressure from the ocean itself, and the ever-increasing volume of material being deposited generate enough heat to form the magma chamber beneath, and the heat starts the chemical reactions that separate the molecules into more efficient bonds. Hydrogen and oxygen are ripped from the oxidized metals and form steam, which then condenses into water and makes the oceans grow larger and larger over time."

"How do plants and animals get there? And why would they want to live on a barren rock?" Joshua had asked with genuine interest.

"Every creature needs to find some sort of shelter. Or rather, protection from the environment. That may be a cave for some who are avoiding the weather, or the camouflage of low brush, or even the isolation of a barren island. Birds and amphibians find these landmasses largely by accident. Swept out to sea by storms, they are driven by the currents to eventually land on these islands. Shellfish and fish in general find the comfort of the porous island surfaces ideal for prospering and propagating, and the birds cover the island with excrement, which creates fertilizer for any seeds that float on the ocean waves to find their way to the island. The birds peck at and eat the seeds and excrete them higher up the island where they are safe from the salt water and able to sprout and grow. It doesn't take long for a barren volcanic island to become vibrant ecosystem of its own." The teacher had spoken as if she had witnessed it a thousand times. As if the pattern were unchanging and too familiar to be refuted.

The bell had rung, dismissing the class.

Joshua's reminiscence ended, and he was again soaring over the waves below as he searched for a place to land.

He spotted it on the horizon, right where it was supposed to be: a tiny volcanic island oozing with molten lava. The charred, black, brittle surface was already covered with birds. They stalked the nearby seas and caught fish to feast on back at the island. Their droppings and the flecks of flesh that fell between the cracks in the surface mixed with the carbon-rich soil, and the churning of their finned feet mixed the soil into a rich fertilizer. Already ocean grasses had taken root. Even with the active volcano, they were able to go to seed and propagate as the flow of lava scorched them in its path.

Joshua found himself taking on the form of one of these birds quite frequently. They were notorious scavengers and supremely adaptable. He knew better than to pick favorites anymore. The Technician would only test them to near extinction. But they needed to be stressed in order to evolve. Why was still a mystery to Joshua, but it seemed in his interest.

As he landed, the few birds he flocked with landed as well, carving out some nesting terrain and depositing the seeds of fruit they had ingested at their last stop. Joshua felt free in this form. There was little that preyed on this species other than opportunistically. Their only real threat was occasional fatal fights. He had been using this form to transfer plants from nearby islands to this fledgling ecosystem. He was creating a habitat but didn't know what for yet. He just liked to see nature fight for survival and conquer the odds.

A little rodent hopped among the rocks picking up seeds from the grass that had blown nearby. This one was generations away from the first couple he had brought to the island. Gripping the tail in his beak, he dropped one off at a time as they bit and clawed at his face. Diversity required sacrifice. He felt the blood oozing from his eye as the rodent thrashed and clawed and bit until his eyeball burst. He felt for the ground with his feet. Once he landed, the pain of stumbling around blind made him give up on this body. He released the rodent, which scampered away to the safety of the rocks and grasses. Joshua triggered cardiac arrest in the bird. As it fell over, he felt that familiar fading: the body going into shock and the brain releasing the chemical cocktail to desperately try to stimulate a survival mechanism, triggering every memory associated with the emotions those neurotransmitters stimulated.

Immediately, he was conscious again, looking down over the island he had left, watching other birds peck at the now lifeless corpse he'd just discarded. Then he found another vessel to carry his consciousness so he could populate the island with more biodiversity.

Of course, Joshua had seen this process taking shape in the formation of the universe. The incomprehensible speeds had made it impossible to see the cause, yet he saw it now. Even more so, he lived it and became a part of the transformation. He wanted to better understand the planet he was shaping, so he could make more-informed decisions on his actions, find creative ways to preserve his favorite creations, and prevent the widespread damage the Technician had caused. He was fully at the mercy of Technician, so that knowledge would empower him in this battle of wits. But Joshua knew the Technician wasn't sitting idle while he learned.

His sanctuaries had kept many creatures safe for a while, but the continued pressure of hunger had wiped out many of the prey, and subsequently, the predators in their starved search for food. Only a fraction of the variety remained of his former menagerie.

His favored rats had survived the apocalypse and thrived. Their success led to intraspecies competition, which stimulated their divergence into numerous subspecies. Tree rats were longer-limbed and more daring in their leaps from branch to branch as they hunted for nuts and berries where they would be protected from the predators of the ground. Ground rats, which hunted for insects and roots in burrows, were developing short limbs with long nails for digging and long snouts for snatching bugs from tight spaces. Surface rats scavenged for all manner of food, living or dead. A strange variety of flying rats had emerged from an environment with little foliage, and many flying insects hatched in stagnant mud pits in the arid stretches of the emerging deserts. The diversity reminded him of the algae forests, and for once he felt that warm tingle and relaxation that only comes after realizing everything would be all right. Life struggled but it persisted, and the apocalypse wasn't total.

He created unique and isolated habitats with all the skill a billion years of practice could provide. With a single seed dropped from a bird's beak, the roots of the plant split a boulder from a mountain cliff that tumbled into the path of a blowing wind, where airborne dust would settle against it and the rains would compact it into a hard mud. This formed a hill, and as ten thousand years passed, the hill stretched three times the distance of the horizon. It curved and looped where the surrounding hills had redirected the winds themselves, always growing as the wind carried sediment to its final rest on the windward end of the ridge.

While waiting for the ridgeline to expand, Joshua redirected a river into the valley formed between the two ridgelines. He guided birds to the area, where they deposited seed and stopped to drink in peace, as there were no predators nearby to torment them. From this, grasses and berry bushes grew and competed for light and water, and the diversification of plants increased in this fertile valley. The foliage followed the river all the way to a connecting river and the surrounding forest. From here the tree, ground, and flying rats made their way upstream away from the pressure of their predators and toward the valley. Once Joshua had them in the valley, he split the ground beneath the river at the end of the valley where it leaked into a salt deposit and dissolved into a flooded cavern.

Over time, this cavern collapsed and sealed the end of the valley off with a giant sinkhole flanked by wide non-traversable cliffs. Though sediment carved out of the river's path was continually deposited in the hole, it wouldn't fill up for a very long time, so the valley was effectively isolated. Any predators that made it into the new ecosystem were hampered by the dense vegetation that hid their prey and the moist soil that made the ground difficult to traverse and were killed by accidents of Joshua's choosing.

In building the ridgeline and redirecting the river, Joshua had created a vast, dry grassland that quickly turned into a desert because of the weather-blocking ridgeline and the lack of flowing water. This ensured that although the vegetation might reach the top of the ridgeline, it wouldn't go over the top, due to a lack of water. Again, he had created a biosphere out of the local environment with a few simple tricks and a little patience.

Moving land, water, or air in a miraculous display only forced them back for a time. They redirected one another and ended up creating pockets of unique ecosystems. While this was useful and interesting for a time, Joshua had long since learned the nuances and subtleties of creating environments and built perfect habitats to mold his creation to his ideal.

The valley existed in a stable equilibrium for a thousand generations. The forests grew taller and more diverse. The waterways supported fish, and even the large reptiles managed to eke out a survival by suffering thousands of years of frail hunger and growing smaller as a result, populating the banks and mud of the river that gave life to the valley. The birds flew in and out but always carried with them the seeds of the plants they feasted on in the valley to the expanse beyond. The world outside began its rebirth, and the valley was no longer as isolated as it once had been.

The forest swelled and burst forth from the confines of the valley. Dieback from the harsh environment outside killed off all but the hardiest, most efficient plants. Those that survived expanded far beyond the horizon in a sea of green when the climate changed and the plants flourished. When drought came again, it all died back, leaving the bleached bones of the forest to haunt the vast wastelands between the isolated pockets, where the forest clung to life. When the climate changed again, those oases were the seed stock that covered the landscape again.

In the valley, each subspecies diverged into several every twenty to fifty generations. Personalities, phenotypes, location, environment, and opportunism all conspired to divide the species until every opportunity for survival in the environment was filled. Once this perfect harmony was established, and the waste and consumption were all equal, Joshua released the occupants of the valley onto the wider world.

He triggered a rockslide on the north ridgeline at a narrow point of the valley to allow escape from the valley. As it blocked the river, the blockage filled with water and began spilling over the top of the dam. It continued on its course, but the constant flow of water and the weight of the reservoir slowly forced its way through. As the dam began to leak, the water pushed through the gaps, and in an almost instantaneous breach, the whole volume of water broke through and flowed down the riverbed, tearing away the trees and bushes and carrying many of the creatures along with it. The torn-away soil reached the end of the valley and cascaded over, plugging the hole where the water had been flowing into underground caverns.

Though the flow into the underground cavern didn't stop, it slowed enough that the hole began to fill. When it reached the top, it spilled this way and that trying to find the path of least resistance, washing out the loose soil until it found bedrock. Then the flow continued all the way to the sea, carrying the seeds of the valley along its way to plant an oasis for the creatures emerging from the sanctuary. The isolated environment in which the flora and fauna had evolved had forced them into the most efficient forms for survival. This efficiency, developed from the competition for space and resources, made them able to dominate the other plant life they encountered along the way. Where the ground was fertile, the species from the valley dominated; where it was not, those of the plains did better.

Rats from the valley had evolved from abundant nutrition but intense competition. Rats from the arid plain were hardy and had been forced to highest energy efficiency by their exposed and malnourished existence. Both found new nesting grounds where they could feed and drink and propagate freely with little danger of predators anymore, as they no longer lived exposed beneath the scrub grasses. These two breeds of rats, unique in the kilns that proofed them, interbred with each other, and the hybrid offspring carried with them greater adaptability and stronger traits than their ancestors.

When the first of the seeds had sprouted and grown tall enough that they could be seen from the valley on the other side, primates and rats and many other animals began picking their way across the cliff faces to get to the side where they could find an environment with less population pressure.

Joshua was particularly fond of these elegant calamities. Like building the ridgeline, one small action led to the same desired outcome he had achieved with great calamities before: one ripple that triggered a tsunami, one echo that beckoned from the unknown, one vibration that started a landslide.

———⊗∞⊗———

The Technician was a master at devising the elegant calamity, a confluence of minor events that reached a crescendo at a critical moment and stunned Joshua with its effectiveness.

The first time the Technician had assaulted Joshua this way, he had felt shocked and awed. The next time he had determined to outmaneuver the Technician, and when that had failed, he had begun to get frustrated. But the incredible array of minor events had been difficult to read and thus impossible to defend against. When frustration had turned to abject refusal to participate, the Technician had not stopped. He had simply grown bolder. The less Joshua had participated, the more the Technician had spoiled.

So Joshua had been forced to play, if only to halt the spread of the cancer the Technician spread.

Diseases had run rampant, rockslides had blocked rivers and diverted them, and whole ecosystems had died off to starved desperate remnants. Even the weather patterns had shifted when the air flow had diverted. The Technician was masterful and well-practiced, ruthless but not reckless.

It was only after giving up for a time that Joshua was able to observe the Technician's methods. The subtle actions that produced such catastrophic results had suddenly made Joshua aware of how light a touch was possible. He had begun to practice on everything. Now, like the pinpointing of the cells of the heart of a creature, he was able to effectively guide the evolution of planets with the movement of single grains of sand.

One day, the Technician started creating a barren desert, turning rivers, one boulder at a time, until a huge swath of land was left thirsty.

When Joshua saw it happening, rather than confront it head-on, he worked in a different area to divert the air before the Technician's diversion could even affect it. The Technician chimed in to admonish Joshua for being blind to his maneuvering, when all of a sudden, a supercell formed right on top of the desert. The rain came down hard. The sandy ground was unable to absorb the water, and it flooded the area before percolating underground. Stress fractures deep underground were lubricated, and the sudden slippage cracked the surface and opened an aquifer, which flooded out and filled the gap, spilling out and picking up dormant grass seeds that took root in the sand. The life cycle started again. The heat evaporated the water and created moisture-heavy, warm, high-pressure air that mixed with the low-pressure air from the mountains. The mixture created more storms and more rain and renewed the arid savanna into a verdant prairie and left a permanent lake.

"You have been watching me, I see," the Technician taunted. "Very clever."

"I'm getting pretty good at this. I think you might have your work cut out for you." Joshua was cocky in his statement, bolder and more confident.

"Oh, that is a certainty. You are becoming quite the master of this world. Congratulations on your small victory. Allow me to set off some fireworks for you."

The Technician punctuated that statement by wiping out a dozen jungle ecosystems, drying up whole lake beds and collapsing mountains with the same subtle triggers, except all at once to show that he was a thousand steps ahead.

Joshua couldn't help but laugh. He had gotten to the Technician.

———— ✖ ————

The rats were supremely adaptable creatures. Without a guiding hand, they had carved out dozens of niches in the food chain and found themselves able to fill in those gaps vacated by other species that had become too specialized and couldn't adapt to changing conditions. The rats had a craftiness and a hardiness. Though they were preyed upon by a wide swath of the fauna that populated the valley, they were prolific in their conquest of the forest. Joshua had to admit they were his favorite curiosity.

A ground rat fed on bugs at night, and another fed during the day. Two distinct species emerged after so much diurnal isolation. There was a tree rat that fed on the fruit that grew in the branches, and another that fed on the ones that fell to the ground. Birds fed on those fruits too, and other birds preyed on the tree rats, but the rats managed to muscle out their competition over time and outwit their predators. There were finite opportunities for survival in the environment, and as the populations grew each species became more and more specialized in their survival strategies. But the rats remained adaptable to *any* opportunity.

Joshua could sense their thoughts and emotions as they were all a part of his being, but he had long neglected them in favor of his chosen few from the asteroid catastrophe. He shut them out as a mild droning in his mind. That made it possible for the Technician to run his own breeding program in the background. The Technician had created animals with hyperspecialized abilities, with more acute hearing, sight, smell, and taste formed out of the necessity of survival in the vast wastelands of the dead zones.

It was the carnivore who dominated the dead lands. All shapes and sizes, from the light-footed mongrels that preyed on anything they could catch to the carrion birds that circled overhead, the land was too dry and sparse to support much grazing, and only a bare few desert rodents scraped out a living and provided nourishment for the predators that roamed.

In his neglect of the wider world, Joshua had allowed the Technician to create some truly fearsome creatures—or rather, allowed him to create environments that shaped these creatures into the fearsome beasts that emerged. These would be a constant bane for Joshua's creation.

As the primates and rats and other creatures adapted to their new environment, they found themselves encountering these new monsters along the way more and more frequently. The more monsters they encountered, the more came from the desert region, following the trail of fleshy "breadcrumbs" who happened out into the desert in a search for more isolated regions to increase their own diversity.

Joshua found that he could reach inside individuals to increase their pheromones so that others of their species found them irresistible, increasing their reproductive potential and breeding specific traits. Unfortunately, he found, after a few dozen generations, that the gene pool became largely homogenous, and no amount of pheromone production would encourage the herd to mate. They became sickly and feeble and easy prey. But he also noticed that those that drank iron-rich water carried more oxygen in their blood and could run farther. Those that ate insects while grazing grew stronger and had denser bones. The environment contributed to the shaping of these animals in a multitude of ways, so over time Joshua simply allowed nature to play out without interference.

His creatures could adapt, but only through much hardship and suffering. He realized the experiment in the petri dish the Valley provided had to withstand the true test of the environment. The world at large would prove their mettle, and those that failed were not suited to survival, no matter their value to Joshua's plans. The biological factory he had created had no quality assurance, no research and development, no market analysis. The product simply existed on hope. They *needed* to be tested, they *needed* to be broken, they *needed* to face the harsh assessment of their consumers to be proven marketable, and that was the role the Technician played.

It didn't matter what the Technician did—the species that lived in the environment with the terrors he unleashed simply adapted, so Joshua stopped engaging in battles over the gene pool.

"So, you don't find this game interesting anymore?" the Technician asked as another pack of monstrosities charged out of the mountains descending on a helpless herd of deer.

"There's really no point," Joshua said flatly, ignoring the massacre of a herd of deer that left a few lucky and quick ones darting away in different directions. "No matter what I do, they just get sick and die. The best way to mold the creatures is to let the environment do it."

"What does that mean for your involvement? Are you going to ignore all this?"

"Essentially, yes. There's nothing you can create that isn't already possible in the environment."

"What are you going to do in the meantime?"

"I'll simply mold their environment and shape them that way.

I suppose the next step is to create a civilization out of one or more of these creatures. That's what I'm going to worry about now."

The Technician was silent for a moment and then replied, "I guess you've passed that test then."

Joshua thought for a moment. He hadn't realized this was a test against anything other than his creation. Then he understood. "You didn't care about the creatures at all? You weren't testing them?"

The Technician chortled. "What do you think? That these dumb, instinctive creatures were the goal? Everyone gets to this point. There is no effort required. That was the test. Whatever you do, the environment tests it, and whatever effort you make, the environment changes the outcome. The most effective at any survival strategy are the ones that ultimately dominate and drive anything else in that niche to extinction or subjugation. The test is seeing when you discover that."

Joshua knew anger was pointless, so he just let it harden into bitterness. *That was the test? My own acceptance of zero effort?* The longer he was trapped inside this prison of the mind, the more he understood the transformation of those who came out. There is no value in the veneer of emotion. It could only harm him. Feelings still remained, but the reaction to them was in vain. The adults weren't emotionless, they simply didn't expend the energy to *show* it.

12

Once again, Joshua inhabited the body of a bird, but this time he did it simply to be free. He wanted to feel the ocean breeze on his face and glide through the air toward no known destination. The discovery of the futility of his own effort left a lot of time to simply exist. He tried life as every creature that existed, living as they would and experiencing what they experienced, to see the world through their eyes and feel what they felt. He was a stag in rut, a bear going into and out of hibernation, a lion on the savanna, and a primate in the trees. He lived every life he could and experienced every death as if it were his own.

He could think clearly as a bird. The waves crashing below drowned out the static noise in his head. The waves sounded similar, and the constancy of their motion helped him get his mind off this prison he was trapped in.

Time is relative. In the experience of learning, it is rapid. In bore-

dom it is a crawl. Yet here in the Machine I have felt the seconds tick away in the lives of every creature that lives. A trillion perspectives for every second that passes. There is so much to do, but I am bored. I don't know how to move forward. I don't know how to get out. I am running a race where the finish line is always just around the next bend. I have tried everything. I have failed, and failed dismally, in so many ways, and in the end the solution was to stop trying?

He ignored the other birds as he flew. As far as the others knew, he had lost his mind. Technically, the bird *had* lost its mind. Under Joshua's control, the bird's behavior was abnormal to what it and all its kin knew to be normal. Joshua laughed at this, his bird voice squawking shrilly. Discordant and obnoxious as he knew it was, he liked the sound of it. Joshua laughed again as he barrel-rolled in the ocean breeze and dove headfirst into a wave about to crest. He emerged with a flopping fish in his beak, flipped it in the air, and swallowed it whole. No sense in running this creature to death.

This Machine is designed to frustrate. It is designed to humble me. To make me crawl bloodied and humiliated through the exit. If the shape creation took is irrelevant, if stopping the Technician is irrelevant, then the only thing that is relevant is getting out.

Joshua needed to create a civilization, but where to start? It wasn't soaring above the waves in this bird, but sometimes a brief escape like this was enough to clear his mind. He knew he needed guidance.

———— ∞ ————

Joshua had become well practiced in developing genetic diversity. Millions of years focused on one species could create countless subspecies, and whole ecosystems of predator and prey, herbivores, omnivores, and carnivores could emerge from a single common ancestor when pushed and prodded with the threat of extinction or rewarded with procreation. Yet this became little more than a curiosity after a while. Even as he had learned all there was about the practice, he was unable to move life forward.

Nothing is beyond the capability of a being with eternity to experiment and too much time to wait for certain projects to bear fruit. Even at the pace of the solar year as a heartbeat in real time, the number of generations and years for any critical project to progress to a point of usefulness is still an eternity in the Machine. So everything that can be toyed with is toyed with. Everything that can be is tried. Everything that can't be is realized. There is no shadow that eternity cannot illuminate.

For Joshua, there had always been a great mystery about how his own species rose out of the prairies and forests to become a dominant species on the planet. It wasn't something any person knew going in. The lesson was vague in school, and the exact tipping point was difficult to grasp. What caused a species to go from brutish animal to developing tools and culture out of nothing? This was an impenetrable mystery to Joshua, but there were five others that understood this lesson intimately.

A group of primates became isolated by a lightning strike that set a grassland ablaze, forcing them to flee toward desert. When the fire died out, they tried to turn back toward their known origin, but vicious beasts of all kinds assaulted them and forced them along the unknown path. This group had no choice but to move forward.

Their flight across the prairie and eventually across the coarse sand of the encroaching desert yielded only more hardship. There was no rest, no refuge, so the hunted moved forward desperately seeking sanctuary.

Joshua was only vaguely aware of these creatures as they made their flight out into the desert until their screams and fearful prayers penetrated the static and drew his attention. He watched them for a moment and then turned them toward a distant oasis.

Predators gnashing at them from all sides left only one route toward any hope of survival. Driving them forward, Joshua watched as predators laid an ambush for these tiny refugees. With a few carefully placed rockfalls and a turning of the wind, the path was cleared, the ambush foiled.

This oasis crested the horizon and beckoned to the thirsty, starved, and hunted primates to find safety in the trees and shrubs. The green canopy rippled and waved in the heat rising off the sand. What first appeared to be a mirage proved to be real. They found an azure pool, lush green foliage, and bright red and white flowers that would soon become sweet fruit.

Isolated and protected from predators, they were able to flourish. These primates could work as a group to complete tasks and thought ahead and planned. Similar to the rats evolved from the valley dwellers long ago, they had been shaped by their environment, and their fragility was offset by an industrious use of rudimentary tools. They used rocks to defend against predators and sticks to pull termites and ants out of their holes to eat them. They built dams out of rocks and caught fish. They used rolled-up leaves as a sort of armor while they harassed beehives for their honey. All this yielded results from basic efforts that seemed comical to Joshua.

This troupe was just a small part of a greater world, a single troupe of a species that spanned the breadth of the savanna they called home.

Then he saw something in the oasis that puzzled him. A lone tree bore fruit that he didn't recognize. How had such a thing come to be? How had he never seen or rather, felt its presence? It had a mysterious elusiveness about it, constantly in sight, yet invisible.

"Where did this come from?"

"I shaped it," the Technician responded. "It is a test."

"A test of what?"

"A test of obedience, of discipline, of shame, of self-awareness
. . ."

"How does it do that? It's just a tree."

"Yes, but the tree is not the test, the reaction is."

As they spoke, a serpent emerged from the branches, and the
group saw it. Not knowing what it was, they fled in terror. Except
one. A lone female stared at the tree and the creature, her beady
eyes pointed forward, her long, pointed ears alert. The serpent
looked her in the face and slowly approached. Cautious, she leaned
over and put her forehand to the ground. Then she took one step
forward.

The serpent paused briefly at this bold action, then moved toward her a little faster. Less cautious.

The female took another bolder step forward. And then another. And another.

The serpent continued forward, but did not lunge or move ag-
gressively in any way.

Neither did the female.

The rest of the group stayed hidden, yet watchful of the female's boldness.

As she approached, the serpent drew closer until they were
within reach of each other.

She reached out her hand and touched the serpent. It stuck
out its tongue and tasted the air around her. It eyed her and drew
closer, looking at her from all sides. She followed its every move,
reading it for any sign of danger, finding none.

The serpent drew closer until she could touch it with both
hands. It smelled sweet, like the fruit that littered the ground beneath the unusual tree, yet bitter like the sun-bleached bones and
dust of a corpse in the desert. She drew close to its face. Touching,
smelling, feeling, and seeing every scale, every pore, every tooth,
and every stripe on its body.

Her group watched too.

She laid both her hands on the serpent's underbelly, and it raised its head, recoiling, but not reacting. It towered over her, yet did not assault her.

She turned to the bushes where her group had fled and started calling for them, assuring them that everything was fine.

The serpent stayed elevated above her, curiously watching the rest of the group slowly emerge from their hiding places. A few at a time took bold steps forward, cautiously testing each step to see the serpent's reaction.

The female moved toward the tree, spotting a large ripe fruit on the ground. As she moved forward, so did the serpent. The rest of her group froze. The movement of the serpent was startling, and most took a step back and waited.

Their leader reached for the fruit, her tiny hands holding the massive ripe orb. She took one cautious bite, spraying juice and letting it drip down her face. She looked up into the serpent's eyes as she swallowed, her pupils dilating, and the catatonia of the visions overwhelmed her. As the universe unfolded before her eyes, it swallowed her, and in one swift move, so did the serpent. His mouth engulfed her and the fruit, crushing them in its powerful throat. She had no time to cry out.

Joshua watched the shocking scene. With swift movements, the serpent swallowed three more before they could gather their voices to sound the alarm. They began to flee, but one more was picked off, and as one more stumbled, he was devoured as well.

The few that remained fled as far and as fast as they could, zigging and zagging to avoid being tracked.

Joshua's mind was reeling at this affront to his effort. He had seen this happen before millions of times, but never had he seen such a well-cultivated and carefully planned trap. "What kind of lesson does that teach? The best of the group is now being turned into fertilizer!"

"It seems they were found lacking," the Technician coldly replied.

"Lacking *what?*"

"The desire to survive. A species that does not first bare its teeth at an unknown threat is not interested in defending their own right to live."

13

Joshua tried to understand this test, the purpose of the tree, the fruit, the serpent. He spent whole lives contemplating it. The tree was an ancient species. It had certainly been part of a larger forest long before the desert was turned on its course. It was the only one of its type left in existence. The chemical makeup of the fruit was not unusual, but for the primates that encountered it, it was mildly psychedelic. The serpent, too, was not unique, one of many of its species, but it was isolated and alone.

It had escaped his attention and still stood in plain sight. Joshua wondered how he had chosen that oasis to begin with. Seeing it on the horizon as a likely place to isolate this troupe made it feel like his own decision, yet it was not of his making.

The population grew, and population pressure made these apes their own worst enemies. They divided themselves into two groups, and each sought the destruction of the other, killing each other over arbitrary things.

Joshua didn't need to choose who would win nor tip the balance in favor of either side. Neither side was particularly virtuous; neither side was particularly different either. The side that "won" was more prone to strategic planning, and by degrees the whole population became increasingly more adept at this talent.

When the seasons changed and food grew scarce, the oasis was a bleak place for such a crowd. On the scales of survival, weighing the risk of starvation against the risk of being eaten meant many were willing to risk death to feed on the forbidden fruit rather than starve to death. The serpent grew bigger, fatter, and faster because of its regular feedings. The group that populated the oasis was quick to breed but short-lived, so Joshua endured birth, life, and death numerous times. Within twenty-three generations, those born were nearly double the size their ancestors had been. In another twenty-three, they were double that again. The cyclical pattern of population growth, ecological pressure, conflict, and regrowth left the population constantly evolving toward larger, more dominant bodies.

Joshua did not neglect the rest of the world during this time. The species in the oasis was unique in their forward, strategic thinking, but that was not enough for him to abandon everything else to the whims of the Technician. Even as this species was evolving to suit the oasis, Joshua sought other creatures that might be worth grooming and experimenting with. Yet he found his attention drifting toward this little oasis and these primates. He was still curious about the test and curious how the Technician might manipulate him and how these creatures would survive the often-brutal tests they were forced to endure.

Over time, as the primates got larger and larger, the ecosystem could support a few less every generation. The perception by the group was that the environment had been changing, that they were themselves destroying their chances of survival, yet the bounty of the oasis remained the same.

The fewer the environment could sustain, the smaller the conflicts. They created rules their society would live by. Though the rules were basic and sometimes arbitrary, they were the foundation of laws, and every generation the primates lived by these laws, the less lawless they became as they enforced the rules by the will of the majority. Joshua saw that the more laws the primates created, the fewer reckless primates there were in each generation. They became more obedient to authority figures, and as the populations continued to grow, more needed to be culled to accommodate, so new, more-restrictive rules were created, and those who rebelled were the first to be eliminated.

What first appeared to be a paradise proved to be a prison. There was no escape for the occupants. There was no freedom of movement. They lived by the tyranny of the majority, and the only punishment was death. Yet even in paradise, death creates more death. At times the water was undrinkable. It forced the group to evolve, albeit slowly, to drink less, eat less, and still grow larger. Their bodies became more efficient to suit their environment and ensure their survival. They lived the first rule of life—adaptation.

Joshua thought back to his class. He now understood his teacher's callous view of nature. Experiencing life and death had become less and less shocking.

"Every creature lives by a few simple rules to increase the likelihood of their survival," the teacher had said one morning. "The first rule is adaptation. No creature survives long in a foreign environment while trying to cling to their former diets, shelters, or strategies. Longing for the past does not secure the future. Those who don't learn this lesson soon face extinction."

The second rule she had discussed was the law of conservation of energy. "The path of least resistance always yields the greatest fruit. Water runs downhill. Flora and fauna follow this flow. Even civilization tends to form at the lowest point near these abundant resources. Our ancient civilizations had their origins along the coastlines and waterways of our home planet.

"Next comes equilibrium with the environment. Any species

that outbreeds their food supply suffers more. Any species that consumes more than they need suffers greatly. Any species that pushes their environment beyond its natural limits invites catastrophe on itself. While the environment recovers easily, the species that caused it harm finds itself suffering catastrophic dieback. Thus, forward-thinking, conscientious effort proves more sustainable for long-term comfort and survival.

"Next comes economic distribution—that every individual determines the rewards and costs of each environment. Higher population densities lead to increased competition for scarcer resources, meaning the cleverest, strongest, or hardiest tend to survive longest. All others migrate elsewhere to lower pressure systems or die out."

As usual, Joshua was watching the birds and insects outside the window that day. But he'd internalized the ideas and was trying to imagine how they applied to what he saw. Each had come to adapt to life in their society but had also struggled to get there. *Which was easier, adapting to the change, fighting against it, or running from it?*

The teacher noticed his distant gaze and tried to bring him back into the lecture of the morning. "Joshua? What do you think about that?"

Hearing his name, he immediately sat upright and looked around, nervously trying to recall the last thing the teacher had said. "It sounds like you're saying economics is a natural phenomenon. That it is a natural calculation of the costs and benefits of each decision rather than simply being a monetary construct."

"I did suggest that, yes. But what do you think about the fifth rule?"

"The fifth?" Joshua's mind raced for any crumb that might have fallen into his daydream. "Food requires . . . um . . . migration—"

The teacher cut him off. "Very perceptive of you. I suppose the fifth rule, that greater utility encourages proliferation, could be interpreted as 'Food requires . . . um . . . migration.'" The class chuckled at this, and Joshua's face flushed with embarrassment.

The teacher continued. "As a population uses a resource, they seek ways to increase the availability of that resource closer to their shelter. As a species faces collapse, the population outliers are the first to be eliminated. Anything that is not practical is eliminated, anyone who does not produce is removed, and any group that stands apart is eradicated."

There were many lesser rules, but these five were primary to every creature's survival. She'd explained they even determined how real estate markets determined value and how people, flora, and fauna found opportunities for survival in every environment.

Now Joshua was watching these rules play out in the oasis.

14

Domestication is compassion, Joshua surmised. The isolation of the primates was like the cities of his society. These creatures were once wild and living brutish and short lives, yet his attention on them, though forcing them to endure a certain degree of suffering, ensured the strongest and biggest and most adaptable had the most success. The rest perished. The heirs of those who survived found life much easier to endure. Those creatures that were controlled and conditioned, selectively bred for specific traits, found their share of survival opportunities expand and become more secure as their specialization assured they dominated in that particular niche.

The fighting and sickness took its toll on this dwindling troupe. Still the tree stood, surrounded by the rotting husks of forbidden fruit. The temptation to brave the ancient curse grew stronger in the hearts of every inhabitant of the oasis.

The original tale was lost. All they knew was the powerful lesson that eating the fruit meant death. The serpent was present, but it was forced to sustain itself again on the fruit, rather than on the group's leaders and desperate rebels.

The population continued to grow, and growth demanded sacrifice. Again murder and death occurred, even in the small community. When the adults faced each other to assert dominance, many died, and in the end only the younglings survived. The youngest babies and toddlers starved, unable to fend for themselves, leaving behind only two self-sufficient children. They were old enough to know what food and drink was, but too young to know the lore or the reason for the rules. The oasis and the experiment remained with the fate of these two.

Joshua was concerned for them. Too much effort had gone into monitoring and breeding them and controlling their habitat to allow them to simply perish. These were his pets, his project, and he was bound and determined to keep their legacy alive.

Joshua finally understood the purpose of the tree. Or so he thought. If the creatures were obedient to their cultural prohibitions, they proved that they followed custom. Custom meant they revered lore, which meant they understood consequences. If they could overcome the prohibition, they proved themselves capable of logical thinking and planning. The real question was whether they could feel guilt, *shame* in defying their culture. It was clear, though, that no matter the outcome, these primates were doomed if they stayed here.

The test of the tree provided a historical lesson for them. They understood that the tree meant death, the fruit was deadly, and the serpent was ruthless. But the fruit had been prohibited so long, and it had grown independently for so long, and the minerals the tree used to produce the fruit were so different from everything else in the ecosystem that these primates could not wholly absorb it.

The two remaining younglings continued to grow and eat and survive on their own. But as they grew larger, the food supply could not keep up. Joshua kept the fruit growing as fast as the environment would allow without sapping the minerals and causing the ecosystem to collapse, but this was not good enough. These two had outgrown their environment. It became a matter of survival that they try the fruit against Joshua's best efforts and desires.

This test was for quality assurance. Joshua could sense the Technician's plan unfolding against his own desires. *He* was predictable, and *his* actions were inevitable. This was all part of the calculus. But what did the test *mean*?

He spoke to them in their dreams to remind them of the rule. They needed to remember the prohibition, and he needed time to unravel the web of purpose the Technician had woven.

15

The tree stood in a clearing not far from the shore of the oasis. Rotted fruit scattered around the trunk. Its long, gangly roots poked out of the ground in various places. A glimpse underground showed that it mirrored the branches above in its depth and span, its rooted mouth tasting the minerals within reach as it wriggled its rigid tendrils into the pits and crevices to find the delicious mineral deposits hidden within. Yet it bore few viable seeds and did not propagate in the oasis, as the minerals it required were exclusively beneath the single mature tree.

The two primates stood at the edge of the clearing, peering toward the tree. They'd been too young when their parents were alive to understand any more than "tree bad," and though the vivid dreams they had warned against it, dreams fade. The bright, tantalizing fruit beckoned to them from the ground, and their knots of hunger collaborated with their instincts.

The male crouched at the edge of the clearing and looked

around. It didn't *seem* dangerous. The words of his ancestors cried out in the depths of his memory. He slowly backed away and went to sit beside the water a branch's reach away.

She stayed, however. She was younger, though not by much, and the words and fear weren't as clear in her memory.

Joshua looked on as the hunger gnawed at her and delivered the final punctuation on the decision. He watched her creep forward, drawn in by a yellow eye on a low branch of the tree. She stopped and watched it continue down the branch until it bowed.

The serpent lowered itself to the ground. Compared to her size, it was no longer than her body and no wider than her arm. She looked at it with curiosity. As the branch sprang back up to its resting position, a fresh fruit broke free and fell to the ground. It bore no bruises and no rot, and its color was a most appealing reddish orange. It was unlike anything she was used to seeing.

She knew nothing of the serpent either, not even the tales. When it looked at her, it elicited no fear. When it backed away or encircled a fruit with its body to entice its prey, she did not know the game.

Though it wasn't a venomous serpent, its fangs could incapacitate and take down prey while they were paralyzed and hallucinating. So the serpent invited the woman to taste the fruit. And she accepted the invitation as innocently as a child.

Joshua had seen the effects countless times before and knew the result. He had spoken to the creatures through their dreams and had encouraged the rest of the fruit to ripen prematurely. He had to watch and wait though. He knew they were intelligent animals. Whether they were *people* was the real question.

The ecosystem was pointless without them, and it was doomed with them, so it was irrelevant whether he pushed the balance of the ecosystem beyond its ability to recover. The experiment was over with or without intervention. *What choice do I have then but to watch and wait?*

16

His teacher's lessons echoed in Joshua's mind as he watched the scene unfold.

"In every ecosystem, a symbiosis occurs—a natural evolutionary process where organisms impact the survival and growth of everything else. As a tree grows, it casts a shadow. The grasses that grow beneath it adapt to the lack of sunlight. The seeds that need more light die off, the ones that need less survive and propagate. That tree needs water. If the grass at its base drinks too much, the tree dies back and leaves don't develop. Thus the grass that thrives in the shade is scorched and dies in the sun. The rot of one plant nourishes another. The toxins of one are rebuffed by another. . . ."

This was the relationship between the tree and the ecosystem around it. The fruit fell and rotted. At its base, most of these nutrients were reabsorbed by the tree, but some tumbled into the nearby water and rotted there. The fruit tainted the water, and the grasses at the shoreline absorbed that tainted water. Those grasses that could not defend against the toxins died off; those that were hardier survived. The grass had developed a natural counterbalance to the fruit. The primates found this grass to be an effective curative for upset stomachs from all causes.

The female gathered a handful of the fruit as the serpent allowed and went to find the male. When he saw what she carried and that she wasn't dead from merely approaching the tree, he was struck with confusion.

"You live?" he grunted, their language little more than grunts, hisses, and clicks, but perfectly understandable to each other and to Joshua. Complex ideas could be communicated through very simple combinations of these guttural noises.

"Yes, serpent not kill. Tree not kill. Not know why stories say tree bad." The grunts and chirps and hisses spun a loose tapestry of language as she examined the fruit in her hands.

Either the stories were lies, or she had overcome death. She assured him that the fruit was safe, that she had just gone to the serpent, and he had given her all the fruit she wanted.

His concern then became, though only partly correct, that the fruit itself was the trouble.

"I not eat. Tree not kill. Serpent not kill. Then *fruit* kill." His final grunt punctuating the statement with authoritative finality.

There was nothing else left to eat, so he chewed the grass, hoping the soothing juices would settle his stomach and help him forget his gnawing hunger. It didn't, so he chewed more.

She sat beside him and laid the fruit on the ground between them. She understood him completely, but she refused to starve to death either. Yet his fear infected her, and she was afraid to try the fruit herself—for the moment. She pulled a clump of grass and gnawed on it as well, swallowing the juices, hoping the same as he hoped—that the curative would resolve the issue for them both by taking away their hunger. It did not.

"Not eat fruit, we dead." she said finally. The logic of the statement resonated, and the male sat silent.

The serpent was on its way toward the pair. Having never left the shelter of the tree's canopy, it was hesitant, but this meal was a long time coming, and it was not going to let the opportunity slip away.

Joshua was not oblivious to this though. With a turning of the breeze, a hawk found the oasis and peered down. It eyed the serpent and began its decent.

With one last grunt, she picked one of the fruits up and sniffed it. It had a sweet aroma, too different from anything she knew, but it was alluring all the same.

She took that first cautious bite and waited.

Immediately the fruit warmed her throat as the juices oozed down. As the nectar tried to paralyze her throat and suffocate her, the antidotal juices from the grasses neutralized it. As the lump rested in her stomach, the grasses prevented it from stalling her heart when it was absorbed through her stomach lining. The hallucinogenic, though, was not stalled.

She began to dream. With eyes wide open she could see the world around her, the symbiosis between the grasses and the tree, the water and them drinking it. She saw the history of where she came from. She remembered the shadows of her relatives in her memory and what they were. She saw what she was—the product of murder and rape and assault and bullying and starvation and suffering.

She recognized that she *should* be more, that she *could* be.

She looked deeply into the face of the male, who sat beside her watching intently for any signs of the promised death. In him, she saw a future where only they were left and would ensure the future of the world.

As she stared, the serpent coiled for the strike from the grasses. Guessing the toxins had had time to take their effect on the pair, it tensed for the strike.

With a flash, the hawk bore down and dug its sharp talons into the serpent. A meal this large would be a boon to its chicks. She carried it writhing in her talons to the cliff face beyond the horizon where she nested.

Though the blur surprised the male, the female was oblivious to it. She fell deeper into catatonia.

She saw visions of the movement of the stars, the planets around the star, the air around the planet, the life cycle of the plants, and her ancestors and the very ground they walked on. Whatever she turned her focus to, she could peer through the depths of eternity and decipher its origin. She knew nothing of the outside world, but the thought terrified her that she had glimpsed the river of time and all those who drank from it. She begged noiselessly for the visions to stop, unable to comprehend what she was seeing, yet the visions did not end. She swam through the air and tasted the colors of the desert, and from that flavor knew her origins were the stones and she was little more than sand. She sensed a stone watching her, judging her, and guiding her. And on that stone a face appeared. It was the face from her dreams. She saw his face in the trunk of every tree, in the array of pebbles at the shore of the oasis, and in the clouds above. He was the trees that swayed and the breeze that swayed them. It was Joshua.

She could see him looking at her, and suddenly she was ashamed.

She was connected to his nervous system and formed the bridge to his cognitive brain. She looked at her own reflection in the water as she bent to quench her insatiable thirst. The vision of her rippling visage shocked her, and she wanted to cry. Deeper into her own subconscious she tumbled motionlessly until she finally found the bottom of her being and peered up at the long bright tunnel toward her former reality. The distant image of her own face reflected in the water and the voices of the world around her echoed through the dark tunnel that surrounded her, whispering their sacred knowledge to her. She felt like an ignorant child. So much knowledge existed, and she could not comprehend it. But knowing it existed changed her.

She determined to seek it out. In that moment, she felt herself reaching out to the image on the water, and the tunnel collapsed behind her until she was once more in the world she had momentarily left. Suddenly she felt more aware of the world she once thought she knew.

While this went on, the man had taken a bite from the same fruit. He, too, was protected from the paralysis, and he, too, experienced the perception-altering hallucinations that left him similarly shamed and shattered.

They saw the world around them differently. They had broken their ancestors' sacred commandment to never eat of the fruit. They knew shame for the first time in its violation. They knew humility in seeing their own brutish origins. But they also knew they could never go back. Their innocence lost, they felt only despair.

Joshua knew they were more than merely intelligent animals now. They were people. Their shame over defying him and realizing their carnal origins proved them to be more.

17

Joshua forced all the plants to bloom, all the fruit to ripen, and all the locusts to sing out where they could be caught. The two gathered and ate as much as they could from the oasis. Seeing the dying trees and the waning shoreline of the pool, they both knew they would have to leave. Even the tree of death had lost its persistent bloom, and spots of brown were visible in the canopy.

They both wore leaves now, covering themselves in recognition of the indecency of their origins. They were no longer completely animal, though they had never thought of themselves in that way before. They had a glimpse of Joshua in their minds. The watchfulness of his gaze shamed them, and they had turned their thoughts inward and had seen themselves for what they were—the carnality and simplicity of their existence, eating, breeding, and fighting. It was what the common creatures of the world did. But they were set apart and had a chance to make their way forward.

Joshua asked the Technician, "So they passed the test?"

"It seems so." he replied in an even tone.

"They weren't so domesticated that they refused to eat the fruit, but they aren't truly animals either. They know they were wrong for violating their cultural prohibitions, but they used logic to justify its necessity." Joshua watched them as he absorbed this new sensation.

The Technician interrupted his moment of reflection. "Like you and I, they are bound by a sense of morality. They think and plan ahead but can also think themselves out of their conditioned states. They have risen above their nature and from here on will be able to utilize nature itself as a tool. They have been created in your image. At least your image of what it means to be people, though undeveloped as they are."

Joshua watched as the two people found their identities again and prepared to face the world outside. They could not stay in the oasis. They knew too much of where they came from to ever be content again living amongst the bones of their ancestors.

Through much trial and error, they created woven baskets. They overlapped blades of grass in cross patterns and then alternated. The weave was loose and lacked a nice hemmed edge, but the wide flat woven mat seemed to hold the weight of the fruits, allowing them to travel with more than a bellyful. Though they would not get very far with what they could carry, they could get far enough to see what there was to see.

As the oasis dried up, and the trees burst forth in their final desperate glory, the pair set off with determination in no particular direction.

Joshua made the flowers bloom in their path to guide their steps toward the nearest river and forest canopy. The woman rushed ahead to pluck the bouquet she adorned herself with. The man smelled each one as he passed, sensing in the blossoms a hint of the connection to the greater world. As it happened, they were headed back the way their ancestors had come from. There was no great savanna and no enormous vicious predators. They encountered some harmless wild dogs and hawks in the sky, but the monsters from their ancestral memories were no longer as fierce. The distance wasn't nearly as long as they had been led to believe. The great desert stretched for maybe half a day for them, and though they were thirsty, they found on the other side an ancient river that flowed clear and cool despite the climate and dust. They even arrived with some of the fruit leftover from their oasis.

Finding other fresh and ripe fruits at the riverbank, they opted to discard their burden and content themselves with the new luxury they found themselves in. They were under no duress, no predators stalked them, and there was plenty of food around. The river had an odd but enticing splash that increased at sunup and at sundown. As the pair watched, they ate, and they mated.

"Flowers look pretty. Not pretty as woman." He flirted brutishly.

She blushed and then said enticingly, "You smell flowers on ground. Not smell as good as these." She gestured to the ones stuck in her hair. "You come smell?" she cooed at the man, and he took the hint. Along the riverbank, with the warm breeze dancing in the treetops and the splash of water on the shore, they secured their lineage.

The influence of the forbidden fruit having long since left their system, and with only a sneaking memory of it, they reverted back to their primal selves.

They were the last two of a unique experiment. They'd passed the test but were scarred by it. Their new purpose was to proliferate, and their progeny would face other tests.

As the first of the lineage came forth into the world, Joshua watched with wonder at what they might become. He saw in the first child all the struggles of the world that had come before him. The millions of years of evolution, the loneliness, the anger, the futility he felt all washed away. The reason for it all became abundantly clear now. This child represented the future. The innocence and awareness in that tiny face told Joshua that there was something worth preserving, something to fight for and live for. He felt something powerful stirring inside him—a tender feeling rather than the cold aloofness he had developed. He saw in this child all the hope of the world to come.

He felt a growing warmth in his chest. His face flushed, and his eyes tingled with threatening tears. In the Machine, this was all just a sensation, but he knew he loved this child. He would love each one who came forth from these beautiful beings. These were his chosen People.

The abundance of food and safety and water provided enough time for mating. Every now and then an idea popped into their heads for something they could do to make their lives easier. Joshua inspired all those ideas. He gave them dreams and visions and guidance in every subtle way he could.

A vessel made from mud and dried in the sun could carry fruit and water away from the river, making it possible for them to venture a little further out. A long stick with a point on it could be poked at the things splashing in the river, providing a big hunk of meat. Their diet expanded, as did their range and their camp. Now, one baby at a time, they had room to grow in numbers as well. No longer confined by their biology, they could travel and explore and thrive.

These two lived much longer than their predecessors had. They still bred prolifically and saw many generations born after them. With no natural predator, their isolation meant they were biologically incompatible with most other species and did not suffer from the communicable ailments and diseases that the rest of the environment contracted. Their heirs remembered them as having lived a dozen generations, yet Joshua knew they were barely into their eightieth year before they died. As the population grew, more exposure to the environment made them more susceptible to the environment's cruelties, and so their lifespans shortened even as they bred later and later.

Joshua could not protect these People forever. As the environment adapted to them, and they to it, diseases and maladies became a bane of their existence. Though their later childbirth ensured they were healthier and stronger before enduring it, it was still the leading cause of death among his People. He struggled to watch without interfering. They needed to endure that suffering so they could grow stronger as a species even as it tortured him to watch the suffering of the individuals.

18

"Every being carries with it a piece of where it's been. . . ." The teacher's words seemed like something from a billion years ago, but they were the truth. Here Joshua could see the dull, colorless lecture play out. He watched each species of tree isolated by environment flourish once the seeds found new ground to propagate on. Some species went extinct in regions they once flourished in, simply because they were no longer suited to that environment once a foreign seed was introduced. Yet some proved more resilient, even against the invaders, once they adapted.

The same was true of the fruits carried from the oasis. The seeds took root in the fertile riverbank of the new home and gradually took over. Other plants couldn't endure this foreign invader at first. It had been cultivated in an oasis, so it was more efficient at using the available resources than the other plants and threw the ecosystem out of balance.

The People, however, saw this as a positive change. The fruit they'd once survived on now grew here as well. Even the forbidden fruit flourished. It still caused paralysis and hallucinations, but the People found that it became a useful tool for enlightenment and divine experiences of connecting with Joshua. And paralyzing the fish they sought meant they were easier to catch. They planned to keep the fruit as part of their society forever.

But over time, it no longer had the same effect. Though the original toxicity had not declined, the People's constant use of it turned the once hallucinogenic drug into a common staple in their diet. Their leisurely pursuit of that experience caused their bodies to adapt to it.

It contented Joshua to see this occur. The drugs had become a distracting pastime for the People, and they were far less productive because of it. The more adapted to the drug they became, the less it appealed to them and the less they saw Joshua. It was better to see them come by invention on their own. Without the drug, he also knew which were relying on a "divine" experience and which had the higher natural creativity.

Eventually, the People took the lesson of the discarded fruits and applied it to the grasslands. They liked the variety of foods available at the river when they had first arrived, but because of their imports, most of this was lost. They opted to bury the fruits of other plants for safekeeping. When these sprouted, they tried again and again and, by accident, discovered farming.

Joshua admired these industrious People and their ingenuity. There was something satisfying about observing a species that controlled its own destiny. While they were still largely at the mercy of nature, as they mastered it, harnessing its power, learning its rhythms, and sculpting it to their will, they conquered it. They did the same with all other creatures still enslaved by nature. As they conquered their environment, the People became autonomous.

Out of a need for prediction, they began watching the stars. They had long ago recognized that the night sky remained fairly consistent, and that as it turned, the stars fell to the horizon. As the seasons changed, the stars they saw seemed different. Certain ones were more prominent. The People broke the sky up into equal parts. They knew when the sun had set for the day. If a particular grouping of stars was visible, they counted on certain natural events occurring.

The rains came with the sign of the fish, so they planted when it first appeared, knowing the plants needed water to flourish. When another sign appeared, they harvested. During the next, they gathered wild berries. Another warned them to prepare for the cold winds.

Personalities shaped in utero by the available seasonal diets became associated with those signs, and the culture grew around the importance of properly arranging couplings and planning events. Marriages, hunts, festivals, and celebrations were planned around particularly auspicious days that followed the natural rhythms of the stars. Out of science grew myth.

The growth of the population, the abundance of food from agriculture, the luring of wild animals also seeking a cheap meal led the People to invention. They could not catch the rats that ate their harvest, so they devised tools to kill them from a distance—snares of woven grasses, rocks and sticks to smash them, throwing stones to hit them from afar, and pointed sticks to stab them with. They ate the meat from these kills, and their diet expanded.

When the People killed wild dogs, they captured and fenced in the pups, and allowed the calmest and most docile to live in the community. They used others as hunters, as guards, or as pest control. The dogs kept predators at bay and vermin to a minimum and allowed the People in the villages to rest easier knowing their loud bark would alert them if the need arose.

Everything about this nascent civilization awed Joshua. Every invention arose from logical necessity, yet all the systems they implemented, and tools they devised, were prevalent around them in nature. When they paired one skill with another, it formed a more complex idea that grew and flourished. It was beautiful to observe, the elegant choreography of these thinking beings mimicking the natural process with purpose and precision and overcoming enslavement to the natural world.

The People began to unravel the natural laws of nature and revealed the fundaments of all the knowledge that followed.

The influence of the Machine was evident in all this, yet Joshua wondered if it had created this phenomenon or if the environment that shaped the Machine provided the laws that governed the simulation.

"What came first, the Machine or the environment that shaped it?" Joshua asked.

"Obviously the environment," the Technician stated flatly. "But if your question is about the laws of nature in the Machine, then the laws existed outside, but the Machine proved them. That allowed us to refine the laws to more accurately represent reality and update the Machine."

"Then the laws that exist here are true to nature and reality?"

"Yes. As true as our minds and society can comprehend. As true as our technology can test and retest and prove. As true as logic can determine from the countless people who have gone through the Machine and proven or disproven the theories time and again."

Despite his adversarial approach to his role in the Machine, Joshua could always count on the Technician to give a straight answer. Perhaps knowing the truth was not as important as knowing how to use it. Joshua had all, or at least many, of the pieces, but he had no idea what to do with them. At least not yet.

19

Barter is the most rudimentary form of commerce. 'I have something you want, you have something I want, let's trade.' The inherent value of an item is in its usefulness and the difficulty of collection. A fruit can be collected and grown by anyone—therefore it holds low inherent value—while a fish requires more skill and equipment, so a fish is worth more. So the barter of a fish for fruit ensures that a bushel of the fruit based on the labor of gathering and the labor of gathering the fish creates relative value for each in relation to each other. This also ensures that the higher value item attracts more labor from the society. Over time, there are more fishermen than gatherers. And so, the value of the fish falls to market equivalency with the fruit.

"The most successful planters grew trees that bore more fruit so they could afford to barter for more fish without having to catch it themselves. More successful fishermen caught more fish. They understood the fish better, knew the secret spots, or developed new techniques that ensured the fish came to them. Likewise, for the hunters, success meant relative ease. Naturally, this left some who were less adept unable to compete and forced them to find more gainful employment. They could not guarantee a fish every day, and they could not find the fruit on their own, so they relied on the rest of the society for assistance or they starved."

The teacher had droned on. Every day a new lesson about something long since passed. That day had focused on economics and the foundations of blah, blah, something, something. She never gave these lectures with any sort of judgment on their merits, only explaining them as a natural process. There was no alternative, no matter what environment. This was simply how it was.

Joshua lost focus frequently when it came to these lectures. Again, the rain falling on the leaves outside the window or the insects taking shelter and fighting against the forces of nature for shelter captured his attention. He looked out the window and saw a cart making its way down the road to the next town, the tarp billowing in the wind and whipping up at the corners, the excess production of the village making its way to the city through little weigh stations along the way.

The lecture droned on. "Barter is the most rudimentary form of economic activity. It is in fact a natural process, the same as reproduction and consumption. It derives from the need to eat, the uncertainty of eating, and the influence of those who never have trouble finding enough to eat. In the wild, animals prostitute themselves for extra portions of food. They pay each other in portions of food for security and protection. Not every animal in a herd devotes itself to finding food. Some solely provide protection. The question that forms the foundation of economic theory is 'what is my value? What can I provide that will make me worth preserving to others?' For females, it may be their reproduction. For males, it is their protection. For others, it is what they can provide materially. Ultimately, each determines their value and trades that for survival within the group, and so becomes the basis of economics."

Without raising his hand, Joshua opined, "That means that prostitution is the oldest profession then, that and guard."

"And producer. There is no oldest single profession. All professions today are merely complex variations of those three. We all today produce something in the fields and sell it in the markets, who pay for guards to transport it to the city where it is bought by those who trade themselves for money. The producer, the protector, and the prostitute are active in every part of life."

"But what about the bandit?" Joshua asked defiantly, "Hasn't there also always been a fourth alternative to simply steal and kill for a larger portion?"

The teacher was not amused and didn't miss a step, "No one who lives solely off the means of others survives long. Yes, they can kill. Once. Then the pack turns on them. They are not trusted. They are not lusted after. They have proven they are more important to themselves than the troupe is, and they can suffer alone or perish. They are exiled, and very few creatures survive alone. Even those who live off the charity of others are expected to repay it somehow. Charity is a loan society gives to the desperate to be paid in blood when the need arises. There has never been any variation on either of these two ideas. And they only arise after the establishment of the aforementioned economic dynamic."

Joshua watched as his little social experiment blossomed into a thriving colony. His People were industrious. Just as the teacher had suggested in a lecture about bartering and economics, all had a role. Sure, there were some who seemed to have no tangible skills. The males could not bear children, so the unskilled were less useful to the nascent society. Females had more natural value to a society for their ability to reproduce. This higher value also went with less risk. They were not expected to venture far away or risk themselves for the collective effort. So they tended to the village life, and the males assumed the risk—and rewards.

Joshua was constantly amazed by the ingenuity and industry of these People. It was the instinct to survive, just as the teacher had explained, that allowed them to thrive. The use of sex as a means of survival was alive and well. If a female failed in other professions, she could always earn a meal by using the promise of paternity. The production of food from gathering, hunting, fishing, and farming, along with exploration and experimentation, was as fundamental to the society as anything. But the society could not survive, could not grow, and could not find purpose in its existence without children, so this became the highest value produced in the society.

As always, the wilderness needed to be kept at bay, so some stood watch over the town day and night. This took them away from otherwise productive efforts, so they lived off the communal resources, a portion of the production of their society that allowed them to maintain peace and keep the village secure.

As the seasons moved, people had lots of downtime, leaving lots of time for experimentation. New technology arose from necessity. Waste was turned into something productive. Rot was made nutritious. Shelters became hardened and permanent. Wherever value could be increased or preserved, these people found ways to do it.

The more inept harvesters were forced by necessity to try the most rotted fruits in order to have anything to eat. Where profit was the father of invention, necessity became its mother. The poor would pick through the fruit and find the least rotted until there was nothing left but the mush.

In order to maximize the amount of food kept, they wrapped it to protect it from the flies and insects. They kept it as high as possible to prevent the rodents from reducing their stores. Their fruit became shriveled and dehydrated over time because of this. Where at first, they threw it out, the smallest harvests in the worst seasons forced some to at least try the shriveled fruit. When the first person didn't die, they went out and collected more and found that they could sustain themselves on it.

Others would take the mush and add it to water. Vessels made of hardened soil were used for cooking. Boiling water took away the chill of the winter air and became a drink of choice. Adding the fruit mush made that water more flavorful. The mush could be cooked without water and hardened into a more palatable portion. This also made it last longer. Moisture was removed, and in a covered container it lasted even longer. When the bitter tubers of the winter were gathered, the paste was used to add flavor and sweetness.

The poor who found themselves starving and suffering wandered into the nearby savannas and forests searching for food. When desperation finally took its toll, they were forced to try anything. They found a sticky yellow goop in a grid made by flying insects. They found wild roots and flowers that all proved edible. These discoveries enabled those individuals to expand the diets of the village.

Inventions improved the lives of the people. Those improved lives flourished and expanded, and eventually a village on a river grew and grew until the sprawl of connected villages pushed the population across the horizon.

The People marketed their inventions to each other. Some were easier sells than others, and those inventions proved the worth of their merits and those of the inventor. The People bartered and traded and improved the efficiencies of their lives through invention. Some were lazy and had to use their wits to prove their worth. Others were industrious and used their perseverance to prove their value to society. Those who had neither wits nor industry found their portion of paternity grow smaller and smaller as the society aged.

Joshua played his part in this age of discovery. He saw in each of these People that first child born after the oasis. He saw the glimmer in their eyes of consciousness, and he loved each of them. He guided the hungry to the foods that would preserve them. Then he watched as they devastated the rest of the ecosystem hunting for that one root, or the next hive, or the special flowers that kept them alive. He loved them, yet saw their destructiveness manifest in everything they did. They were clever, but they were selfish.

20

Joshua continued developing other creatures and plants and manipulating the environment as he had before. But it was the People that he took the most interest in. Splitting groups and isolating them and growing them into two distinct subgroups no longer brought him joy.

"I don't find any pleasure in this anymore," Joshua said to the Technician.

"Who says there's any pleasure intended?" the Technician challenged.

"What I mean is, it's no different than the environments. The animals are shaped by the environment. The plants are shaped by the climate. And the climate is shaped by the environments elsewhere. There is no real point in shaping a creature to take on a larger or different niche because the vacuum they leave is filled by something else."

"There is nothing new under the sun, I'm afraid. You are correct, but it is your responsibility to yourself to evolve. Those creatures with the most diverse capabilities in any ecosystem are the ones that are capable of becoming a civilization. But science is the replication and repetition of the accidents of nature. You have only one civilization, and I had to trick you into creating it. You still don't know intuitively how they are created, so you have not finished the lesson yet."

The Technician said this with an air of threat. Joshua had no idea what form that threat would take, but it seemed his people would be at risk if it weren't taken seriously.

"What is the next step then?" Joshua asked, capitulating.

"Replicate the experience and repeat it until you understand how it works," the Technician said with finality and went silent again.

Joshua began to replicate and repeat the experience.

He learned a number of interesting things from this. His observations proved true over and over again.

Two species of different origins could be forced into environments and, while competing for the exact same resource, would find their genetic code converge until they were able to reproduce with each other. The environment and the resource made them compatible over time. Their evolutionary paths converged.

There are only a finite number of possibilities in a finite system. No matter what Joshua tried, there always seemed to be a drive to fill the vacuum. Where only one species existed, that species became both predator and prey, mean and kind, strong and weak. They filled all the available opportunities of the environment they lived in. Only with Joshua's guidance did they take a path he chose for them.

If he wanted to create more nimble creatures, he created opportunities for the less nimble to fill that void, killing off the nimblest martyr the rest would emulate. All the remaining creatures saw the opportunity left behind and fought for that position, which had its own survival benefits. Competition creates efficiencies and forces equal competitors to find a competitive advantage. By degrees, the whole ecosystem could become nimbler in their pursuit of the opportunities of that niche. He saw that creation of a moral society required martyrdom, a polite society mayhem, and a creative society oppressive order.

Joshua contemplated these lessons as he molded the next batch of would-be civilizations.

Now was the time of replication.

———⊗⊗⊗———

Joshua had isolated numerous other creatures in the same way as in the oasis. All different in their origins, yet all were isolated in similar style ecosystems—an oasis in a desert, a cavern in a frozen wasteland, a verdant plateau in a volcanic hell, and an island on the vast salt oceans. He had many of each, all large enough to contain the nourishment the creatures needed and isolated enough to prevent nature from interfering. He had to devise ways to prevent the actions of the Technician from spoiling their biospheres, which was a struggle of learning in itself.

In some ecosystems he forced multiple species to coexist, finding natural symbiosis and seeing what emerged. In others it was a battle royal, where the most vicious carnivores vied with each other for survival, breeding fast enough to supply each other with food, small or large enough to be sustained from a single kill, until they eventually became a symbiotic braid. All became the same size, evolved to equal each other's speed, and were able to breed with one another. A short-term advantage went to those with interspecies reproduction. The offspring took on the strongest traits of each parent and were able to dominate the others, yet this strategy was replicated in the other species as well, a part of the symbiosis. Eventually the original competitors went extinct, and the emergent ones were hybrids of the others. They could all reproduce with one another, though their offspring were sterile at first. Their increasing cohabitation led the offspring to become increasingly viable, and then they were able to reproduce freely with either ancestral group. Joshua found that any number of creatures isolated would eventually homogenize as a single creature as long as they competed for the exact same niche in the ecosystem. This he replicated tens of thousands of times at every scale in every environment.

While he watched the oasis with fascination, he also developed the same pattern, and what emerged had similar results of varying qualities.

Joshua watched impassively as the work to create a new civilization from a river lizard failed spectacularly. "They don't have the capacity to make or use tools, and they don't see any consequence in killing the last survivor of their species."

"They are doomed to nature, certainly," the Technician said. "Some creatures are simply tools to shape others. Just as some systems, religions and people are. They have no purpose other than that. This lizard is no different, but anything else that lives in its environment must learn to adapt to its presence, so it is as much a part of the environment as the stones or the prevailing winds are."

"So not all creatures are equipped to become civilization."

"Any creature *can* be, at least to a very rudimentary level before they descend back into nature. The amount of effort to make an alligator into a farmer, though, would make the endeavor pointless. And frankly, I'm not patient enough to allow you to force that outcome."

"I think I'm content knowing how the process works now, then."

"I'm content knowing that you do."

21

The desert oasis was the first successful experiment but not the last. Out of the tundra of the north emerged another group developed from herd animals whose tree of death was the blood of their kin. Another developed from sea creatures too lean and dense to swim when climate change trapped them on an isolated island far from the land. Their tree of death was a slowly learned fear of the water and their habit of drinking the salt water that caused hallucination for them.

This was the case in each oasis. Only in overcoming their object of fear could they experience a paradigm shift in their own self-awareness that would catapult them into a different level of society.

For the most part, they did not develop as rapidly or cleverly as the people of the desert had, perhaps a testament to the Technician's uncanny skill in devising such tests. Many died off despite Joshua's best efforts to nurture them. Others were simply incapable of adapting after their release from captivity and died off when the oasis's ecosystem collapsed around them. Others were not adequately protected from the machinations of the Technician. Each habitat was a game of chess. While the Technician didn't seek to destroy any specific specimens, it wasn't hard for him to do so. This forced Joshua to be thorough to avoid the Technician exploiting any of his failures. The result hardened Joshua to the emotions of failure and made him more honest with himself about the shortcomings of his work.

Yet those that did emerge with many of the qualities that Joshua sought thrived in their respective environments. From this trial and error, Joshua was able to determine the best traits for survival. These virtues were difficult to manifest totally though. He found a natural drive in all creatures, an inherent desire to destroy themselves. They would overeat and hunt their prey into extinction and starve to death themselves. They saw what their brethren had and tried to take it, triggering unnecessarily fatal conflicts that left many injured and weakened. Others forsook their desires for food and health for self-gratification. They spent all their time pursuing simulated reproduction instead of activities that would make them more fruitful. Even when their behavior was primarily virtuous, they often strayed, making decisions favoring their self-destructive behaviors.

Joshua had no direct prohibition against any of those sins. He learned through trial and error that leveraging nature created the appropriate reward-and-punishment dynamic necessary to shape a creature's behavior. It made no sense to him to eliminate every desire for fornication or the willingness to fight over trivialities or the ability to kill or the desire to eat too much. Each had its value in certain situations, but these persistent proclivities prevented the species from achieving their potential. Joshua found that without direct attention, those who were more virtuous would be destroyed by those who weren't. The same happened with their offspring—the violent quickly eradicated the nonviolent in one-on-one situations.

The best solution was to find those who could meter their violence, their consumption, their lust. Those with self-discipline plus the capabilities of the sinful were the best survivors. They were not dependent on the bounty or scarcity of nature. They could measure their response, what they would take, and what they would leave.

While these colonies of creatures continued to grow, they occasionally encountered one another, and the reaction became the next catalyst of growth in their cultures.

Joshua used this to drive his creatures together. Their conflict became their binding. Some groups were completely dominated by others. Subjugated and enslaved, they fought for survival at the bottom of their conjoined society. The genetic overlap took thousands of years before they began to merge. The result was a single species.

It was this dynamic that had played out for those from the desert oasis. Joshua was proud of these People, but they were still selfish and weak, and though he loved them, he felt they needed refinement.

One day a group of hunters was on the fringe of their territory. They stepped into unfamiliar land while chasing game. They tracked the game to an isolated valley and sent one of their members back to let the village know. As they approached, they found an eerie scene, a clearing that not long before had been trampled by hundreds of feet. Not feet like theirs, but longer, wider, and with only three large toes. The footprints didn't belong to the game they chased. The signs of fire in the center of the clearing suggested a group lived and hunted from there.

At that moment a branch broke, and as they turned to look at the noise, creatures twice the size of the hunters and covered in dull black feathers emerged from the shadows. They had vestigial wings with claws at the ends that they used as arms.

One of the hunters cocked his arm back to throw a spear at the closest attacker and was struck in the ribs with a javelin thrown from the shadows. He fell. The others circled in a defensive posture, wide-eyed and uncertain what to make of these creatures. From the forest came a volley of stones that struck the hunters head to toe, incapacitating all of them. As they lay bleeding and stunned, semiconscious, the bird-beasts lashed their hands together around a long pole and tethered the hunters together by the ankles, one rope for their left ankles and another for their right.

Over the next few nights, the Birdmen picked off and captured all the villagers except a few lucky ones who'd left town immediately after people started going missing. Those spread the viral rumor and mobilized the other nearby villages to the defensive.

Those captured were enslaved, first broken of their will to fight, then broken of their hope for escape, then broken of their will to live. They toiled in the valley, reducing the cliffs to sheer walls and digging a hole deep into the ground in search of whatever these birds deemed a treasure.

Yet when the Birdmen tried to take captives of the next village, they met stronger resistance, still capturing more slaves but losing some of their own in the struggle. Once the rumors spread and the rest knew what they were fighting and where they came from, villages mobilized and stopped the birds. The struggle continued for centuries.

In the end the slaves became too numerous to contain, and the fight had been too long and draining. When the slaves revolted, they managed to kill their captors. The simultaneous assault from villages pushed the Birdmen deep into the mountains where they came from.

Sometimes years passed without incident, but people always disappeared near the fringes of their civilization. When people started returning, hybrids of the People and the Birdmen, they weren't welcomed or trusted, and many were killed outright. But they kept coming. Shunned by the Birdmen society and by the People, they became creoles without a home.

The creoles set up villages of their own on the borders of the others, and over time, they became part of the world. They held no sympathy for the home they had left behind, and as their strength grew, so did their anger for their former homelands.

When the People went on the offensive again, the creoles went with them, their tender alliance hinging on their mutual hatred for the Birdmen. When the war finished, the Birdmen were too few to rise again, and the few who remained were captured and enslaved. The People found that the slaves they liberated far exceeded the number of people in the villages. The Birdmen deemed it prudent to breed more slaves rather than capture them, so they increased their numbers tenfold over what they captured and threefold over what was already in the villages. The Birdmen were taken prisoner, but over several generations, the creoles absorbed them, and the People absorbed the creoles, so the two societies merged, and the genes of both were strengthened.

Over and over the same pattern played out. Sometimes the result was surprising. The tactics used for one group to dominate the other varied dramatically. One group might use sex appeal to manipulate the other, thus conquering them with peace. Others used violence or deception. The dynamic was always the same though: the meek overcame their oppressors.

To Joshua, this pattern became tedious. He'd mastered the creation of civilizations, and now he had mastered their merging. Yet he still held a soft spot in his heart for the People. They were the first, and they proved to be resilient despite numerous hardships. They emerged stronger each time and more confident. He admired them as a parent admires their child for learning and mastering a new skill. He loved them more than all the rest.

22

A thousand times a thousand times, Joshua repeated this process. His original People still thrived. As they encountered a new group, they conquered them. If they were enslaved, they usurped their masters. Some groups were completely annihilated, like the Giants, as he referred to them. For a brief time they dominated because of their size, but the smaller, more nimble People learned the weaknesses of these behemoths and, after a brief era of slavery, overthrew their masters and killed every one of them.

Some encounters turned cooperative. The northern herd people encountered the desert people and after a brief conflict accepted each other's presence. They had villages populated by people from both cultures and knit together a mutually satisfying culture. The resultant offspring were never acknowledged as desert children, but the hybrids continued to mate with them. Plagues exterminated the remaining pure-blooded northern people, but their genes were still carried forward by the hybrids.

These People were not deterred by any environment, and they used both the cultural innovations they encountered from other species and their tools. They learned to use the skins of other creatures to augment their own as a buffer against the weather and to make artificial skins from grasses and crops they had encountered in other cultures. It came to be that every person on the planet was descended from the original two that emerged from the desert oasis. While there were other subgroups that maintained a prolific population, the desert people had traveled far and wide enough that every one of the subgroups had been able to reproduce with them. Though the desert people conquered from time to time, it was because they themselves were conquered and suffered at the hands of many masters that they were so widely dispersed.

Slaves were ever present. Because the conditions were the most severe, only the hardiest survived. They were proved in the kiln of misery and emerged as a group much more resilient. The subjugation stripped them of their pretense, the trappings of freedom like wealth and beauty, and whittled them down to the essence of their beings, the kernel of identity deep inside their souls that showed who they really were. The subjugation actually made them *more* attractive as the survival traits were stronger in the slave than in the master, so the master's daughters were often found sneaking around the slave quarters.

Joshua was enamored with these slaves. He found ways of preserving their genes. They spread throughout the planet, interbreeding with other races and leaving the trace of their common ancestor in each civilization they served. Though these civilizations remained in place, they shared no commonality with the other master races except through the genes of the slaves.

The slaves thus formed an extensive network handling and trading goods. The more dependent the masters were on the slaves, the more skills and knowledge the slaves developed to perform more complex tasks. The slaves shared their knowledge with each other, and the skills spread. And so did plagues.

The slaves were long-suffering in all parts of the world. Where some were hybrids of their masters, they shared the bacteria and viruses that were largely benign in the region the plague originated from. Those viruses stopped being deadly to the slaves. The slaves and hybrids fared much better and fewer died, and the world became a little more homogenized with each pestilence. The slaves inherited the world.

This outcome surprised Joshua. Their humility allowed them to silently accept their persecution, and their self-discipline prevented their inner violence from striking out too soon. These were qualities he wanted in himself. To increase them, he would need to increase their numbers. He would cultivate his chosen People against the rest of the world. Slavery, as an economic tool, ensured that their masters would find ways of obtaining more, and cheaply. Buying them, breeding them, and depending on the slaves more and more ensured their survival and reproduction. The traits they were chosen for were their endurance to work long hours in the weather with little food or drink, their passivity to stay quiet and accept their fate without complaint, and their perceptiveness in picking up skills that their masters favored.

The cost of inheritance ensured that the masters themselves produced fewer and fewer offspring. And those offspring were born by political necessity and the ravages of mortality in order to merge two houses and their assets. Frail and weak, predisposed to lethargy and narcissism, they applauded themselves as they lost their inheritance to foolish endeavors. Then they lost their lives to the slaves they thought they dominated.

23

The desert was ideal for forcing the People to deal with scarcity and high temperature. The cultures they encountered provided the technology that allowed those same People to deal with the cold. Nature forced their adaptation to the highest extreme, and intelligence enabled them to endure the lowest. In this way their conquest of the world was preordained. But there still survived the isolated gene pools that dominated the tiny oases they had emerged from.

The world continued as it had all along. Each enclave had specific advantages and disadvantages, but with the People enslaved throughout the world, those traits were transmitted into their genes. The best traits were nourished, and the worst were starved out. The more the slave resembled their masters, the better their conditions were. The more they were bred, the more the genes of the master race were transmitted to those of the slave. It was one particularly cruel enclave that forced Joshua's decision to finally liberate the People.

In the far northern tundra, an empire arose that saw the People as disposable. They had the wealth of furs that the other cultures sought, and in trade the People were once again taken as slaves. They were not well fed or given appropriate clothes for the harsh environment. The masters forced them to chip ice and stone from glacial peaks for days at a time without respite. Their hands and bare feet frozen black, their bones shattering from the impact on the glassy surface, they were whipped and beaten until death. They were doomed.

The cruelty of this practice made Joshua hot with fury. He no longer erupted as he once did; he burned low and hot, a blue flame at the coals. He could see the People in every enclave of the world and knew they would be the most likely to survive a cataclysm.

It was time to liberate these slaves and create an apocalypse, to lock in the genetic diversity that made his People special. He needed a cataclysm to do this, though, a shock that would release the built-up tensions of the planet without permanently altering the established conditions.

He found a suitable fault line and, with a single fallen rock, redirected the flow of a river to the soft sediment over the fault. As the water percolated down, the fault was lubricated and began to slip, little by little. When it finally broke, the surface shifted in a sudden jolt, and a tsunami of water rushed across the ocean triggering other earthquakes that broke the planet's surface in predictable ways.

The static pressure of the planet unleashed, all at once, the tension on landmasses from the constant pressure of the ocean causing the frictional energy that liquefied the underlying rock, and they tore open. Violent eruptions took place. The edges of continents—undermined by the constant pressure of great depths tearing away at the footing, the tilt of the dry brittle land leaning over the depths—broke free, unleashing earthquakes that crumbled mountains and split the continents. New pathways for water flowed, and the mixture of cold oceans and warmer seawater created massive storms that blacked out the sun's light. Wild winds tore at the forests and landscape, permanently displacing topsoil, sand, and populations of plants, animals, and people.

The soot from the volcanoes across the world, the massive storms along the coasts, the earthquakes dislodging rocks and debris caused the widespread death of huge swaths of the planet's flora and fauna. Those who survived looked out at a barren and dying landscape and felt their hopes disappear. There was no food and very little clean water left, and as the seasons changed, the moisture in the air from the massive storms formed even more massive blizzards that blanketed the poles and lower latitudes with snow and ice.

The snow and ice reflected the stars' light rather than absorbing it. The death of so many plants prevented the moisture from being absorbed, and losing so many animals meant the greenhouse gases that prevented the planet from freezing were now in short supply.

Joshua guided the People where they needed to go. Not all of them survived, but all of them were now free. The slaves were saved by the inhospitable nature of their labors. The high mountains where they froze were oozing molten lava. The glaciers melted and the lahars wiped out the towns of their masters. In the deserts, the tsunamis were rapidly absorbed by the thirst of the sands, and their masters, tangled in their fineries, were washed away and battered to death while the People were naked and stood unharmed after the flow ebbed. In the hills and mines and quarries, the mountains themselves provided shelter from the tumbling debris that crushed the masters in their tents.

The slaves endured because they had nothing, because they were prolific and ubiquitous. As the world stopped shaking and the tides stopped surging, they emerged from the wreckage. When the few surviving masters tried to bind them again, the People rose up and destroyed them. They massacred every one of their tormentors.

And then they started their journeys to new lands away from the raging storms and plummeting temperatures.

━━━◦∞◦━━━

Each year found more of the polar regions succumbing to frozen death, and fewer people and animals ventured there. The mass exodus of survivors headed to the equatorial region. The population of the whole planet would be packed into a tight band that maintained temperate conditions year round. Yet the wind still blew, the storms still raged, and the moisture continued to freeze and fall at the poles. The sea level fell, and the salinity increased as the water evaporated and got redistributed. The fish died off, and huge areas of land were exposed from the receding water. Ice covered much of the world. The few survivors found refuge in the lowlands and valleys within twenty-three degrees of the equator.

Though there were survivors outside that band, life was harsh and sad. But in every low area, water flowed, and once again the People could find refuge in an oasis and adapt and survive.

━━━◦∞◦━━━

Joshua guided a small band of stragglers from the encroaching glaciers of the north where they had toiled and frozen under their former masters. With no one to crack a whip at them or beat them, they took their survival in their own hands.

Each day they moved with the flow of water and animals downhill and toward the equator. Each village they came across was similarly destroyed or vacated. Even the few survivors of the masters' race did nothing to halt their progress, most just staring with hollow eyes and sadness as the world they knew was destroyed around them.

The path ahead was well worn by the tracks of similar bands of refugees. Some of the masters moved on. Most were too devastated and stayed behind hoping their world would re-emerge from the ashes overnight. They fell victim to this errant thinking. The People migrated en masse wherever the world guided them.

Joshua had very little to do with it other than to ensure there were wild berries to be plucked and small game to catch to provide the nourishment the People needed to make their way to the refuge of the valleys they would make their new lives in.

He guided others toward a single giant valley. It was an enormous scar across the landscape. It had once been full of water, but that water evaporated or froze and turned to ice in the upper highlands. Initially the people were forced to live at the edges of the giant lake that stood there facing the elements and the frigid winters. But as the lake receded, the people were able to move lower and lower. The ice walls climbed higher and higher behind them, isolating and insulating the valley from the oppressive storms that raged high above. The ground proved fertile and rich, and they were able to establish communities in a temperate lowland.

Eventually, only rivers flowed into the vast green valley, and those rivers pooled in a lake far down the valley. Even that became smaller and smaller as populations and plant life grew, using more of the tributary waters before they reached the lake far below.

The rules of population migration predicted the movement of people, plants, and animals. The path of least resistance was down. The valley became a dense and diverse ecosystem that stretched one hundred times the distance from horizon to horizon. It became an ark for the world and enabled the People to become a more unified genetic composite. The animals, too, became more unified among those that shared certain niches in their isolated habitats previously.

Like a river of people, the settlements down the valley perimeter marked the paths of their migration. The constant effort to find easier living and more temperate climates than the harsh upper reaches put most of the population pressure at the waterfront.

These former slaves brought their hardiness and skillsets and conditioning to their newfound freedom. Their children kept multiplying and moving away. Unused to the notion of family, they left when they were able. Before long the whole valley was full of people. Wild animals were pushed into the harsh extremities, and only domesticated livestock and pets were kept in the community. The people themselves began the process of selectively breeding these animals. Once-towering beasts used for their lactation now stood waist high. They were selected for their milk, so the smaller beasts could produce as much milk as their ancestors could. The world was forced by increasing population pressure to become more efficient.

—⁂—

Joshua had guided one troupe to the water's edge. Abandoned boats and ropes from what had been a fishing village remained, and the People were able to put them to use. Though none had fished before, they had cast nets and used ropes for their labor. Joshua gave them the visions and dreams they needed to see how to make it all work for their purposes.

Before long the troupe of refugees had established a foothold. They had food to eat and water to drink, shelter and tools to make a life with. Though they faced the cold bluster of the wind, their past life in the glaciers meant they had endured far worse conditions and were not uncomfortable where they were.

The village became a burgeoning hub of activity as more people straggled in from the frozen lands to the north. Even as the shoreline receded, the town grew, and the village chased the waterline farther and farther. While the population continued to grow and expand, the remnants farther inland continued to feel the pressure to seek refuge, but while those on the water's edge had stable lives, they were fiercely territorial and pushed the latecomers out.

The most violent were most successful at holding the waterfront, but they were the least suited to the patience of catching fish. The least aggressive were also the most adaptable. They simply moved down the shoreline until they could find a spot to get in.

Joshua was ever watchful of these People. There was an admirable quality in both strategies on their own. But Joshua was much more sympathetic to those who moved on. They weren't deterred; they weren't cowering—they simply saw easier opportunities elsewhere.

The water receded slowly at first, but then much more rapidly as its reservoir narrowed. Those who had fought too hard for the space they claimed found themselves stubbornly left behind by the waterline. Where they failed at fishing, they found the newly churned soil arable and springing to life. They began the difficult process of producing farms from the remnants of the cultures they had escaped.

Generations came and went, and no generation walked on the same shoreline of their forebearers. Those who were once fishermen found their lives ending as farmers. Those who fought for space on the shoreline found the crowds grow denser and denser as the waterline continued to recede. Those who fed themselves from the sea found the catch getting slimmer and slimmer as the volume of the water shrank. The entirety of the surviving population pressed into the valley, and when both sides of the sea finally met when the water level fell far enough, there arose a city like two waves crashing and thrusting upward.

All the People carried with them the remnants of the fallen civilizations they once served—all the foods they could eat, the animals that could be domesticated, the plants that could be cultivated, and the tools and skills that could be leveraged came with them. The variety and the diversity of the population and the vast array of technology and products ensured that the most effective and efficient and popular would flourish. And industries arose around replicating those tools for wide distribution.

The crush of people ensured the transmission of the ideas

that recreated the cultures that had died out. Even the genes of those cultures were carried through the People, and though they faded out almost entirely, the ghost of those myriad people lived on through the People. The dominant traits expressed increasingly throughout the population.

―――∞∞∞――――

The growing population increased the heavier-than-air gases that created an insulating layer throughout the Valley and ensured that the winters were not harsh enough to do much damage, despite the towering ice cliffs that lined the Valley. The gases helped to melt off much of the surrounding ice. The result was an increase in water that helped saturate the soil of the Valley and keep it fresh and green despite the massive population and now burgeoning cities that emerged.

The ice walls, too, helped insulate the Valley. The gases couldn't escape, and neither could the evaporated moisture. Because of this, the Valley had its own weather patterns. It created its own storms from the falling cold air off the ice cliffs that penetrated and swirled as it mixed with the warm moist air below. The storms could be massive, sometimes devastating, but the water it unleashed ensured that the whole Valley was fertile and moist and food was abundant.

The population pressure constantly moving down the Valley ensured that there would be a cultural collision at the epicenter. With pressure from all sides, this epicenter sprouted up in the middle and rose tall and dense. Murder was a constant nuisance. Disease and filth were everywhere. People lived in squalor and could barely find work to pay for food that trickled into their sectors.

They died by multitudes. People banded together to make sure that even if everyone else suffered and died, they at least would remain. They wouldn't have much, but they would have enough to survive. These bands fought other bands openly, claiming territories in the crowded ghettos. They committed all manner of depravity and sought every means of escape from their misery—anything that would allow them to forget the world they lived in. Death did not worry them since life was no great pleasure.

For thousands of years the people in the Valley existed this way. Even as great efforts cleaned up the ghettos and improved conditions in one place, the constant flow of people meant another would emerge elsewhere to replace it. The People had forgotten the history that came before. It was locked up in the ice beyond, and they had no reason to remember. To them, the Valley became the only history, and they were able to forget the horrors that brought them there.

24

Joshua observed as the valley's population exploded. The salted and sterile soil made planting difficult, but rains flushed the salt out and vegetation sprouted. Crops flourished.

The People were as diverse in appearance as they were in personalities. He could still see in them the traits that reminded him of the cultures he despised, including the personalities of cultures that allowed such brutality. Yet they remained resilient. They had survived, largely without his aid, so he saw each one as a hero. He looked deep inside them and tried to figure out the qualities that made them so hardy. Where their fellow slaves had perished, these survivors were the progeny of those who had not. There was something special in each. But despite his love for them and sympathy for their suffering, they weren't all good.

The brutality that had served them in the mines and slave fighting pits did not translate well to freedom. They merely increased the suffering of other refugees.

Joshua sought to eradicate this trait. But the more complex personalities who reverted to that behavior only in times of stress were not wholly bad, and that conditioning could be cured. At least he hoped.

———————⌾———————

Joshua was stumped. He wanted to keep these tough individuals alive so they could toughen all the People, but the suffering they created far outweighed the benefits.

"What can I do?" He spoke aloud, hoping the Technician would answer.

The Technician did reply. "You are beginning to see why those you love must be culled or destroyed, even as you cherish some of their qualities."

Joshua replied haughtily, "Did I not kill off millions of the People in the cataclysm?"

The Technician was not stymied. "Yes, but that was a broad stroke. What you did tested the survivability of all of them without regard to their talents. You are better able to see the individual merits of each survivor. Their dominant traits are more readily apparent and can be assessed and culled as need be."

"How do I do that without destroying everything around them? I can't just drop a boulder on them. They'll only begin to fake the behavior that pleases me. Then it's tougher to identify truly bad qualities." Joshua was annoyed by his own inability to see the solution.

"They are no longer animals. You can use the systems they create to cultivate the traits you want and weed out the ones you don't. They will create sports to attract the strong and fast and limber. Their enterprises will attract the greedy and ambitious, and their politics the most sociopathic. They will create institutions that are attractive to every trait you can imagine, and then they will compete with one another until they face their end. You can shape the society to eliminate anything you want through some social custom or another. Religion is a very powerful tool for this end." The Technician almost seemed giddy as he spoke.

The notion of sculpting a whole society did seem exciting. Joshua felt increasingly hopeful that there would be a surprise end to his experience in the Machine.

Yet the memory of a lecture long ago drifted into his mind. He had no understanding of it then, but the Machine had made it clearer, and the objective now made it suddenly relevant.

"In every environment there is a roughly equal distribution of biomass in each niche within that environment. In our society, there are roughly equal proportions in agriculture, manufacturing, commerce, and government services. As such, our 'ecosystem' of society is in equilibrium." As the teacher had said *ecosystem*, she raised her hands and simulated air quotes. Joshua interpreted this as meaning that an ecosystem was more than forests and deserts, that the ecosystems of society where diverse identities competed for dominance were just as legitimately considered ecosystems to be molded and studied.

"When one part of that ecosystem is disrupted, a vacuum occurs. All who are capable compete to fill it. Their former positions are then vacated, and the next tier competes for those positions. Whatever they leave behind is filled, and the whole of the ecosystem moves steadily toward that single niche.

"In religion, martyrdom of saints or holy men creates that vacuum. Others seek to fill it, thus creating a flow from all other parts of that society toward that moral perspective. Society thinks and acts more morally, at least for a time. If a vacuum is created in government, others compete to fill it as well, and the society becomes more ordered and more bureaucratic. If there's a vacuum in industry, all similar businesses and industries compete to find the most effective way to fill that void, creating more products and more efficiencies." She had listed a number of other voids and how they create an attractive force for the whole of society.

"As a caveat to this idea, however, is that not all of the ecosystem, or society as we are using as our example, are attracted to the vacuum. Since all opportunities need to be filled equally, only the most available and capable will seek to fill the void. This in essence extrudes those qualities from the rest of the ecosystem, and the other niches are purified." The teacher had made a gesture in the air, openly splaying her fingers and drawing her hand downward as she closed her fingers into a point. "Only the most susceptible are attracted. Yet no matter what, that niche will be filled."

Joshua had been intrigued by this philosophical concept. He could point to nothing directly to represent this idea, but it seemed to explain the purpose of so many tragedies they had read about and the subsequent rebirth of the societies they occurred in. He had asked with a curious look on his face, "So if all opportunities or niches must be filled equally, and you create a vacuum in one area, does that mean you will never completely eliminate an opportunity from society?"

The teacher had nodded as she replied, "Yes it does. There is a survival opportunity in our society. But just as there is competition in every aspect of life, there is competition within every sort of criminality. The best criminals rise to the top and eliminate or subjugate their competition, and the worst criminals are eliminated in the process. One eliminates the other, and the replacement is slightly less adept than the one they replace, making them an easier criminal. The more violent the criminal is, the noisier their ascent, thus making them easier to identify."

This idea had excited Joshua. "But you just said the rest of society flows toward that opportunity. Doesn't that make the society more criminal? How can you ever eradicate something like that?"

The teacher had smiled broadly in the exaggerated way she was used to, showing her approval for the question. "Well, Joshua, you can't. Yes, the society flows toward criminality, but only in equal parts. Though the opportunity exists, the opportunist must weigh for themselves whether they would be successful in that endeavor or whether they would be better in a different one. The trick is to starve that opportunity so it becomes less attractive. This is best done by establishing clear, focused laws with consequences and alternatives. A society like ours has very little criminality because our laws are not so invasive and our people are so vigilant."

Joshua had then wondered aloud, "So do we have criminals in our society?"

The teacher had laughed and stated flatly, "If we didn't, we wouldn't need government."

———⸎———

Joshua looked down at his society and the people forming tiny communities wherever they could. He needed to get rid of the malicious behavior without completely destroying the trait.

The only way he could think to do this was to eliminate those that met a certain threshold. If stress was the catalyst, then it wasn't the trait itself that needed to be culled, it was the reaction to stress. The lower the people's threshold for stress, the sooner those traits exhibited themselves, and the easier they were to cull. The population pressure was the most effective natural force for increasing stress he had available, so the traits that needed to be culled needed to be rewarded somehow to draw them into the most stressful environments. Once there they would face others with similar personality traits, similarly under stress, and the result of the two fighters facing each other would be to make the toughest survive the other. By halves, the population would have their stress threshold increase, while at the same time the negative traits would be removed. Evil destroyed evil.

25

Does anyone know the supply chain of our town?" the teacher asked the class. "How, for example, the food and products of our town get to the city and beyond? Why does the city need the food we produce? And why does this archaic system continue despite our advancement as a society?"

This was another of her lectures on the timelessness of certain qualities of civilization. The school day had started with a lesson about history and the nations that succumbed to starvation. They'd learned why sieges were effective in war, then progressed to the discussion of the natural hydrologic process and why food grown in nature was more sustainable than hydroponics. The teacher had also covered the proper ratio of farmland that was needed compared to industrial, commercial, and residential uses to optimize growth of a society. How many acres were required per person to sustain them? Why was hunting an inefficient means of sustenance for a large population? Each lesson, from history to chemistry to statistics, all centered on the agronomy cycle for her lesson about the supply chain.

A female student in the back of the class called out part of the answer. "Our farmers grow the crops, then sell them to the distributors at the market for the best available price. The distributor takes them to the rail station and ships everything to whichever city is offering the highest price for the day."

"Very good."

The girl bragged, "My father took me with him to the rail station one day, so I got to see the whole process."

"Very observant of you," the teacher commended. "And why do we want the highest price?"

Another student chimed in. "Because prices are a reflection of demand. It tells us where the food is needed most."

"True. And where is the price typically the highest?"

The same student continued. "In the city, since they don't grow anything themselves."

"And why not? The city is full of potential space for hydroponic growth, and it would eliminate the demand for our product. Prices would fall considerably, right?"

Joshua heard several murmurs in the class, but no one knew enough to disprove her.

The class waited for her to explain.

"The space in cities is limited and is used for the highest economic value per square meter. Governments collect taxes, and utilities are paid based on use, so the production of that square meter must be higher than the cost of that same space. With hydroponics, vast amounts of water, electricity, and heat must be used and regulated to be used productively. The produce grown must be of higher value than all that. Additionally, living organisms are destructive to every building system and will increase repair costs. Therefore, it is impractical to grow produce in the city from an economic perspective. What about the merits of hydroponics?"

Joshua looked around, waiting for someone to answer. Again,

the class was silent. Their families all grew from the soil, and hydroponics was never discussed outside class and theory.

"Hydroponics still requires land space. It also needs carefully measured nutrients and lots of electrical energy to control climate, as well as precise understanding of the plants being grown. We also know that hydroponic plants are almost completely nonviable in the environment and are highly susceptible to disease. It is useful for certain environments or for feeding people who don't have arable soil, but it has been proven unwise for sustained reliance as an agricultural source. So why are soil-grown plants better?"

Nobody could answer that question either.

"Because they are hardier from exposure to the environment. The wind strengthens the stalks, the sun scorches the leaves, the fluctuation in the temperature changes the growth rate, and the minerals in the soil change the chemistry of the produce itself. It remains viable year after year and allows for product differentiation and endurance. Each environmental stress forces the plant to become hardier and tougher, and the flavor of the root or stalk or fruit changes as a result. The plants are able to adapt, and they don't die off from a single blight. From this we can figure out how much people consume daily and how to maximize caloric value per square meter of land."

She drew the cycle and all the nodes of distribution and projected them for the students to see. If the soil was too poor for crops, a farmer would use livestock. The feed cost for slaughter animals was higher than for those that provided milk. Milk was more productive as cheese than as milk, since the milk spoiled. The cheese could be marketed, and prices varied by region for quality and texture, making it a much more efficient use of the land. To reduce fertilizer costs, the farmers tended to specialize in crops that were most suited to their local climate. The finished products of dried grains or milled flours carried higher market prices and lower storage costs, so they could be shipped more efficiently. The silage replenished part of the soil as compost.

Each product had an evolution and purpose, and with the increased efficiency, fewer farmers were needed and less space per farm.

While she never came to a specific conclusion about perfect ratios of land use, there was a very clear requirement for vast swaths of land left for agriculture versus those used for everything else, regardless of the advanced nature of a society.

"This is why we will never see a society that exists without arable land, or at least one that is not subservient to a place that has it. Society is made or broken by its access to food, and so every society must protect, preserve, and empower agriculture, or it will face the same fate of those who suffered the effects of siege warfare—starvation and disease and horrible deaths. Those who know the land will never go out of style. It cannot be fully automated or legislated. The environment constantly reshapes itself, and only those who live in it can make it productive."

Joshua thought of this lecture as he watched the People form the society. Each fell in where they were most useful and specialized and maximized their own value.

The food that the farmlands produced made its way to a market to be bought in bulk, loaded onto carts, and moved to the market at the outskirts of the city. From there, smaller vendors would buy enough to fill their carts and travel to their distribution areas. Each tried to find a market to maximize their profits while paying the expenses of the logistics and passing their incurred expenses on to their customers, with a slight markup to ensure they could afford the next shipment and a little extra to expand their business.

Yet this complicated network could never make it into the places where food was so desperately needed. Joshua had seen them try, but those living in that squalor could not afford the prices, opting instead to steal and hijack. This prevented all but the most idealistic and freshest grocers from attempting it. It was impossible to make a difference without deliberate, targeted distribution at a price the people could afford. For hundreds of years, the people in these areas suffered. All the filth and all the dregs and all the broken undesirables of society migrated to these places, and they were left there to die. Anything of value was stolen or broken and sold for next to nothing. Still, people survived here. The pressure making rare gems of the people stripped of all their pretense, they became the essence of who they truly were, and the saints shone brighter through the gloom to Joshua. So the suffering was tolerated.

The bands and gangs eventually took larger and larger territories. One became so dominant that it could keep order and prevent senseless violence. The leader of that band was the de facto chief of the region and could exert enough authority to send groups out into the wider territory and bring back what they needed. Raiding parties would go out and take whole shipments of produce on their way to the market. This food went to the borough's chief, who extracted his expenses from the people. But when the only cost was to organize a raid and guard the goods on the way back, the price fell significantly, and the people could afford to eat.

It always started with the most well-meaning, boldest grocers. Their carts were closer and easier to haul away. Very few could afford to start up again once gangs robbed their cart. Most gave up a portion of their produce as a tax to the gangs. This of course caused prices to rise, causing more suffering among those trying to survive. Few could afford to be generous or gentle. Everything had a price, everything demanded repayment, and families needed to be protected. They became hard and shrewd and suspicious of everyone.

While most paid the tax, a few sought retributions. Without government, moral institutions, or cooperation, most were alone in their suffering and bitterness. A few who had been jilted banded together and retaliated. They attacked bandits directly, risking their lives. Many were killed in the attempt. Over time, they found it was much more lucrative to simply provide security for those setting up shop in dangerous areas. The more successful the protection was, the more grocers wanted to guard their wares, the more guards were needed. Higher expenses and food costs at the end of the line increased the rate of hijacking and the demand for guards. Anyone who could find a stick and sharpen it or swing it could earn a living.

This led to other lines of business for the borough chief, raiding with one band and protecting with the other. All the wealth flowed through him; he was the center point between two competing services and grew fat from their positions. Before long, this borough gang leader *became* the law.

In this way the crime and justice dynamic began to emerge. Neither side wanted to die, so neither side pursued the other too vigorously. But if someone went too far, they became a target and a threat. The vigilante who survived long enough always found the blame come full circle. The criminals they pursued led them to their boss, who led them to the leader, who led them to the guard's boss, and then they found the orders they followed conveniently serving the interests of those they pursued. Likewise, the thug who pursued too vigorously without obeying the rules of their code became a danger to the whole dynamic.

Yet the borough chief over the ghetto was despised by those who lived further out. Those parts of the city, where people were better off, banded together and developed their own bands of guards. The syndicates of criminals that ran their neighborhoods were much more sophisticated in the methods used. Rather than stealing food carts, they encouraged burglary and vandalism of anything that would be necessary to replace. They then would run the shops that provided the replacements, often selling back the very item they stole. If there was a threat or someone didn't pay their tax, they might leave a marked cart near that person's home and pay off someone to say they witnessed the theft. The wheels of fabricated justice would punish that person and destroy their life.

The borough chiefs frequently went to war with one another. The poorest areas had the manpower to cause great damage, often inciting riots targeted at certain areas in order to maximize disorder and dissatisfaction there, increasing costs for their leader. Raids and murders of prominent citizens was bad publicity for leaders, so anyone who had a name became a target. Yet when this happened, the other boroughs responded by starving the poor areas. The subsequent death and hunger and disease from bodies rotting in the streets forced the leaders to acquiesce. The tide shifted back and forth. Always death and theft and expense forced one side to make concessions to end the misery. All sides suffered—especially those at the bottom, the pawns of the machinations of those with power.

This forced these leaders to form coalitions with each other, against others. The more pressure they could put on one borough from all sides, the quicker they could end the conflict. Other, unaligned boroughs took advantage of the situation, selling food at a premium to blockaded districts, allowing safe passage through their territories for hit men and raiders for a fee. There was always opportunity created by conflict, so all sides conspired to manipulate the others into conflict.

This happened in every city across the Valley. Everywhere a natural barrier stood, a new city formed. The poorest pressed and packed in tight at the point of greatest pressure like grains of sand in a river. The poor flowed the furthest downstream the fastest.

When these cities became too overrun with poverty and violence, borough chiefs felt pressure to come up with new ways to relieve that population. The more other cities expanded, the more they encroached on the territory of others, and that meant diminishing profits for the affected borough chiefs.

As it happened, a few affected borough chiefs lobbied for the others to support their efforts against the encroachment. There were spoils to be had, and the apportionment tipped in favor of whoever had the least interest in the venture. If another city encroached from the north, only the northern boroughs would be affected. There was no incentive for those boroughs in the south side to expend resources to the effort. So the incentive had to be given in terms of division of the spoils. The most affected areas often earned none of the spoils, but the territory they maintained would be recovered, so they still benefited.

The city-states waged wars in this fashion for hundreds of years. There was always reason for war, and the more they found their citizens were pacified after the war, the more war was waged. The ghettos and slums would be cleared of citizens. If every tenth male was drafted, the most densely packed areas were affected the most. In a borough of ten thousand, a thousand would be recruited; in the neighboring borough with nicer homes and a smaller population of one thousand, that same tenth would be called up, but only one hundred would have to serve. The impact was equal, but the poor were always the majority of those in battle because the poor were always in the majority in life.

26

The Technician became very active in twisting people and creating the events that would ensure the highest quality. But Joshua discovered that suffering made people behave in unwholesome ways even without the Technician's manipulation. They destroyed each other fighting over rotten scraps. The evil they exhibited was brutish. A man dying of thirst wouldn't hesitate to murder his own children to have a sip of water, so the manipulation of these souls became too easy and only lasted while they suffered.

Finally, Joshua had to ask, "What is the purpose of all this?"

"There is no purpose," the Technician stated flatly.

"Then why create more anguish?"

"Are you suggesting I am doing this? No, this is the natural process. Why don't you do something about it?" The Technician goaded Joshua. "Why are you allowing it to happen?"

"I've tried to change things, but it's like scooping water from a rushing stream. The void is immediately filled, and the suffering never ends." Joshua hesitated at this idea. He had just blamed the Technician for something he knew was unavoidable.

"I have no stake in increasing misery. Nothing is gained by it. It exists. That is its nature; that is the nature of *nature*. I merely shape individuals and institutions. I push the limits of the laws and turn them inside out, and I take individuals and turn them into hypocrites. Suffering happens on its own. But the more suffering there is, the more rapid the change to upend it. Likewise, the less there is, the slower the change. I am here for your growth." As the Technician spoke, one of his minions lit a fire that became the largest in the city's history. With thousands dead, a hole emerged in the heart of the city. Yet it created an opportunity for regrowth. The city came together and built a series of monuments and public buildings. The ghetto that once stood was dispersed, and the people found their lives slightly easier outside the crush of the city.

Joshua observed this and disdainfully retorted, "Do you think you are doing me favors by this destruction?"

"I would say so, yes. You clearly don't understand the balance that exists between destruction and suffering. People languish in their squalor. It's often just as easy to destroy the environment that creates the suffering as to remove the sufferers from the environment."

Joshua thought about this. It was no different than the ice age he created. He wiped out many of the civilizations that enslaved the People in order to give a better life to those whom he cared most about. Destruction on a smaller scale could cure the problems that led to the suffering of his people, if he were only strong enough to use it. Destruction came with its own traumas. He had traumatized himself with the ice age. Yet it was necessary for the freedom he sought to give the People. Everything was a lever that moved something else.

"So clearly it has a purpose. But what?" Joshua asked after assessing the world and all the enclaves of despair he found, all the oppression that was wrought, and all the souls who flowed head-long into those conditions without regard for the misery ahead.

A note of appreciation came through in the Technician's voice as he said, "When people suffer, they withdraw into themselves. How they behave demonstrates their core identity. With plenty of food, water, shelter, entertainment, and free time, anyone can delude themselves into believing they are strong, smart, righteous, or kind. It is only under the pressure of misery and suffering that who they truly are emerges.

"Some find a form of expression. Writing, sculpting, painting, music—anything that allows their voices to leave the confines of their prison and allows them to leave behind the immortal piece of themselves. Something that will make generations after them hear their voice.

"Some find solitude in pugilism. No matter how bad the world gets around them, they can escape themselves and fight back against the unseen force of oppression, suppressing their suffering in the repetitive, ritualistic, controlled violence. They prove to themselves that strength lies within and they can conquer the misery that oppresses them. They find the will to carry on and silence the voice inside that perpetually tells them to give up and give in to the misery." The voice of the Technician drifted off as he seemed to be living the hell he was describing. "It is *my* voice they hear in their minds, though, that voice that tells them to quit, to give up, that they'll never be good enough . . . Some heed that voice. Those who don't become true masters of their fate." He punctuated this statement with a reverence Joshua had never before heard from his adversary.

After a brief pause, the Technician continued. "Some find peace in books and knowledge and learning. They can hide from the world and escape in the adventures they read or the mysteries unraveled far away in a real-life fantasy they could never hope to see for themselves. They absorb the collective, distilled wisdoms of whole lives condensed into a few days' literary consumption. Too uncoordinated, too weak, too unattractive, too easy to victimize, they practice their talent and find protection in their isolation."

Joshua listened closely as he explained that these were the only ones who escaped with any true character.

Joshua fell silent, the thought weighing on him. The Technician merely manipulated people and scenarios to force him to explore new ideas and stymie bad ones. He leveraged selfishness in individuals and used their fatal flaws against them. It cost him nothing to enrich a monster who would serve his purpose for a time. And it cost him nothing to throw away any of these monsters he created. There was no bargaining with him. *I'm the user. The people are refractions of my personality. When I emerge from the Machine, there will be nothing left for anyone but me.* So the only acquiescence or resistance was against the Technician. Only reward or suffering. But the reward meant nothing because acquiescence meant weakness and flaw, and flaws were meant to be eradicated.

The Technician ignored the long silence and left a final point hanging in the ether. "Pressure makes diamonds. These diamonds are rough, but your family's job is to seek them out and preserve them. That is the only way you will become the best version of yourself."

This was the first time Joshua had heard of his parents or their role since he entered the Machine. For the first time, he didn't feel alone.

27

When diplomacy and economic manipulation and incentives fail, war is a last resort. As a force of nature, it is no different than the packs of wild dogs who patrol and defend their territories or the primates who hunt each other in troops to expand their domains. War is a natural process, and every excuse for its justification is used to convince the population that it is righteous and they are morally right," the teacher explained. As she cited examples from their history, she emphasized the given justifications for the conflict: encroachment on the traditional territory of one nation, the need to destroy the false god of another tribe, to sabotage the production of a product, the bad guys caused the drought that killed the harvest.

"War is justified because people always need to believe they are in the right," she continued. "They need to know that the gods are on their side and the authors of history will favor their conflict. Every person wants to know they lived honorably, and when their nations were called, they fought honorably, and their brothers in arms died honorable deaths. Yet the willingness to fight a war roughly once every generation, whatever the reason, proves that the justification is not as important as the need for a violent release. Societal stress builds and builds to a crescendo, and any excuse becomes good enough to face the brutality of war."

As she spoke, she looked each class member in the eyes as if it were an accusation against them. "Each person has a self-destructive need to demonstrate their value in hard times—to prove their merits in the hunt. To confirm with themselves that they would stand tall against the arrows of their enemies and not falter or retreat. That they are stronger than their mortal fears. Many are not. But every generation or sooner, the people always demand the opportunity to find out, so they seek an enemy."

She started walking between the rows of desks. "It says a lot that there is always an enemy willing to fight. Whatever the difference, be it religious or cultural, a nation looking for an adversary will always find one. And for those in power, war has always been an effective means of population control. The ideal is to use it as a means of controlling your enemy's population more than your own, but it could hardly go unnoticed that after the rigors and mayhem of war, fewer men return, and there are fewer social problems as a result.

"The conflicts between gangs, boroughs, cities, and so on have always replicated the dance of convergent evolution. Two different species target the same prey or produce, and over time they become equal in their capabilities. One may dominate for a period, and then the other. There is no true winner; they are merely becoming more aligned. To defeat an enemy, you must think like them. When you think like them, you become like them. When you become like them, they cease to be your enemy. Thus, the nature of war and conquest."

For the first time in many days, Joshua was enthralled by the topic at hand: The movement of armies, the glorious battles that colored the mundane flow of time in the history books. The psychology of the soldier who stood and fought, and that of the coward who ran away or fainted. The way soldiers were trained to see enemies as targets instead of as people, the conditioning on the practice field that desensitizes them to the rigors of war.

He raised his hand.

"Yes, Joshua."

"Why isn't there ever a winner in war? Wouldn't that mean that the justification is always wrong too?" He hoped to get the teacher rolling on the subject.

"It would, but to say there are no winners in war means that everyone becomes a casualty of it. We tend to think about the soldiers who die and the wounded. But those who sustain no physical injury sustain psychological wounds that never truly heal. A soldier sees his best friend maimed and broken by a battle. The blood that drenches a field between two armies stains that soil for generations. The population sends its future and its strength into the fray, loses its productivity, and gets back a fraction of what went away. Disease ravages armies. The weather devastates spirits. The longing for home and the thoughts of family, spouses, and children distract them. They miss the moments that make life special, only to find themselves haunted by the proof that it is not.

"As far as the justifications? There is seldom an excuse good enough short of the enemy at your doorstep. Yet every person must know if there is something in themselves that is worthy of the life they've been granted. And so any excuse will do until they know what they want to know."

"Can you name any wars that have been justified though?" Joshua asked pointedly. If the teacher found no justification, the wars of freedom were just as illusory.

She surprised him though. "Absolutely, yes."

When she didn't elaborate, he goaded her further. "What makes a justification worthy of war?"

She forced a smile at Joshua, but then she went somewhere

far away in her mind as she began to speak. "War is justified when the truth and the propaganda are the same. War is justified when the price of dying is less than the cost of living with yourself. It is justified when the horrors of what is possible are no less than the horrors of what is happening. Most of the time though, it is not."

She looked at him again. "There have been cultures that sought to exterminate other cultures by virtue of their heritage alone. Monsters have sought to sterilize whole landscapes for the sake of their own cultural dominance. Demons have looked to the plight of their own people, and rather than find a way to feed them, they enslaved and murdered them. Cultures have sought to cleanse the world of others without seeing the fault in themselves. And the worst of all are those who have watched all that happen and saw no reason to intervene. Those are the ones who see cancer and allow it to metastasize. They know what the face of evil looks like and allow it to survive because they don't have the courage to face it alone."

"Who would do such a thing?" Joshua asked.

"All of you would." She looked around the room at the shocked faces. "That is why we have the Machine."

Joshua watched two armies clash. Like two wrestlers, they pushed and pulled at each other, using whatever tricks they knew to gain the advantage. As their ranks rapidly dwindled, one finally broke. The momentum of the opposing army carved through the fleeing forces and flanked those who remained, sending the army scattering for sanctuary. Half had fallen; the other half fled. The wounded were gathered as prisoners and ended up as slaves. Those who fled picked their weary way back home, where they spread the virus of fear and retaliation, and the war effort took on a more desperate tone.

Slavery was a major part of the society. Each city had different standards for how long a person should remain a slave. Most made it a life sentence. The slave women were used for domestic service, often bearing children of their captors, growing the population of their enemies while passing on their own genes in the process. The daughters of the enslaved were sold into prostitution, the mothers served in the fields, the fathers served hard labor until death, and the sons were castrated and used wherever they were useful or desired. No longer people, they lived on long after they perished. Their children were free. Though they were reduced to the bottom in the ghettos, they rose to prominence. They were orphans who from the start were forced to face the injustice of the world, but survival meant they were tougher than their grandfathers had been. Each hardship was a test that hardened their resolve. Each test made them stronger and proved their discipline.

These slaves became the genetic glue between the societies and eventually conquered their captor states from the inside out. The more often two cities fought, the closer their genetics became. A soldier might be enslaved and have a child born free in the captor's society. That captive soldier's genes infiltrated the society he was enslaved in, and his great-great-grandson might wear the uniform of the city he fought against. The bloodline shifted back and forth, stitching the two cities more closely together.

Joshua ensured that the slaves endured and provided solace to them in their dreams. They drew his face crudely on the walls of their quarters, just as it had been drawn on the walls of the caves of their ancestors. In their dreams he consoled them and promised he was there for them. He reminded them that their suffering was not eternal.

The society became too bottom heavy. The many poor and enslaved banded together, overthrowing the city's leaders, whom they executed in a violent display. The cities all around them supported the revolt with weapons and blockades, and the surrounding farms turned their produce toward other, more peaceful markets, thus increasing the suffering and increasing the anger. All the well-off families were massacred. And all those who took sides against the populists fled to the surrounding country.

As with every fire, once the fuel was removed, it quickly died. They had eliminated the leading families and pillaged everything they could, but they couldn't eat the goods they pillaged, so their hunger pacified them. The other families had to negotiate for reentry into the city in order to return home, so concessions had to be made. Agreements and contracts and rules and laws were created. The people had to extort their equality and dignity. Yet that was still not enough to change their fate.

Much like their emergence from the desert oasis, when the People were removed to areas of less pressure, they tended to thrive, and those qualities proliferated. There was always a way for them to escape their birthright, and if it suited Joshua's purpose, he made sure they found that escape. Those left behind were made useful in other ways. The constant external pressure kept pushing inward toward that epicenter, and where one was removed another took their place.

When cities and people got too bad, Joshua built a new society from these dregs. The dispossessed and desperate coalesced around the hope he propagated, and their new affiliation and identity secured their status as founding revolutionary. They saw the villainy of those who had abused them. These new societies and nations carved out their territories from the cancerous world around them. When a city needed to be destroyed, there were new nations that served the purpose. They had the personal motivation, the moral justification, and Joshua's approval and guidance. He used these armies to excise the cancer of people and cities that had gone too far astray.

Joshua discovered that there was value in war after all, and he used it effectively against the worst parts of himself. The teacher would say that these wars were justified. A tumor must be excised, and there was no tumor greater than a hedonistic society that abused the People.

The man walked down the street, taking a different route than he had the day before. The destination was the same, but there was always the suspicion that after all these years someone might come back from the dead and seek revenge for his part in their fate.

He limped slightly; the old wound that forced his retirement ached in the cool of the morning. He was fortunate to still have the leg, but the fight had been intense, and the memory of those desperate moments still echoed in his mind. His longtime friend was run through fatally, while he escaped with his life, though they fell side by side. Trampled by the melee around him, he watched the life fade from his friend's eyes as he struggled to pull them both out from beneath the struggle above them. It was too late for his friend, but to carry his body to safety was all he could do to honor the life they had spent together serving their city. The trinket he always carried, a symbol of his faith, scarred from where it stopped an arrow long ago, was lost in the dust and blood-soaked mud.

They spent years facing the enemies of their homeland, neither one knowing anything but that life. The men they served with meeting similar fates or simply moving on once their youth had been spent and the cause they fought for was corrupted by the politics that turned enemies into friends overnight and friends into enemies. The tide constantly shifted, the next war always on the furthest horizon and the struggles of carrying their whole life on their backs in the most miserable weather in the most desolate places for the most superficial reasons.

For most it wasn't the battles that made them lose their spirit; it was the attitude of an ungrateful populace that made them walk away: "You murderers can go elsewhere with your business." "It was men like you who made my grandfather a slave and raped my grandmother."

Even the patriots in the population seemed to give hollow thanks for their sacrifice. Though material support was often given, it was the moral support that was lacking. Whatever horrors the soldiers saw in the service of their city, they were expected to be the toughest minds and the toughest hearts in the toughest bodies, and despite their orders, their actions were always their burden to carry long after the fact.

He always left at this hour, before the world had woken up fully. Before the judgment could be seen on the faces of those he passed in the neighborhood. Before the flag-waving patriots could scowl at his weakness. Before the bleary-eyed peacemongers could muster the saliva or words to assault him with their hypocrisy. The other early risers were courteous enough to their neighbors to keep their activities quiet, and the old soldier felt less jumpy in the soothing requiem of the night that the noises of the city played while waking up.

Even the early morning had its moments of chaos, but the accidental slamming of a door left few people around to see him duck and reach for the blade he always wore strapped to his thigh over the old wound, where at least it would provide some cover from the ambush he was vigilant against, and he could keep his dignity. This morning, though, he felt like all eyes were looking in his direction, and he hurried to escape the gaze of the emptiness around him.

Joshua watched the old soldier with pity. He remembered this man as a child, knowing his life was meant to serve the city. He would help around his father's shop carrying stacks of lumber, pretending it was spears for the front lines to replace those that had broken. He carried sacks of flour for his mother, pretending they were his comrades fallen in battle. He took his first job as a courier for the city guard so he could run from post to post and make his body ready for the next call to arms when he would have his chance to prove his worth. Everything in his life was oriented to that single purpose. At night he would bus tables at the favorite bar of the local garrison and listen to the tales of courage and triumph those men boasted of. The memories of their lost friends toasted and memorialized in their drunken mirth. They would settle their tabs with one last ritualistic toast, "To the boys who go to war, and the men who don't return!" They would solemnly finish their glasses and leave the bar in a disorderly staggering column. Joshua saw all that devotion and love still, an immortal youth trapped in a broken body with a heart full of sadness and pain.

The soldier still could not shake that feeling of being watched. He ducked into a bar on the corner just opening for the breakfast crowd. It was one he'd passed a hundred times on his way, but one he'd never set foot in. As he walked through the open door, he assessed the scene and found a suitable booth with a bench against a wall with a sliver of a window to watch the road through and a full view of the entrance.

The bar was empty save for the barkeep, a middle-aged man with graying hair, a grizzled face, and grease-stained apron. He was clearly well fed, but there was a hardened air about him too—someone who had been embittered by life but still took pride in his work and cared for the people he met. When the old soldier came in, he looked him up and down and put down the towel he was polishing the counter with.

He filled a cup with a steaming liquid, a strong aroma emanating from it that awakened the senses and relaxed the mind and body. He brought the cup over, approaching the anxious-looking soldier head-on, both hands occupied with the cup and a slate for taking orders. He set the cup down and took half a step back and to the side to keep the soldier's view unobstructed. "What're you having today?" he asked in a jovial and unconcerned way.

Slightly distracted but not wanting to be rude, the old soldier simply said, "The special."

The barkeep dropped his slate slightly, looking slyly toward the door to see if anyone else could hear. "You probably don't want that today. The special has become extra special over the last couple days, if you catch my meaning."

The old soldier turned his gaze from the street outside to the barkeep and raised an eyebrow as a smile broke through the ice in his eyes. "Well, what do you recommend?"

"Here? Probably just the tea." He chortled at his own joke before continuing. "But if you're hungry, I'd say the eggs are fresh and the bread still has some spring in it. I can bring some cheese and jam too if you'd like."

"That would be fine. Thank you, sir." The old soldier watched the barkeep shuffle away. A slight favoring of one leg over the other betrayed an old injury. "How'd you hurt your leg?" he asked, assuming a banal story of old age and missed steps.

"Oh, I accidentally took an arrow in the knee." The barkeep smiled, knowing the soldier assumed far less.

The old soldier chuckled at that and said, "I had a similar nuisance injury myself. Someone in a yellow tunic mistook me for a rabbit and put a spear through my thigh."

The barkeep smiled broadly. "Where was your unit stationed?"

"We were out of the northeastern district, but we trained at every post in the city. What about you?"

"The south gate. Did ten years before my career was ended." The barkeep nodded meaningfully to his leg as he gathered ingredients for the meal and began warming the pans.

The old soldier nodded with understanding and answered the unasked but intended question, "I was in my twenty-first year. Reconnaissance. We were in enemy territory, and we were discovered by a patrol. That patrol stalled us long enough to get a runner back to their encampment, and then we spent the next ten days being pursued and skirmishing. Barely half of us survived. I took the spear through the leg but escaped with my life. A good friend of mine died next to me." As he continued the story, his voice trailed off and his eyes grew distant as the memory again flashed through his mind, obscuring the world before him with the vivid colors and smells of that battle.

The barkeep only nodded in understanding as he brought the hot meal and set it before the old soldier. "I imagine they gave you a pension for your service at least, right?"

The soldier's eyes were still distant before he blinked away the memory. "Yeah," he scoffed. "Enough to pay rent in a shabby apartment and eat out a few times a week." He smiled and pointed his chin at the barroom around him.

The barkeep shook his head in commiseration. "You give so much for the city, and in the end you just get thrown away. A pittance to pay for the sacrifice you made, and the scars you carry are never deeper than the ones in your mind."

"Yeah . . ." The old soldier took a bite of the meal in front of him. "You can't get those years back. You can't unsee those horrors, and you never get to know what else you might have been."

The barkeep grabbed his own cup of morning brew and sat down across from the soldier. "The people we protect will never know those horrors. They get to live innocently. They get to judge you through their lens only, based on what they believe reality to be. We are foreign to those who never have to experience what we did. I spent a lot of years after my service wondering what it all meant, what it all was worth, how many people lived freely because of what I did for them without their knowing. There is no thanks they can give, there's no trinket or meal they can buy that replaces that sacrifice. You could have been something much greater; you could have been a city leader, but instead you chose to bear the burden of protecting a society that never understood the true cost of your sacrifice for them."

The old soldier only stared at the barkeep. He felt these words personally, and to find someone who could finally speak them made him love this man as a brother.

The barkeep continued. "You can never get back what you gave up for them, and you can never know what you might have become instead. The scars you wear and the traumas you carry in your memory can never be undone." He took a sip of the steaming brew in front of him. "But you are not alone in that burden. Everywhere you go, you have brothers who know your suffering. You aren't alone."

The old soldier shook this off. "No, I know that. I just don't like to feel like such a broken husk. Everywhere I go, I feel that silent judgment. I just want to be back with people who knew those hardships and endured them with me. I just want to be that younger version of myself that was still fighting fit. I just want to be that version of myself that could still hold my head up high." He stopped short, his eyes starting to glisten from the memory. His voice showed every sign of breaking, but he continued. "I was a hero once . . . Now what am I good for?" As he gestured to his wound, the streaks of his tears marked his face, and he turned his head in shame to regain control of himself. *I used to be much stronger*, he thought as he wiped his face with the back of his hand.

The barkeep nodded, pretending not to notice the tears. "It's not the body that makes a man a hero. It's the mind. It's the heart. Despite where you've ended up, I guarantee if you were given the choice a thousand times again, you would never change that decision. Despite every memory you carry, like a thousand bricks in your rucksack, you would never ask another person to share that load. You wake up each morning and carry those burdens with dignity, with enough energy left to carry the memory of your fallen brothers and do them honor by pretending it doesn't bother you. By absorbing the judgment around you and keeping your blade sheathed against those who will never understand your suffering. You never stopped being a hero, brother. You fight those old battles every single day, and at the end of the day when you have exhausted all your will to carry on, you lie down and dream of the moment you can finally escape this life and tell those stories of your courage once more with your brothers long since gone.

"Every day you awaken and bravely clean yourself up and carry that burden once more through the land of the living. For us, we knew death too intimately to ever believe in living a normal life. When the mission was bleak, you accepted your death and carried on. You gave up all your hope and accepted whatever God had in store for you. And when you emerged alive, you were empty. There was no more future. All plans and expectations had been abandoned the moment you accepted death, and now you're just waiting." The barkeep turned his cup in his hands, knowing the feelings the old soldier bore.

He continued. "It took a long time for me to find something to occupy my time while waiting for death. Nothing is as satisfying as heading to battle with your brothers. Nothing is as meaningful as training a young soldier in the skills that will keep him alive. Nothing is as real as the blood, the sweat, the tears, and the carnage of the fight. And everything that seems important to the people back home just seems like an illusion. How fragile the world truly is and how unprepared those people truly are for the chaos that can erupt in the world they thought protected them.

"I was angry when I first came home. How dare they not know the violence inherent to our being! How dare they judge me and pretend that I endured what I did because I had no other options! How dare they not bear my trauma! *How dare they patronize my sacrifices!*" The barkeep slammed his fist on the table, causing the hot brew to slosh out a bit.

He pursed his lips at this and reached into his apron pouch and pulled out a fresh rag to soak up the mess as he continued to talk. "But then I realized that my sacrifice was entirely so they *wouldn't* have to know. Our role isn't to be the heroes at the front of the parades. Our role is to allow the world we sacrifice for to know the joy and happiness and kindness that only comes from the naïveté of lives lived without the horrors of the world outside the city walls. The privilege of judgment they exercise is solely possible because we did our jobs so well." As he said this, a woman walked by with all the colors of those disdainful of public service. "Besides," he said as he finished the last of his own cup, "they still need us to protect them from reality. Even if we don't wear a uniform anymore, reality always intrudes on the fantasy societies are built on. And we are the only ones who know how to deal with it."

The old soldier finished his plate and sat looking at the barkeep. "I wish I had your wisdom to see that. I'm tired. All the time. And I don't have the strength to protect these people anymore. It's time they saw for themselves; maybe then they'd understand us."

The barkeep just nodded solemnly. "I promise you, that time is always coming. We can only protect them so long before their contempt of our kind leaves the gates unmanned and the outposts abandoned. You can only do so much for the ungrateful."

The old soldier reached into his purse to pay for the meal. The barkeep held up his hand. "Your money is no good here. You've already paid your debts. Besides," he smirked as he spoke, "I think the bread may have been a little older than I thought."

The old soldier chuckled as he put the coin back. As he got up to leave, he reached out to shake the barkeep's hand. To his surprise the barkeep met his hand with a little trinket, similar to the one his friend used to carry. Even the scars on it were the same.

He scrunched his face in confusion as he walked out the door staring at the little medallion. The barkeep called to him as he left, "Just take that as a reminder that God shares your suffering. He will always listen to you. Stay strong, brother." He waved his hand in the air as acknowledgment without turning around.

He heard a door slam open behind him, and he flinched as he whirled around. A strange-looking man had flung the bar door and tucked a *Closed* sign under his arm as he hung the *Open* sign in its place. The old soldier just looked at the unfamiliar man standing in the doorway of the bar he had just left, the puzzled look making the man uncomfortable.

"Can I help you, sir?" the man asked.

"Who are you?" the old soldier asked. "What happened to the barkeep I was just talking to?"

"Look, sir, I open the bar for breakfast every morning at the same time. I have been doing it for thirty years. I am the only one here, and you were just passing by, so I have no idea what you mean. If you want some breakfast, come inside; otherwise, I've got some work to do."

The old soldier looked at him, confusion plain on his face. He looked in his hand, and the trinket was still there, his belly was still full, and he could still taste the brew on his breath. He finally stammered a reply, "N-no thanks. I've already eaten." He turned again to walk away and tried to recount the last hour he'd spent in that very bar talking to the old veteran serving as barkeeper. *Did I imagine it all?* He couldn't be sure, but he wasn't going to invite a question about his sanity from this stranger.

He continued walking to the destination he set out for that morning, the veteran's cemetery and memorial where his friend was buried. Suddenly he stopped and looked closely at the trinket in his hand. On the back were inscribed initials, just the way his friend's were written, in the same shaky scrawl he used to carve them. The same initials as his friend's. This trinket wasn't just eerily similar to his friend's trinket. This *was* his friend's trinket.

As the flood of realization struck him, the old soldier looked up to the sky and could feel that same sense of being watched wash over him. Joshua stared back at him. *God shares your suffering.* The old soldier felt the comforting warmth envelop his whole body as those words reverberated in his mind. He no longer felt alone.

28

The class began as it always did: looking at history and the rise and fall of kingdoms. Today's subject was: What makes a person a leader, and why do others follow? The revelation that even the great leaders were fallible led to a discussion of the forms that governments take.

"Societies always formed the same way," the teacher said as she began making bullet points on the screen. "First there is anarchy, or rule by none, and justice is at the whims of individual powers. They have no justice because they have no law. Instead, these societies have vigilantes and bandits. Those who create suffering, and those who hunt them. Justice is based on how oppressed a person *feels* and how willing they are to do something about it.

"In times like these, people seek any sort of stabilizing force. Often, a strong man emerges, and though they may be cruel, they are at least predictable and consistent. In the interests of keeping their power protected from usurpers, they maintain some semblance of law and order.

"Tyranny is the next form of government. It always creates a yearning for something in the middle, leading to a democracy, then oligarchy when that fails, then finally a republic. Like a swinging pendulum loses its momentum, the society's last breath is as a republic, recharged only from the great energy of tyranny and anarchy that emerges from the stale and stagnant bureaucracy that stifles any movement and suffocates the society under a blanket of laws, rules, and regulations. Oppression takes many forms.

"Of all the types of government, democracy is the most fragile. It relies on the vote of a majority, typically a simple majority, but often a larger portion is required to make laws. Voters can be bribed, intimidated, blocked, or otherwise prevented from voting for their own best interests. With enough public manipulation, enough propaganda, the voters can be convinced to vote for anything. The most violent regimes in history were elected by a vote of the people. The most horrific crimes against people were endorsed by the people. Purges of minorities are often approved by the will of the majority. The most emotional collective decision-making is made through democratic vote, and those who know how to manipulate the emotions of others control the vote. And the slowest reaction to any threat is a vote. Then the democracy is conquered before the votes have all been tallied. And then the next vote is for a dictator to lead them out of chains."

Then she covered oligarchy, which was essentially the rule of strong men who formed a council and made mutually beneficial decisions based on their own interests.

"All governments start on a sliding scale between total chaos and total power. Oligarchs appoint one of their own to rule over the council, effectively empowering a dictator. Democracies vote in a strong man populist who they then vote to hold that position for life, empowering a dictator. Republics eventually beg for a king to make command decisions that the laborious process of the law prevents them from doing. In the end, a succession of kings, dictators, tyrants, emperors, and other monarchist leaders rule all nations. And when those leaders are killed, either through coup or age, there is usually a war for succession. In that time the land is ruled by anarchy. And so the pendulum swings."

Joshua thought about the lessons in the history books. How many people had died in the wars for colonization? He tried to imagine life as one of those people caught up in the fray only to find their efforts used to empower someone without their interests at heart.

The wind blew outside and tossed the leaves on the shrubbery violently. He imagined each leaf as a soldier serving the root ball of the shrub. Not a single leaf was important, and if the root thought it better to cut energy to a branch and kill the leaves, the leaf could say nothing about it. It just died. The life of a soldier was no different, he guessed.

Someone in back asked a question that Joshua didn't hear. His teacher's voice shook him from his tale of leaf soldiers.

The teacher replied to the unheard question, "Yes, these systems can involve complex combinations. Kingdoms can be led by kings or emperors or tyrants that also have a leadership council. For example, they might have ministers to lead agriculture and defense and whatever else. That is a sort of mixed system. They may have a set of laws to govern the society that they themselves don't have to adhere to, which undermines, but at least introduces, the idea of republic. A congress of the people gives the people a voice to express their issues. These civilizations still have crime and wilderness and anarchy. All systems can coexist together."

She explained how similar system existed in families. "Each of you have parents that lead your homes. This is a microversion of the communist ideal. This is what idealistic fools have sought to impose on societies since the concept was founded."

The same was true of socialism. "In our extended families we find reason to help our cousins and grandparents. We may give them resources to aid them in difficult times with the expectations that they will do the same for us. This is the idea behind socialism.

Yet it works in families and homogenized societies only, because these people carry the genes that we share and care about.

"Every town has a set of rules, and beyond that town is the wilderness, thus the dynamic of republic and anarchy. Even our society has individuals who have special influence on the empress herself and form what could be called an oligarchy. Oligarchy is not necessarily based on resources. The poorest wretch can be an oligarch if they are best friends with someone in power. It is the Machine's ability to make us all leaders that keeps our society from the corruption and decay emblematic of these systems throughout history."

Joshua could see the political evolution play out in every household and village that emerged. The jockeying for power and wealth and influence made every system come vibrantly to life before his eyes.

He could feel the stories his father told him taking shape. Yet those tales paled in comparison to the reality before him. One city in particular was a shining example of the failures of the natural process. It took no extra effort on the Technician's part to make it so. It was the corruption of the People who lived there that made it come to life, but every experiment needs a control, so he simply observed.

The city had formed the way all cities did: from a crush of people fleeing from desperation toward opportunity. The slums and ghettos formed, and those without conscience sought dominance over the desperate. A government formed afterward to provide structure.

The strong men ruled and robbed and abused anyone with anything of value or anyone who showed any sign of resistance. The people sought heroes to eliminate these gangs, but all they could find were mercenaries who insisted on compensation up front for risking their lives. When this wasn't enough, or when they got greedy and realized there was more to be had, they created their own opportunity and established themselves as kings. Each gave generous handouts of food and money to the people as a bribe for their loyalty, each was overthrown by another king, and each granted more and more liberty or rights to the people but seldom enough to change their lives.

The more power these kings obtained, and the more loyalty they could buy, the less they were willing to give up. Though the people were happy to at least have order and consistency of leadership for the time, the kings took a piece of every transaction. Then they redefined a transaction and required a fee, a permit, a tax, or a license to perform it. Public gatherings of more than two nonfamily members constituted a meeting, and the king required meeting notes and a fee for the administrative processing of that meeting. Speaking louder than a whisper constituted a public speech and required a license for oration in a public setting, ostensibly to finance the translation and transcription of such an important and impassioned sermon. This kept the noise from the bars to a minimum, so the people were content with the peace and quiet, but it kept the markets from establishing fair pricing as the noise of negotiation forced both vendor and buyer to pay the price of a license.

When a leader took power, they promised noble intentions, but as they inherited their predecessors' wealth and position, they always found that it was much easier to conform to the old standard than to give anything up and start over.

The people always met their breaking point. The king always overshot that mark in their avarice, and the people always rebelled. A bloody revolt destroyed the king, his spies and tax collectors and his servants, who themselves had grown fat from their role in the extortion. And then the people had the power again to give it to some other tyrant.

Once they established that rule, they were content to develop the laws governing the society. They all agreed that they needed some structure, but there were huge differences in what they found necessary. The majority wanted to ensure that they got bigger parts of the whole. The few who had much were reluctant to give up anything to those who hadn't earned it. Yet the majority deemed it necessary for their social satisfaction that they all earn enough to feed themselves.

They deemed to rule through the best interests of the community, so all were required to contribute half their possessions and property, which would be divided up based on the greatest benefit to the whole. Those with nothing contributed nothing, and those with much were forced to give up much. The majority poor realized they could take from the rich and continued to do so. They held the power of force over them and took everything they could until the rich merely left the city or became impoverished themselves.

Misery, poverty, and hopelessness were distributed evenly. The wealth of the community was put in the hands of the few who managed these funds on behalf of the community. Those who had never had access to such wealth squandered it. To feed the people, they overspent on the produce of the land. What didn't spoil went to the few again for distribution. The majority continued to starve. The rich, who had earned through skill, departed the community, and those capable of managing these issues were long gone.

In the interests of the community, a few individuals rose to prominence. They blamed those who left for sabotaging their great experiment. They blamed the weather for the poor harvests. They blamed greed for allowing their neighbors to suffer from hunger, and they blamed the world at large for not understanding and helping their efforts to give the power to the people. It was out of benevolent intent that the few would alleviate the voting that was such a distraction from real production that would strengthen the people and their great experiment. When a few in the community objected loudly, using their rights to free speech, they were soundly silenced by thugs and angry mobs of people hired to create public spectacles. The people retained their right to free speech, but they had to be willing to face public beatings and murder for it. The people grew silent while the few in control seized more power.

Remembering what happened to the kings before them, the prominent few used the thugs they hired as examples of why weapons needed to be collected from the people: "They are too dangerous in these desperate times to be trusted." These anarchists were examples of the dangers of an armed populace. Thugs and hapless citizens who had something to be leveraged were sent to sow chaos and fear. Those on the payroll were sent on their way, richer. Those who were blackmailed were executed for their wanton villainy as an example. The people then begged for their weapons to be taken away. They begged for the madness to end and demanded order. As soon as they got what they wanted, they stopped financing the chaos, and order restored quickly. It was incredible how quickly peace could return when the money spent sowing chaos could be redirected to other public works. And even more amazing how quickly the people realized the true virtues of the system they now lived under—silent consent and toothless conformity.

Without weapons, the few established themselves as the rulers and leaders of the community. They silenced free speech altogether and justified it by saying the sowing of discontent in such desperate times was not beneficial to the community. The community agreed through its silence and enforced it through their own hunger.

The few continued to rule, but it was only satisfying for those with real positions of power. They sabotaged and undermined one another to highlight the incompetence of their competition. When the eliminated members wouldn't go away, they had tragic accidents. They cut their bellies and throats wide open while harvesting vegetables, accidentally stabbed themselves multiple times in the back and vital organs while hunting, or committed suicide by shooting arrows into their own backs from the grief of letting down their colleagues and the community. Eventually, the same sort of people as before rose to power, only they were much crueler and more devious because of their competition with others of the same ilk. Once again, a king claimed the throne.

And once again, the people reached their breaking point and rebelled and took hold of the reigns of their own destiny.

———✵———

"Another political collapse, another decade of suffering. Do you have no decency?" Joshua asked in the fury of the moment of watching a lynch mob topple the justice system of another city-state.

"This city is a flea on the back of a mongrel dog. It is nothing, and it will recover. In fact, it'll be stronger for this experience."

"Why don't you guide them to the right conclusions instead of corrupting those they turn to?" Joshua felt himself screaming into the atmosphere, facing down his adversary. He felt helpless as each system was corrupted by the technocrats and hired thugs and lawyers and marketeers who painted the illusions that drove the emotional response of the people to self-destructive actions.

The Technician had the lilt of laughter in his voice as he parried this jab. "Why don't you?"

Joshua was furious. But the Technician was right. Why hadn't he done something about it? Why couldn't he?

Again, a city fell to chaos and the destruction of the temples, the monuments, and the homes of all the people, good and bad. Any hidden talents he noticed, cultivated in the pressure of their despair, were caught up in the fray and destroyed or tainted, spoiled by the excitement of the mob.

What could he do, though? The people needed to find their way. The strongest, most resilient legal systems needed to face the withering assault of time and technicality to find the weakness inherent to them.

Joshua's frustration subsided with this thought. There was nothing to do really. Not in a macrosocial sense anyway. The city was one of the many ecosystems that were destroyed and rebuilt and destroyed again by the Technician.

"What happens if they don't reform? What if they simply dissolve?" Joshua was surprised by the realization that he controlled himself much better now. He'd quickly gone from the state of fury to acceptance and understanding. Had he matured?

"As you know, this city formed from the flow of people from the villages higher in the Valley. If that flow doesn't stop, this is where they naturally collect. The city will re-emerge. Whether they choose to learn from their mistakes is a matter for you to decide." The Technician cut off in his typical way and focused his attention on some other devious scheme to ruin something else.

Joshua understood. Only the evolution of the ideas that formed the city, not the city itself, was of value. The people were the same. They reacted the same way as always, but without the wisdom to make the change, he was as responsible for their fall as the Technician was. But he was the only one with something at stake from it.

When the embers of the old regime finally cooled and the sapling of the next emerged from the ashes, the people were determined to never be fooled again. Freedom of speech and assembly again became their priority. They insisted that the king should hear the complaints of his subjects. But the right to remain armed was the only way to enforce this. The king's thugs could silence any speech they didn't like, and thus that right was eliminated through intimidation. An armed populace was the only way to even the odds.

This time, though, the community was not the primary beneficiary of the law. The mistakes of the past had deprioritized the individual, so the individual had become expendable to the community. The individual was now the focus.

Where the individual was the focus, the market boomed. The price of goods fell over time as more sellers sought to take advantage of the competition and supply outpaced demand. Every product found its true value as individuals competed with other individuals for the same goods. The goods that came to market increased in quality, and there was less waste because the most desperate-looking goods could still find a discounted price and be used for other things.

In governance, the individual was granted power in their vote again. They continued to vote for their own interests based on their experiences of the recent past. Yet again, they were manipulated and cajoled by those with wealth and interests different from that of the sovereign kingdom. Most voters found that their votes were worth something. The more secure the voting process was, the more they were worth. It was this that became the target of those interests outside the democracy. This is where the Technician pried and pressed.

All that was required was the majority to agree with anything, and it would be codified as law. Resistant to kings or committees or bureaucrats, everything became an issue worthy of a public vote. Yet this grew wearisome. No one had time enough in the day to vote on every procedural thing. Few really cared what the name of a public building should be, and no one cared who should be the city pest control chief. There were too many items that demanded too much attention, and productivity suffered as long as there was too much tedium.

People went door to door and made sure everyone eligible in the city should get out and vote. It was their civic duty. They didn't want a return to the tyranny or anarchy of the past, did they? People turned out to vote, but the more everyday life interfered with the social responsibility and the fewer items that held any real significance were voted on, the more people made excuses for staying home.

Certain boroughs had a consistent voting pattern, and when something was proposed that certain people needed passed, those boroughs were targeted to either increase their vote or suppress it. When one law got rejected, the authors would dissect that same law into several different pieces and have a vote on numerous laws that no one cared about; but when combined, they became the very law they all rejected to begin with.

With enough people uninterested in voting, the lawmakers could have noneligible voters fill in. After all, the number of votes cast only had to be fewer than the number of eligible voters. In order to increase the number of voters, they expanded citizenship rights to people uninterested in being citizens: birthright citizenship, market-right citizenship, occupancy citizenship, even growing the size of the city to incorporate rural areas completely uninvolved in the happenings of the city. They sought by any means the growth of the voter base. Only in that way could there never be a true census of the neighborhoods of who actually voted for a law that was passed.

Other competing cities and kingdoms took notice of this liberalization of citizenship standards and began using their own citizens as a means of affecting the neighboring kingdom. If their citizens could vote in another city, they could put self-destructive measures on the ballot and have their own citizens vote for it in the other city. They could ensure the collapse of their competition by using their own lax voting standards against them. While the voter rolls were expanded for limited purposes, they continued to expand to serve the fluctuating interests of the authors of the election.

As always happens, the people got suspicious, and the electors were held to account. As always, one took the fall for the habitual deceit of the many. As always, trust in democracy was eroded by the individual desire to institute their own benevolent goals against the ignorant will of the people.

And the whole cycle began again.

Joshua saw that the votes of the people caused democracy to fail. Dictatorships failed with the oppression of the people. Oligarchy failed because of the greed of a few. Anarchy failed by the insecurity inherent in it. And republics failed from lack of resolve. All are undermined by external forces; all are destroyed by internal strife. Eventually their fates lay in the people's lack of confidence in the fairness of the system, and that too was the target of the Technician.

———⊗⊗⊗———

A lone grocer stood on the corner of a deserted street. The mobs had rushed past him in a frenzy, and though they took everything he had for sale, they left him at least with the cart and the money he had earned before the riot broke out. He set his cart upright again and tightened the wheels and started to push his way back up the street to his home, where he would tell his wife about the misfortune of the day and try to figure out a plan for the next.

He stopped for a moment to tie his tunic tighter around him when he looked down and saw a flash off a copper coin. He chuckled at this. The wares he'd lost to the mob were worth at least thirty gold pieces. A single copper was all the gods deemed worthy of payment?

He bent and picked it up and ran his thumb over the muddy image of the front of the coin—the latest monarch ousted by the frenzy of a fickle mob. As he thought about it, he wondered how this particular individual came to be in power. There was plenty of evidence, scrolls and books talking about the democracies and republics that came before them. None mentioned why things fell apart or how they came to this current state.

He began pushing his cart again and entertained his thoughts with the rise and fall of empires, of the failures of the systems as he knew them, and the state of chaos he now saw at hand. What was it all worth? How could a simple grocer have anything to say that might change things? He would be hungry for a while. He knew that.

As he passed a corner, he heard a muffled cough from behind the scattered waste of a ransacked restaurant. He saw a dingy, muddy cloak covering some wretch and felt the pang of pity for this poor fool. Even the mobs had no use for him.

He pulled out the copper piece and thumbed its image one more time. Then he walked over and handed it off to the wretch. "Here you go friend. There's not much left to be had, but maybe you'll eat for one more meal."

The wretch peeked out from behind the hood of the cloak and said, "Thank you kindly, sir. Them folks didn't have much kindness to spare and took what I normally enjoy from the scraps here." He gestured widely to the scattered debris. Only then did the grocer realize the trash was devoid of any scrap of food. It had been picked clean.

The wretch looked dismayed. "It might all be okay if we could figure out how to keep this mess from happening. But people are fools. Even the experts wrap themselves in titles of authority, only memorizing, regurgitating, and picking at the bones of the ideas of other experts. Why, even a humble grocer like yourself can carry some wisdom greater than all them combined. You see the state we're in? All their pretty words are worth nothing." The wretch spat as he said this.

"Well, I suppose that's all true. It would be nice if someone would get this stuff figured out so we can stop overturning the whole world every few years."

The grocer began pushing his cart again. A conversation about politics with a beggar wasn't the sort of distraction he needed right now. He needed to tell his wife what happened and figure out what to do.

"I guess you need to be going then. Let the missus know everything will be all right though. I'm sure your ledger is empty, so maybe there's room for a humble grocer to tell the world what he thinks." The wretch cracked a wry smile.

The grocer stopped and looked hard at the wretch. "What do you know about my ledger? Or my wife?"

"I know that you didn't sell much today because the mob took everything you had to eat. And I know you've been here every day despite the discontent. And every day you have a full cart. I know you are smart and organized, and this is just a small hiccup for you. How many of these riots have you seen? You know how they affect you, and you know when times are easy and when they are hard based on what is going on with the political situation. I think you are wise, and I think you have knowledge the world may like to hear, something that will help keep it from falling to this state so often. You may die tomorrow. Perhaps you have something worth saying before then." The wretch flicked through a pile of parchment and found a heel of bread missed by the mob. He pulled it out and took a cautious look and sniff before he shrugged and shoved it into his mouth whole.

The grocer just stared at him for a moment, a perplexed look on his face. He said nothing as he pushed away.

The wretch smiled through a mouthful of soggy bread and called out, "Be seeing you, grocer." He removed his cloak, and the filth that covered his crooked body fell to the ground as he vanished.

Joshua decided he would need to do this more often. It was the only way to be proactive about molding these people. If the city, the environment, and the individuals were not important, then Joshua needed to get the right people motivated to spread that knowledge. If one small stone could build a ridgeline, one mind could reshape an empire.

The grocer did not look back as he heard the last remark, so he didn't see the wretch vanish. But what he had said was all true. How many times *did* he see this same thing happen in his lifetime? He had a knack for feeling the mood of the market, he had the words, and he knew how to write. Maybe he was the one who needed to write it all out. As vain as it was, he might have something useful to say.

As he came through the door, he greeted his wife. She was making onion soup again. But this time it smelled sweeter. Everything felt different. He kissed her on the cheek as he put the ledger on the dinner table and hung his scarf on the hook on the wall.

"How was the market today?" she asked, eying the purse and knowing the weight of the coins didn't match the produce he should have sold. "I heard there was quite a commotion."

"Well, the mobs took everything but the cart, the ledger, and the coins from the morning." He sighed heavily as he looked down at the tab that opened to the day's page, almost blank save for the few purchases before he was cleaned out. He wondered whether he should tell her about the wretch on the way home. He decided against it and simply said, "Everything will be all right."

He began to write that evening, and he wrote long into the night. The next morning, he got up early and started writing again. He wrote and wrote and wrote until the ledger was full. Then he took it to his friend the scribe and had him make a hundred copies. Political theory was born from what he wrote. His book was read and absorbed and analyzed by all who had time or interest to spare for the ideas that molded society. Nobility and nobodies alike read his words, and though he was wrong in many ways, and overly verbose in others, and his writing style was not appealing to some, he found a way to communicate the lessons he had learned, and his readers were inspired to think about the ideas he imparted. He fulfilled his promise to his wife; everything *was* all right.

29

S upply and demand—the basis of every economic transaction." The teacher had drawn a grid on the screen and two lines representing a supply curve and a demand curve. Their intersection point represented the market value. "It is as much a law of nature as the laws of physics that bind us to the planet's surface and the planet to our star. Though the ancient people may not have had currency in the traditional sense, they still knew that the few berries available had value. Every animal understands this fundamental principle. An ape will trade sex for grapes when they are scarce, but as soon as everyone gets grapes, the number of grapes to get sex increases substantially. When a banana is introduced, the banana suddenly has the most value—even if the scientist running the test knows the bananas are cheaper by the pound than the grapes. The relative supply and relative demand create the artificial scarcity that gives them value."

It wasn't until the Machine that Joshua saw supply and demand for the natural force it really was. No matter what ecosystem he looked in, a form of natural market emerged. In every society that arose, one of the first inventions was currency. It was different everywhere, but it existed nonetheless. In one place, creatures used a certain tree nut that most of them coveted. Its caloric value made it possible for them go longer between meals and spend that extra time preparing other things. The nut was also durable and easy to transport or hoard, so it could serve as a proxy for stored labor. This ultimately was the purpose of money—a tangible representation of stored energy or labor. Even before Joshua could identify it, he was seeing the glimmer of its presence in his little world.

One village found in their little brook a particular rock that was smooth and white and had the same basic virtues as the tree nut. Once the next bend of the brook revealed that they were as abundant as the tree nuts, the rocks ceased to serve the purpose of currency. Besides being rocks with no inherent value of their own, they were often heavier than the items they were used to purchase.

But as the rocks were picked through, one piece of them proved rarer than all the rest. It was just a tiny crumb of translucent green stone, but its scarcity made it valuable. It was small, so it was easy to transport, and impossible by their level of technology or knowledge to reproduce. For the rest of the life of that village, and eventually their society, that green stone remained the currency of those people.

That society came in contact with another one that had red stones. When it became apparent that red stones were more difficult to find, the green stones lost market value. People could still use them to buy things, but only a fraction of the items they could get with the red stones.

When it was discovered that the producers of the red stones had made a grand display of the difficulties of finding them—that they were actually much easier to find than the green stones—the poor who had saved their green stones were immediately the wealthiest people in the society. Yet the sudden change in the perceived value of each currency made all farmers and merchants stop their activities. They no longer knew the true value of their goods in terms of red stones and green stones. The confusion caused people to go hungry, and even though the poor were the richest in terms of their stones, they had few provisions saved or stored that could hold them over through the artificial shortage created by the market uncertainty. A single meal cost three stones, when previously one stone could buy ten meals. Once the market stabilized, everyone but those who provided the food were impoverished again.

When the market collapsed, merchants held back their merchandise, farmers held back their harvest, and the fishermen caged or dried their catch rather than sell it. Regardless of the new currency, they all had food for themselves and their families. Other trades were not so lucky. The miners had stones for buying food from the merchants, but these ran out quickly. Woodsmen, brickmakers, weavers, and fabricators were dependent on the vitality of the market to survive.

Their services were no longer in demand because without circulation of currency there was no need for construction, so the brickmakers were all unemployed and hungry. With so many unemployed, there was no need for baskets and woven goods as none were used enough to be broken, so the weavers suffered. The fabricators and the potters had the same problems.

Ultimately the value of the currency was decided by the merchants. When one fish sold for three green gems, that was the highest value in green gems they could find. When one similar fish sold for nine red gems, that was the highest value in red gems they could find. The lowest value was one red gem for one fish, and three fish for one green one. At the end of the day, all the merchants would go home and count their gems. They consistently had three times more red ones than green ones, so the value of the gems was three red ones for one green one. The market determined the value of the currency, and from there the market began to function again.

But Joshua also saw people learn to take more precautions. They bought less perishable food and stored it longer. They kept a little of all the different currencies in case the values changed again. The vendors built more-secure hard structures instead of using carts for their trading. The farmers planted more of whatever lasted the longest so they wouldn't lose as much food to rot while the market decided what it valued most. And the fishermen built smoke shacks to preserve more fish for the next depression. These precautions laid the groundwork for the revival.

The weavers now made fish traps to keep their stomachs full during shortages. The potter made bricks and tools, and the woodsmen turned to hunting in addition to their regular labor to subsidize themselves.

The miners learned as well. When the various gems were found, most relied on luck to stumble on them. Their single gem was not much, but it added to the growing number in circulation. In a village of one hundred, each person might find one gem every quarter year. By the end of the first year, there were four times as many gems as people. Everyone had gems; thus, the value of the gems fell.

Yet some people consistently found gems. They learned the trick of where they came from and established themselves in those areas. They scratched out a bare living, always paying more for simple things like the food and the pots they carried water in, since the land they lived on could not support that sort of industry. But they had the entire money supply beneath their feet.

Since the mines all relied on the production of gems to survive, they were all forced to come to an agreement that would keep the process of production a secret and regulate how much of the gems to put into the market at once. They all leaked news that the mines had stopped producing. They began selling the broken stones—the refuse—as building materials to replace the ones that were pulled from the river. This became their primary purpose as far as anyone knew. Stone was strong and effective as a building material. Thus it enabled all people to have strong homes, and the mines made enough money off them to trickle more gems into the money supply.

While the purpose of the mines shifted in the eyes of the public, they still actively pursued the original intent. They even changed the perception of how the gems were located. Simply by washing them in the brook, they appeared to have found them there. The rest of the villagers, seeking an easy fortune, tried panning for gems in the river. There was enough success that the rumor grew that this was the way it was done. To encourage that rumor, the mine occasionally lost some of their stones in convenient places for other people to find.

The brook grew wider and wider because of the mining activity, and over time the water ran dry. The rate of flow never changed, but the wider the river got, the shallower it was and the more surface area for evaporation. The people hardly noticed the difference from day to day, but Joshua did. For the fishermen, this was their livelihood being destroyed. For the rest of the people, this meant thirsty times. For the farmer, this meant no water for the crops, which for the rest of the people meant hungry times.

The problem originated from the search for gems. When stones were removed from the brook, they left a mud hole. Then the people would come with their clay pans, scoop the mud up, and let water run over the mud as they shook it. This carried the loose, light sediment away with the current and left behind the sand and the stone, and if they were lucky, the gems.

As they did this, they removed the stones from the stream to use as building material for their homes or as walking paths throughout the village. These stones had held the mud in place, and at least to a degree, protected the softer soils underneath. With the steady flow, the exposure of new mud and soil, and the continual sifting through the mud, this sediment was carried farther downstream and away from the village. Wider and wider it grew over time, and deeper and deeper the streambed grew, while the stream itself grew shallower.

The villagers never stepped into the same brook twice. Even their very footsteps would disturb the sediment, forcing it a little farther downstream to be deposited behind a boulder, and eventually the brook was turned on a different course.

The impact on the village was gradual, but like a tree bough weighed down with snow, it was forced to either shed its load rapidly or break. And all of a sudden, a slight deviation in the climate caused a cataclysm that devastated the village and the people in predictable ways.

A dry summer, a dry brook. Crops died, fish died, and people were thirsty. Thirst drove them to drink from acrid pools of filth that made them sick. This sickness weakened their immune systems, and the chilly nights introduced bacteria that were themselves seeking a warm host in which to live. These bacteria proliferated, and the weakness of the host ensured their deaths came with great agony. There was not enough money in the system to bribe the rainclouds, so the money became worthless. The mines were no longer able to withstand the forces of nature brought about by the pursuit of wealth, and as the workers died off and the labor stopped, the people abandoned the village to find other areas. The mine owner held his ground until the end, when he finally starved to death holding in his hands the riches of the land. When his corpse decayed to a pile of bones, a trove of gems was found beneath his skeleton. He had, in his final moments of starved desperation, tried to eat the gems.

Joshua began to see the benefits of diaspora. After escaping the despair of the village that had been lost to the environment, his People carried with them the knowledge of their societies. They made use of their currencies, lessons, building techniques, and natural knowledge. The bacteria that had killed their village was still present in them, but they were strong enough to resist it and better equipped to find food and water to keep their strength up. They carried all this on to the villages that surrounded them and shared it. The bacteria was not deadly anymore—it had filtered through the immune systems of the survivors and emerged in a more symbiotic form. The knowledge they shared allowed the surrounding areas to thrive with the help of new foods, new techniques, and new ideas.

The diaspora spread lessons of the past far and wide. Those lessons became parables and histories that ensured they would not be forgotten. The consequences of avarice were paramount in the lessons shared.

R eligion is a tool to divide populations without genetic differences. It allows us to isolate subgroups based on beliefs
and exclude others based on theirs. In this way, a subspecies can emerge . . ." The teacher droned on about the utilitarian
aspects of religion as she segued into their value.

"The value of religion is in its ability to shape otherwise hedonistic creatures, guided by baser desires and needs, to restrain or
temper their instincts. As such, the population is able to develop
more complexity because of the forbearance of such traditional
'sins' as gluttony, lust, avarice, pride, envy, wrath, and slothfulness.
Each of these is a base emotional reaction that erodes the productivity of a society, so we always see in nations with a multitude of
religions, all competing for adherents by liberalizing their moral
positions, a rapid slide into decline and collapse."

Joshua keyed in on this idea and interjected, "So that means
that the specific religion doesn't matter, only that the nation is unified in its beliefs? All people need to be the same religion?"

"Not everyone needs to have the same *religion* per se; they simply need to have the same moral values, the same ideas of right and wrong. And these must be meaningful moral virtues. The institution is irrelevant, much like a business in its structure and motives, except the currency is morality rather than money."

Having satisfied the question, she moved to the screen to write the sins she had enumerated previously. "Simply declaring something a sin does not carry enough weight on its own to justify it. You can create a prohibition for an animal to learn the boundary of a fenceless territory through classical conditioning and create a ceremony around it, and you have the makings of a religious dogma or ritualism. But without real and clear consequences, that religious prohibition does not carry the timelessness of the notion of sin; thus, without enforcement, that animal will gradually learn it can ignore the prohibition. The same goes for religion."

As she spoke, she began to draw a Venn diagram. "We can look through history and list the specific prohibitions that each religion enumerates. Most religions fail after so many generations because of a lack of merit. They stop trying to increase true logical morality and instead increase the number of sins so much that they dilute the true sins. Either that or they fall victim to the sin of avarice."

She drew a second Venn diagram with less overlap in the middle. "The first circle represents nature and survival, the mistakes a creature can make that reduce its lifespan, and thus its opportunities to reproduce." She colored in the part of the circle not overlapping and continued. "This area represents things out of a creature's control. Things like natural disasters and famine, things attributed to God or the *gods*." Then she pointed to the overlapping portion. "This represents the portion within a creature's control. Things that would make another creature want to kill them. Things like stealing food, being too ostentatious in their appearance, and taking another creature's mate for their own. All of these will lead to their own demise, either through violence or ostracism and banishment, which in nature is the same as reproductive death."

Then she pointed to the other circle. "This represents the behaviors of a creature that are not altogether deadly but are more self-destructive. Things like poor hygiene and health habits or antisocial behaviors. These normally aren't sins per se, but they are self-destructive and lead to the same result as the deadly sins over a much longer period."

She pointed to the second diagram with less overlap. "This one represents a failed religion. All else being equal, this religion does not advise against all the sins within a creature's control. It allows some to slide, so it enables the death of its adherents by endorsing preventable behaviors, effectively killing its followers."

She paused for a moment, thinking, then drew a third diagram with more overlap than the other two. "This is another example of a failed religion. By accepting too much responsibility for the unavoidable, its adherents either ritualize every aspect of their lives in a futile effort to appease the gods, or they blame the religion itself for the wrath befallen on them. If the rituals do not work every time, then they are false. The religion that preaches them is then proven false as well. Religion is intended to answer philosophical questions for the people. When it can't, accurately, it loses validity."

She scrolled back to the list she had created earlier. "So let's go back to these seven sins, or sin subgroups. Can anyone tell me why they think greed might be a sin?"

A few hands went up. The teacher called on one of Joshua's classmates. Her voice chirpy and confident, she answered, "Because greed attracts greed. Others who are greedy will compete for the same resources and try to destroy one another." She smugly put her hand back down and waited for the teacher to confirm her statement.

The teacher nodded curtly. "Yes, but that is not the whole reason."

The girls face fell and her shoulders slumped.

"Greed represents an excess of resources. Someone who is greedy takes whatever they can get at the expense of others. Impoverished thieves are greedy if they aren't stealing what is necessary for their own survival. While it's true that the upper tiers of society are often greedy, the wealth they acquire is not necessarily a result of the sin of greed. We want the best of our society to rise and succeed and reproduce to make our species stronger and smarter and more capable, but what we don't want is for those people to squeeze others for their resources until they have nothing. A king who taxes his subjects too vigorously reduces their ability to survive happily. Hoarders of wealth are also bad. A greedy animal that kills everything it can, for example, or plucks every berry without eating them, prevents others from eating and allows the stagnant wealth to rot, serving no one. Currency, even, must be circulated. It generates more economic activity and improves more lives. Hoarded currency serves no one, not even the owner. Saving for a rainy day is noble, but too much money saved is money poorly invested."

She looked around the room and caught Joshua doodling in the margins of his notebook. "Joshua, can you tell us why this would shorten someone's life, and why greed is antithetical to survival?"

He looked up, dazed and searching for the question or even the topic in the echoes of the half-heard lecture.

"Why do you think greed could be considered a deadly sin? How could it lead to someone's life being limited or their opportunities for reproduction being reduced?"

He looked around the room and couldn't find anything to focus his thoughts. He started rambling. "Because . . . um . . . people don't like others who are . . . um . . . too focused on one thing, like money." He stammered out this axiomatic statement and hoped it satisfied the teacher's inquiry, unaware that he'd basically repeated what his classmate already said.

She pursed her lips and shook her head before explaining, "That's part of it, but not the whole answer. Greed does repel people, that's true. Taking what you can from others at their expense is not seen as a positive social attitude, which certainly reduces your reproductive success. But greed has a way of isolating a person, from within and without. That person rejects others to protect their hoard. They partner with others whose motive is greed, and as was mentioned before, greed destroys greed. One person takes from their partner to have it all for themselves. Their children, if they have any, wait impatiently for the fortunes to become their own. When their parents die, siblings destroy each other trying to consolidate it for themselves. But little by little, the gene pool eradicates those sins from the population, along with all that goes with it." As she punctuated this point, she swirled her finger in the air representing water circling a drain.

She continued like this for the other sins she had listed, each statistically and demonstrably bad for both society and the individual.

"And so," she said as the lecture ended, "the key to religion is setting the rules and explaining the natural consequences. If it's done right, there is no need to enforce anything. Nature does that itself. The one who rules by force dies by the same."

Joshua thought of that lesson from eons ago. He could see in the communities throughout the Valley the nascent bones of religious thought—the notion that there was a right and a wrong and that certain behaviors were disastrous to the individual and the society around them. Some behaviors were caustic and toxic but not completely destructive on their own. They were symptoms of rot rather than the rot itself.

Yet the deadly sins continued anyway. Joshua had time to think deeply about these ideas. Why were these sins so deadly, and why did they proliferate so much? The examples were all around. As he watched the colonies of People grow and interact, all the sins were evident and their deadliness true.

Gluttony was pervasive where food was abundant, and life was easy. The rural areas saw this all too often. Excessive food, excessive drink, excessive drug use. But that wasn't the only problem. The gluttons took more than their share, their addiction robbing others of comfort. Someone else might starve, but they fed themselves lavishly.

Joshua saw an innkeeper with a rotund belly and grease stains on his shirt berating a scrawny barmaid pushing a mop. As he spoke, food flew out of his mouth and splattered the girl. He threw the browned core of an apple at her, which bounced into a corner and immediately picked up the dust and filth hidden there. As he waddled to the back storeroom, he rubbed his chest and shoulder. A slight pain started to radiate.

The barmaid rushed over to collect the core, and after picking the hairs off and wiping some of the dust from the moist surface, she bit into it hungrily and devoured it stem, seeds, and all.

The innkeeper reached for a bottle of brandy at the top shelf and felt the stabbing pain through his chest. He spun toward the door catching himself briefly on the shelf, and then collapsed face first, the bottle shattering by the door.

The barmaid heard the commotion and crept over cautiously, afraid to incur his wrath. When she found him lying face down, her shoulders relaxed, and she walked away to finish her chores, waiting for him to die. If she went for help, it would take four men to carry him. He ate and drank away any revenue the inn earned, so there was nothing left to even pay for a headstone. She just looked on, and as she worked, she smiled joyfully at the release from this burden.

Joshua looked to the cities and saw lust everywhere. A private party of the idle wealthy exhibited every sin imaginable. Men ran after men naked. Others ran after women, and they harassed and fondled the child servants who could do nothing but endure and hope to avoid their advances.

In the streets two men held each other, groping and advertising for all to see, their sexuality foremost in their self-identification. The pedophile, always obsessing about their fantasies. The adulterers, always sneaking into the bed of their lovers; the closer they were to being caught, the more exciting it was for them.

All used others. All identified themselves by their particular fetish. They became susceptible to disease and infection. When their obsession was widely known, others kept them at arm's length. The hedonists used others for their own gratification. Those who were used by them, or those who cared most about those who had been used, returned with vengeance in their eyes and cut short the lives of the lustful.

The avaricious took from others for personal gain. A lender charged exorbitant interest, ensuring the borrower was always worse off for the loan. The slum lord charged more rent than the apartment was worth. The salesman bought goods at less than their value and sold them at predatory prices. The vultures preyed on desperation and disaster, squeezing every coin from their destitute purses.

All their relationships were based on their desire for wealth. All their friends were of the same ilk. All their lives revolved around the swindle. And every one of their relations sought to separate them from their money. Their lives were often, though not often enough, cut short by those who coveted the wealth they secreted away.

Joshua saw the prideful spend their lives advertising themselves. They had the most beautiful women and the most chiseled men, the biggest houses and the most luxurious toys. Their favorite conversation was themselves. Everyone around them saw their arrogance and ignorance. Some were repulsed by their vanity and ostracized them. Like a vacuum in nature, their boastfulness highlighted to those around them their gross and obvious flaws.

Their vanity forced them to expend all their labors toward exalting their own image. Products for their hair and skin, made from the finest snake oils. Cosmetic alterations, carrying with them the infections and diseases that low-budget fixes usually do.

Their identities were so wrapped up in their own appearance that they subjected themselves to horrific transformations, sometimes dying for their beauty as a result. Some were ridiculed for their bizarre appearance and killed themselves. The women among them seldom reproduced, as that meant their bodies and budgets would have to change to support another life, a parasite they couldn't tolerate competing with for the attention owed to them.

He watched the envious. Neighbors who coveted one another's property or good fortunes. Former friends wishing ill will on one another. Joshua heard the daily prayers of many seeking punishment for those who angered them simply by being blessed. The damage they'd commit to others' property, and the planting of evidence and falsifying statements to authorities to exact the punishment someone else deserved.

Joshua watched one woman sneak over to poison a fruit tree so the neighbor couldn't enjoy it. Then she stole an ax and went and hacked down her own tree that was puny and frail and, in the morning, called on the local magistrate to witness the violation. The other neighbor was oblivious to the acts and admitted the ax was probably theirs. They had to pay for the fallen tree plus recompense for the emotional trouble caused and for the magistrate's time.

He watched another neighbor lie to a government clerk about his neighbor building without approval from the county. Another who blamed someone else for redirecting a small brook toward the home they had built at the bottom of a gully. Each attempted to punish their neighbor for the good fortune they had. Each blamed others for their own misfortune. Each attempted to ruin every joy and blessing of those they envied. For every bad behavior, someone was willing to return it in kind, and every death was a relief to someone else.

Their marriages were bitter and hateful. All couples could agree on was the target of their collective venom. Their hollow lives decayed. Their latchkey children were abused. Their labor was too expensive for employers, and their skills were never lucrative enough to endure. They became a cancer on their societies.

Wrath was everywhere Joshua could see—in the cities, in the country, in the streets, and in the homes. Rage, violence, and irritability cut through society like a knife, and those who wielded it eventually ended up alone. They berated their wives, abused their husbands, beat their children, and picked fights with everyone they could. They screamed at strangers who represented a perceived enemy of their emotional well-being. They took personally every misdeed of those who had power over them.

The slothful were the least useful of the whole society. They were lazy and indolent, apathetic and idle. They left as much slack as others could pick up, and their relationships were characterized by immaturity and filth. The squalor they lived in was as diseased as their caretaker allowed. They never lifted a finger to help, only consumed, and contributed to the mess without doing their share of the cleaning.

Their frail and soft bodies could barely sustain modest activity. At work they did just enough to get by and not enough to be invited back. Their spouses were the ones who bore the burden of any more lives they created. The sloth was too frail to try, so the kids they observed their spouse raising were seldom theirs.

The bitterness of caring for one more charge ensured that their spouses would enable the behaviors that led to an untimely death. An extra portion, an extra glass, a delayed bath, or a damp wardrobe ensured disease and poor health took them.

Joshua was not sympathetic to these sinners. Their lives were a burden on others and were the root cause of the cancers that metastasized within the society that represented Joshua's being.

Joshua thought aloud, "I wonder what the inverse of those sins is? What are the virtues that ensure a life propagates?"

Without hesitation the Technician chimed in. "Think of the people of our own society. What behaviors do they exhibit?"

Joshua could only think of his parents at the moment. "They don't consume anything in excess. No overt sexuality. People give their time and energy to the community. No one is very boastful. Neighbors don't pick fights with one another. I've never heard of any fighting. And no one takes more than a day off from work or responsibilities."

The Technician indicated his approval by summarizing. "So the inverse would be moderation, modesty, charity, humility, grace, patience, and industry. How do these qualities benefit society? How do they benefit the individual?"

Joshua thought for a moment and responded, "Well, all of them are selfless traits. People want to be around those who think of others first. They are always good hosts, always clean and kind, usually working on some project, so they are interesting. They are busy, but never too busy to make time for those who need them. They are happy in other people's successes and downplay their own achievements. They show others how to achieve the same and are delighted in trying something new and productive. Every small success is shared. They are a delight to be around."

"All true," the Technician replied. "They are the ideal, and they are protected and cherished by others. They find love easily, and though they are often victimized by the sinful, they shed those burdens easily. Even I have no effect on them. Their souls seem untouchable and light."

It became clear to Joshua, as he considered the prayers and behaviors of the People, who carried this lightness of spirit. Their prayers, meditations, and focused minds shone brightly. They could set their minds on a single thought and ask for guidance or clear their minds around this one specific issue, and in the echo of the emptiness around it, Joshua could answer.

The sinner, on the other hand, prayed differently. Their trivial

questions demonstrated their lack of true comprehension. It reminded Joshua of his own prayers and hopes from long ago, before
the Machine.

"Please make them like me best."

"Please give me more."

"Please protect the things that I value."

Seldom did prayers go beyond that. When they did, their words
were banalities and generic.

"Please help Mommy and Daddy and the dog and the flowers
in the garden."

It was those searching for understanding rather than solutions
who found answers. In the quiet of a peaceful mind, he could help
even one who was suffering understand why things were the way
they were. His global machinations often caused collateral damage.
Other times, he simply could not hear the suffering over the din
of the countless voices crying for help all at once for things they
couldn't control and those they could.

Yet those who asked to see the plan were not disappointed.
Joshua knew their hearts, and he knew those who would use information the right way. He also knew how far each voice would carry,
and those who would not impact the plan were the ones to whom
the plan was laid out. He could speak to them in their dreams,
where the noise of the world was silenced and his voice would
echo in their minds. He could hear them through their prayers and
meditations and show them what they sought, and they merely
absorbed the whole process.

These were special minds. Some, whose personalities kept them
more grounded to the practical, never allowed their minds to seek
greater knowledge. Concerned only with their day to day, their
small prayers reflected the small worlds they thought about. Others

were less inclined to thinking in general, so even if they saw something transformative, they weren't curious enough to explore the idea and make a transformation in their lives.

The correct alignment of curiosity, intelligence, and solitude made it possible for people to have deeper experiences and find answers. These were the people Joshua communicated with most. They were unafraid of exploring dangerous ideas because they had limited social networks to object. Their intellect allowed them to grasp the tenuous relationships between different events and where those events pointed the whole grand design. It was from these eccentric loners that true religious understanding emerged.

But it was not without its hiccups.

People asked Joshua, "How do we devote ourselves to you?"

He replied in so many ways, "Give your heart to me."

Some societies took this quite literally and created a cult of sacrifice where the hearts of great figures were cut out of their chests and presented as an offering to Joshua. This was a disturbing turn of events. Those societies met with rapid destruction to prevent that misunderstanding from taking further root.

Others asked, "Where can we find you?"

He communicated to them, "I am in all things."

This led to the worship of rocks and trees and animals, where Joshua was said to be living. While it was more benign than most other misinterpretations, the propensity of a society to take things literally meant they eventually declared a different god in each object. The most accurate ones still did not understand and claimed that each thing represented a different face of Joshua. They worshiped the parts they favored and discouraged worship of the parts they didn't. The god of lust and the god of harvest seemed to be the favorites, whereas the god of war, disease, and despair attracted fewer adherents of a much darker disposition. It was useful for eliminating those qualities in a society Joshua abhorred, but it still missed the point. He sought different ways to mold the People to understand his purpose better. This notion that Joshua was in all things, though true, deified his worst flaws and created the tolerance of the evil in the world that Joshua was seeking to eradicate.

Through it all Joshua was there, hearing, though not always listening. Watching, but not always seeing. Feeling, but not always sensing. The constant din of pain and suffering, mayhem, and destruction kept him from focusing on individual lives, so he focused on how people dealt with those constants. Over billions of years, he learned how to listen for the sounds of the danger and mourning that signaled the troubles he needed to address. It was not the single sufferer that he spent his time helping, it was the *signal* suffering that forced him to change a path of events. This was how he knew when to intervene; this was how he picked those who represented his future self.

With the religions that emerged came only more strife. But it was necessary. Each served a purpose in his grand design. It was for the good of the species that they disagreed. Where one religion was created to carry knowledge of health from one era to the next, another was created to badger them and force them to remain apart, their dogma and culture isolating them and ensuring the knowledge, maintained through blind tradition, never eroded. Where one religion spread the philosophy of moral living, another preached hatred and vengeance. Where one taught to do no harm, another taught that Joshua honored those who harmed outsiders. Atheism told Joshua what the moral baseline was, and agnosticism served as a check on the logic of the religions. All created barriers between each other, all serving a purpose. And through it all, the moral instincts of the People, their innate sense of right and wrong, were proved by their willingness to deviate from their religious norms, while their inherent obedience was proved by their dogmatic adherence to them. Both were useful to Joshua—and the Technician.

Joshua offered prophets, shamans, and priests a mere glimpse of different pieces of the whole truth, and from that glimpse they extrapolated the rest, mostly incorrectly. Most, fearing the loss of their privilege from the loss of their communication with Joshua, made up whatever they could not remember. Any inconsistencies were hammered out, and the parts of the truth that were inconvenient to their core construct were ignored.

The rules they created were meant to inspire the most awe toward Joshua, answer the great questions of life, and guide them on a moral life. But those rules often led to corruption of the institutions that upheld and enforced them. Rules were changed to put offerings into the hands of the priests themselves, ensuring the privileged position also became a very lucrative one. The religious succession plan made it impossible for even the most faithful founding prophet to ensure their successor would hear Joshua's words, so eventually Joshua stopped talking to them entirely.

For the most part, religions were harmless. He could guide each one through periodic visions in key figures who added to the growing tomes of rules and perspectives. When the progression of the dogmatic following of one idea left a gaping hole in their understanding, Joshua inspired a visionary to speak to the issue. This helped them to understand the purpose of the rule. Unfortunately for the People, these prophets seldom survived their sermons, as the powers they confronted were not receptive to losing their privilege or admitting the faults that the prophet pointed out. So the evolution of faith was an internally and externally bloody path, as everything else in nature was.

The more visions he gave to any religion, the more vehemently that religion believed it was the only true one. The visions he'd given to those in other religions were falsehoods, and their profaning the name of Joshua was a death sentence. Whole societies clashed over these misinterpretations.

The People rarely chose their own religions. Chance, convenience, and community chose it for them. People seldom changed their religion from what they were born into or subscribed to anything but what their community allowed them to. As long as it answered the eternal questions for them, they never had a reason to stray. All they needed was a reason why things happened. So every religion offered their reasons, and whether they had *the* reason didn't really matter to most. An answer, *any* answer was satisfying enough to pacify the questions of the heart.

And so it went. Religions became a unifying force within a society. When the rules were fair and just, the people were kinder to one another. They were more civil, humbler, and more resilient against the misery that coincided with Joshua's plans. Though he did not seek to increase the misery, it could not be avoided. Religion explained the unavoidable, unchangeable, and unpreventable. And the people found solace in their connection to Joshua.

"R eligions always start the same way—through true spiritual inspiration," the Technician said to Joshua as the world moved around them. "It's curious how often those who found a religion are little more than the product of the sins they railed against. A murderer of town guards, a rapist, a slave trader, a bandit, and on and on. These are the people who are easiest to mold in their escapes from justice. They are the most willing to use the mind-altering substances willingly, and they are trying to find the darkest hole in the quietest corner of the world to escape their troubles." The Technician found such a person to imprint with some notion of homicidal martyrdom as a pathway to salvation. "It is their sociopathology that enables the message to coagulate into a proper religion and spread. Though they aren't the sorts we should admire, they are useful for this purpose."

As the Technician said this, the religion began to spread, visibly to Joshua and the Technician but imperceptibly to the People, at least at first. The corrupting influence was a signal of the frailty of the systems in place. The rot and corruption of the religion infected everything. Like a drop of oil on the water, it spoiled everything it touched.

The society of the Valley was tolerant of it at first. All religions were accepted and welcome. When it stalled the economies in the regions it spread to, the government and immorality of the other religions were blamed for the hardship. When the adherents of the new religion seized control of legislatures and councils, the laws were revised to endorse their ideals, and the violence the new religion perpetrated spread the religion through fear rather than ideology.

The Technician continued to speak passively as Joshua watched the decay. "When you abandon them, they won't notice. They are too busy spreading the word they received. But after a while, their questions yield no answers, so they make things up. It is their lives as criminals that enable them to spin the web of lies that rationalize almost anything. The creativity with which they frequently do it is rather amusing." The Technician chuckled at this cheap entertainment. "This is why you use these sorts of charlatans and brigands. They are so good at building the infrastructure around their version of the truth."

Joshua watched as the infection spread further and further through the realm. He watched as the effort, the learning, the sacrifices made to create this perfect little haven evaporated with the single lie told to the perfect vector. The Technician was not cruel in this test. He simply proved that Joshua's love affair with this Valley was ill founded. They could be broken with very little effort.

The Technician continued his speech as the infection spread through the society. "Much like the nations that form and the species that merge, each forms pieces of a new religion. Each one brings with it the single piece of truth that validates their religion, each conspiring to infect the other with the 'real truth' so that it can carry on in spite. These religions would fight until the death of one or the other, and it is only out of that secret conspiracy that the last priest would give in to the new religion. Their tokens, idols, and sacred words are smashed and destroyed, but the kernel of truth that represents their foundation survives to infect the new religion."

Even as he spoke, the last priest of a dying religion pleaded for mercy from the new zealots, offering the golden relics and the secrets of their founding. The zealots laughed as they ran the priest through with a spear and took up the bounty. The gold was melted down, and the other relics were burned. Only the single sacred cup of the founder of the religion survived the flames. The simple clay hardened in the fire and held its form. The single inscription—the only words Joshua ever shared with the man—remained etched into the clay as a reminder to remain humble. When the fire died down and the zealots left, a child picked through the ashes and found the cup. He read the words and felt their power. He carried them with him through the rest of his life, sharing them with all who would hear. So the religion survived.

Joshua saw this and felt some satisfaction. The veneer of lies built around that single revelation was gone, and all that remained was the truth. It was proofed in the flame, literally and figuratively, and so it remained and became wisdom. Uncontrolled by any forces of idealism, it was free to grow on its own.

Joshua saw more and more of his message emerge this way. As the infection of the false religion spread, all the temples and religions in its path fell the same way. Where before he might share a thousand individual sentences, paragraphs began to emerge when they were combined. His truth could emerge in whole before it was all over. His truth spread like weeds through the minds of the People, and all knew the wisdom once coveted by the religions.

The test was clear. The society was not healthy, despite the effort he put into it. The infection spread too far too fast and proved the society wasn't truly resilient. It was hollow, so it would be filled with the most passionate. Government stagnates and rots when it tries to appease everyone. Society becomes indecisive when it tries to protect everyone from every insult. Religion becomes insalubrious when it tries to appeal to all lifestyles. And economies fail when hindered by notions of compassionate intervention. The society proved to be dead already.

It was time for another apocalypse.

32

efore the Technician's diseased religion arrived, the Valley was at peace. At its heart was Lant, a lustrous, industrious city that stretched from one horizon to the next. The trials of its early years had been worked out. The city center, once a fetid and diseased ghetto, burned and rebuilt, provided a natural place for government to grow. It had its share of corruption but was in balance.

The government concentrated on the greatest areas of need. A single dictator wrote edicts and directed the soldiers of the state. A council approved or disapproved the edicts and controlled the militias of different territories to counter any dictator who posed a threat. The council was hounded by the district governors, who as a body approved or disapproved of the council's decisions and forced them to readdress the issues and had guard forces under their command to counter the council's assaults. And the various commercial entities ensured their needs were heard by providing financial support to those governors and paid spies and assassins to ensure things got done with their interests in mind.

The people had neighborhood councils with elected representatives who caucused at the district level. They retained their rights to defend themselves against all other layers of government and bore the individual responsibility of that right. Every voice was heard whether or not the speaker said something worth listening to. A cautious balance with a hint of violence ensured this mutually beneficial arrangement.

The religion of the Valley was a unified conglomerate. The monotheist religions were content to allow the pantheists to exist—whether they worshiped an aspect of Joshua or Joshua as a whole, they were still worshiping Joshua. The pantheists were satisfied that the monotheists embraced nature, which preserved their individual gods. The atheists respected each person's right to their own understanding of the truth. Everyone else accepted that the atheists' lack of belief had no bearing on Joshua's existence or belief in them. The holy book reflected this conglomeration, and Joshua saw to it that it contained everything he wanted spread and the priesthood was only as corrupt as they could get away with.

The economy reflected the stability of the government. Unification of the Valley's empires had eliminated all economic competition from the outside, and plenty of small cities and towns still depended on their resources. The currency was unified and the supply routes well established and patrolled. They had plenty of active farmland. The efficiency had increased a thousandfold, and a narrow strip of land held enough to feed a family and a half, so the surplus fed the urban dwellers. With a well-established and stable economy, there was little or no need for technological advancements, only improving efficiencies. Resources were in steady supply, and the needs of the people remained basic and satisfied.

To sustain the continuous growth, new areas were explored high in the hills near the ice walls. Mines in the north brought iron to the foundries, and gems were brought in from the south to supply the currency. Farmlands to the east supplied the majority of the food, and to the west the salt mines provided the vital dietary aid that kept neurons firing and bodies hydrated. It was in the latter that the beginning of the end emerged.

The society had grown very large. The population's breathing, moving, and just being, created a huge amount of heat. When this heat combined with the icy air from the high walls, storms formed that kept the Valley rich and fertile. The heat from the growing population melted the lower ledges of the ice walls and eroded them. Little rivulets of melting ice formed the streams, brooks, and creeks and merged into the rivers that ended at the central lake that served as the primary water source for the Valley's largest city. The more the population grew, the larger this lake grew from the lack of absorption by the flora that had once proliferated. Though it was certainly not helpful to the city that rising water levels in the winter could potentially flood the lakeside districts, it also washed away much of the filth that collected there.

But as the new religion took hold, institutions were toppled and freedom stifled. The population fell into rapid decay, and blood flowed as freely as the rain. The pall of darkness descended on the Valley. Those who weren't displaced by the new religion adapted to it, then adopted it as their own, considering that the most prudent thing to do. It resonated with some more than others. Even the lies that Joshua recognized satisfied many who knew deep inside that "the truth will clean the slate." The poor especially found a new voice in this religion and a place to channel the frustration and passion that their conditions had stifled.

Through it all, the ice wall continued to recede, the climate and nature largely indifferent to the machinations of one group over another. An ancient landscape slowly emerged. Ancient flowers bloomed once more from seeds that had lain dormant for thousands of years. Under the ice, rocks with bright green and red rust became visible, and more than that, veins of precious metals were exposed. The till revealed precious stones of all varieties waiting to be collected.

Whole industries were developed to collect this bounty. They set up villages on the frontiers and housed enclaves of scientists in facilities near the rich resources. They monitored the ice wall and took measurements of all manner of things: The opacity of the ice, which to them revealed the internal temperature of the ice and was altogether a nonsense reading. The surface temperature of the ice, which remained constant. The flow of melt off, which could never be fully captured. The height of the ice, which could never be accurately measured at all places. The ambient temperature, which changed with the seasons and reflected nothing of consequence other than the change of the local climate.

The population continued to grow, which kept the demand for the water high. The system struggled to provide it, but with the increasing population, the Valley grew wider and wider as the ice receded and melted away. This ensured that land for the population also grew.

Scientists sounded the alarm at numerous points in the population's advance.

"The rate of melt off will flood the Valley and everyone will die," they claimed.

The population instead grew larger, making use of the increasing moisture in the farms and faucets of the Valley. When they set up at a higher point, the temperature continued to rise, and scientists sounded the alarm again. Again, the population grew and people adapted.

When the Valley walls continued to climb and the ice continued to recede, the population continued to grow, the scientists relaxed. Most of them had only known the climate they'd grown accustomed to in their lifetimes. The heat made the climate much more comfortable, and heavier moist air helped the population grow healthier. Instead of sounding their alarms and making predictions, they simply reported their findings and analyzed what they saw.

These weather stations became libraries full of government scrolls, news articles, religious texts, and reading materials that ranged from salacious smut to dry biographies of famous persons and their modest achievements. The scientists spent the days analyzing various aspects of their society in the same way they'd analyzed weather data. These stations expanded and began tutoring people on the knowledge of their world, and as the growing population surrounded these once-remote stations, full-fledged universities were born, with libraries full of ancient scrolls stretching across the hills of the Great Valley.

These universities produced a prolific amount of innovative ideas, and the tinkerers of the engineering departments created devices that improved the world they lived in by leaps and bounds. The scientific method was applied to every aspect of their society and improved crop yields, farm efficiency, animal husbandry methods, mining methodology, and geologic records. They analyzed the forms of government that were most effective at producing the most good. Their findings were published, and every university and library across the hills and Great Valley had a copy.

The best of all the research, the most current, the most comprehensive, were even to be found in the frontier weather stations. It was this that provided the foundational knowledge for the next era when the old world was swept away.

As the false religion spread, many of the universities fell silent. Many burned. The heretics they housed were found to be spreading anticanonical falsehoods and were publicly tortured. The research stations that had not yet taken to teaching simply fell silent. Others raided their own libraries and became nomads, chasing the ice wall and leaving the world they knew far behind in an effort to escape the tyranny of the evil.

Joshua saw these Chaldean scholars as the seeds of the new world. They carried with them the tale of their fallen empire, the great city of Lant had fallen to the tyranny. The knowledge that "At Lant is death" drove them forward to the expanding horizon.

33

The same tale of diseased ideals spread throughout the world, proving the necessity of the collapse.

When the world was covered with ice, the vast oceans of water were condensed into highly salinized bands across the equatorial region. Water flowed freely beneath the ice over the poles, but the ice was so thick that the majority of the ocean was displaced toward the equator. The Great Valley was isolated from this ocean by the wall of sea ice that blocked the mountains on the western edge. As the ice receded around the Valley, the same was happening around the rest of the planet. The populations that had inhabited the lowland regions throughout the world grew beyond the confines of the regions that isolated them.

The inhabitants of these sanctuaries of civilization were all different from each other. They had become homogenized within the confines of their isolated regions. The DNA of the slave people unified them all, but they were all slightly different in their phenotypes and looked different from one another as well. Even the creatures they domesticated were different. Where one valley used dogs as domesticated guards, another might use large felines with ferocious roars. One relied on horses while another used elephants for the same tasks.

Joshua had named these creatures based on what they resembled from his world, and in thinking so, the people called them by the same names. There was an innate connection between Joshua's thoughts and the actions of the beings that represented his refracted self. At will Joshua could see life through their eyes and interact with the world as a person, experiencing their actions as his own, along with their lust, hate, voice, and personalities. He retained his own consciousness, yet the people never knew he was there guiding their actions. He did it through the touch of a single neuron at a time, and it was this link that enabled him to shape the people into the tools that shaped the world.

⎯⎯ ⚬⚬⚬ ⎯⎯

The ice that receded only invited more problems. While the oceans' levels began to fall slightly, the wall of ice receded rapidly. As the miners in the west went about their normal business developing new salt mines for operations, they opened up a fissure that exposed the salt to the moisture a horizon beyond their mine. The great ocean worked its way through the rocks and under the ice, and while the total might of the ocean was contained, enough of it seeped through that crack to begin the process. The salt began to dissolve. The already salt-heavy water still had not reached peak salinity, so it absorbed a little more as it pooled. The immediate solution for the mine was to drain the water off. They were used to rain and snow and melting ice in those high reaches of the Valley, so water in the mine was nothing new. The salt water was nothing new either. All water that touched the salt became salinized. So there was nothing new about the situation that warranted any other action. They cut drains where the infiltration occurred and continued as normal.

The land beneath the salt mine was a wasteland. Nothing grew, and everything had a perpetual white film of crystalized salt. Yet with the infiltration of the salt water into the mine, there was now an ever-present standing pool of salt water on the ground. When someone was told to monitor the flow of the water, it didn't matter what season it was, they found the flow never stopped. When they started taking measurements of water that was flowing in, the flow proved to have increased each time. When they tried to stop the flow, they found other places where it started percolating through, before the stopper was washed out. The drain grew ever larger, not from deliberate boring, but because the salt the drain was cut from continued to dissolve.

Eventually the pool beneath the salt mine became a stream, and the local government was forced to step in. They tried damming the stream with huge blocks and piled aggregate and mud. This helped for a while. The water that percolated through lost much of its salinity as it reacted with the soil that filtered it, and it carried further into the Valley.

It carried death wherever it went. Farmlands were abandoned and the owners forced to leave with only partial compensation for their losses as a reward. They would have to set up far away where land was still cheap or take up life in the city with what remained of their life's work.

The salt poisoned the waters, killing fish and disrupting the ecosystem, killing the grasses wild game fed on and poisoning the water they drank. The only saving grace was the rainfall that decreased the salinity and washed away the stain from the soil. Most creatures died when their water sources were poisoned. Others managed to find a tolerable balance. Some fish, long adapted to clean fresh water, were slowly becoming used to the low salinity far downstream. Some tolerated more, others less, but many managed to adapt and survive.

Eventually even the dam overflowed, and the water, now supersaturated with salt, was able to flood over the top. Larger dams were built, and eventually a whole area between two hills was dedicated to holding back the water.

The government blamed the salt mine. It was, after all, salt water. The farmers sued whoever they could to get their recompense, and eventually the mine owners were forced to shut down. They lived the rest of their lives as ruined men.

Yet the flood continued unabated. It actually increased after the mine shut down because there was no one actively working to stop the flooding. The steady drip turned into a trickle, the trickle into a gush, and the gush into a roar. It took almost no time for the dam to become unstable, requiring the lower valley to be evacuated. When it finally broke, the salt water rushed down the hillside, destroying everything in its path, its roar echoing off the hills all around.

The poison finally reached the great lake and instantly killed all the fish in the westernmost quarter. The dilution of the high salinity by the fresh water enabled some fish to survive. Some had been washed downstream and adapted to moderate levels of salinity. These fish survived off the corpses of the dead. And with the dam gone, the upper reservoir overrun, and no one in the mine to stop the flow, the water continued to flood in.

The salt water was not drinkable, so very little of it was used. This meant the lake continued to rise, and the people of the harbor districts, who could no longer make a living off fishing, left the area to move uphill to the highlands where land was cheap and the water pure from the flowing springs. They were no longer fishermen, but they could find other work. Except the whole of their borough had met the same fate. Now people numbering in the tens of thousands fled the city to find work elsewhere. Some moved only as far as necessary before settling down again.

Still the water rose. Icy salt water met with the warm river water and a constant storm brewed. The driving wind and rain flushed more of the desolate hillsides into the lake, filling it with debris and forcing the water levels to rise. With no grasses to hold the sediment in place, the hills leading up to the salt mines were scoured down to bedrock.

This process continued for two hundred years, reaching a point where the history became legend, and the legend became myth. The people of the area had always known the lake was salty. There were fish in it but not many, and they were not good to eat. Things progressed the same way until the ice wall, far above the salt mine, finally split. There were few people to hear it, but its initial earsplitting crack shook the little remaining ice far to the north, and the subsequent explosions from the stress deafened all to the sound of the roar that followed.

A mere drip had turned into a deluge. The ocean had worked its way to the last few spans of ice and, with a final crack, came cascading down the mountainside at a force unknown to the people of the Valley in all their eons of natural serenity. The water wasn't much at first. But as it tore at and dislodged the fracturing ice, its volume increased immeasurably. It crashed into the slopes of the western valley and destroyed what remained of the sediment and the scraggly plants that clung to life.

The roiling mass moved unabated toward the city. The greatest city in the world watched as the whole ocean flowed through the gap. Some fled in terror; others stood hopelessly watching in awe as the leading edge of their world was ripped from its foundation and battered the next area. Death was coming for them. There was no escape. A few had boats, but those boats were worthless against the torrent that cascaded toward them. The horror unfolded before their eyes. As the water continued to rise, they took whatever they had and fled as far and as fast as they could. Many were overcome regardless. Some managed to cling to debris for a while before slipping beneath the waves, caught up in the undercurrent that pulled hapless victims beneath the surface and bludgeoned them against the wreckage of their world.

One hundred horizons from the breach, a great storm approached. The rains started to fall, and the winds began to howl. Though the high plains were cold, it was no longer cold enough to snow. Joshua had commanded one of many prophets to create a refuge—static structures and rafts of all kinds to weather the coming storm. All the preserves of the glorious society of the Valley would be stored in these vessels and sanctuaries until the storm passed.

This storm raged for one-ninth of the year. It finally quieted. The waters receded back to the Valley where the final resting place of the great society lay still, beneath the salty sea. Obliterated and covered with the displaced sediment of the churned valley floor, it was a stinking, muddy, bloody horror, beyond anyone's imagination. But it was over. Those who remained had found shelter higher than the ocean's water could flow.

A few weather stations survived, high above the valley floor at the frontiers of the empire. A few defeated souls emerged alive from the sea, bruised and battered but alive. The mines of the northern hills were now isolated from the rest of the people of their shattered empire. The farms of the fertile plains to the east were now barren and desolate, the soil salted and worthless, the farmers forced to move further eastward in hopes of finding untouched land, ending at the first freshwater river they found. The gem mines of the southern hills were isolated from the rest in the same way as their brethren. The land salted and barren, no longer able to sustain life. They were forced further south, where they mingled with the people at the headwaters of the great river, a high mountain valley on the equator where the snow could not persist.

Even for Joshua, the carnage was unexpected. He had planned it and calculated the results and was mostly correct in his measurements. But the brutality of the scene, and the filth that filled the valley where he once directed his world for refuge, was shocking. Still, the cancer of the false religion had been eradicated, and what remained would quickly be consumed and destroyed by the desperate. He vowed to never again use such a flood as a means of population control, at least not at that magnitude. It was fortunate that the remaining ice, if melted, could not create a deluge large enough for Joshua to renege on that vow.

34

Eventually the ocean and the valley reached equilibrium. The force of the flood rushing through the gap in the western mountains slowed, and the valley became a sea—a permanent fixture for those who survived—and the scar of that terrible event reverberated throughout the millennia afterward.

Yet the waters receded and left the remnants of the towns the waters had engulfed in the highlands. The bloated corpses left behind by the ebbing tides were quickly devoured by carrion predators.

The scattered survivors continued to suffer. In fact, the flood was only the beginning of their suffering. Nothing grew in the barren wastes covered in salty mud. Stunted crops had been drowned and poisoned. Still, the rats and the birds tried their luck with whatever they could find and managed to find nourishment.

The people who fled from the horror and carnage went as far as they could, the shock visible in their faces as they trudged head-long into the unknown. Most were not adapted to living in the wilderness. Most had had good jobs as tradesmen and farmers, and while hobbyists were able to find food here and there, the stress of long-term survival caused most to flounder and fall. Most had their whole worlds ripped apart—fathers, mothers, sisters, brothers, children, and spouses killed before their eyes, loved ones ripped from their desperate grasp in the force of the flood—and now they wandered with nothing left to return to and nowhere to go. They wandered into the barren wastes where the salt water had destroyed their civilization and headed for the horizon where there was still some green left to explore.

They occasionally came across other survivors. Some were co-operative. Others, too desperate to think clearly, either became a liability or a foe. They were forced by circumstances to kill each other, the victor often making the repulsive choice to consume the body of the fallen. In these desperate moments, the memory of the smell and flavor of that seared flesh reminded them of the popular domesticated meat animal they used to eat with nearly every morning's meal. For some, that made the choice easier to repeat, and cannibalism became their survival technique. For others, the horror left them hungry, but they retained some sense of their personhood. Yet every survivor tried that forbidden meat and were changed by it psychologically.

Of the hundreds of thousands who survived, half died off in the first few weeks. Another half became food for other survivors or died alone. It went on like this for months. Those who survived did so by the grace of Joshua alone. A sickly bush on their path would bear fruit out of season, and the survivor was able to eat for one more day.

The cannibals eventually ran out of food and preyed on each other. They ceased to behave as the people they once were. Their lives as farmers, brickmakers, and weavers became distant memories, and their joys and identities from before were forgotten. Eventually, having found no other food source as Joshua made their paths ashen and bare, they died alone and became food for the scavengers.

This was a test of the fortitude of the survivors. Joshua had laid the plans to move them out of the city and into the far stretches of the Valley. Those whose farms were ruined by the salt water were sent to the far end to start again. The nomadic librarians were pushed ahead of the melee to preserve a record of the knowledge developed in the Valley for those thousands of years. The miners who were working on the frontiers managed to survive the floods, being too high in the hills to be overcome by the waters. The stores of supplies that they were left with dwindled rapidly, but they rationed and held together long enough to survive before the waters receded.

The ice wall rapidly receded at this point as well. The salt had undermined the wall, and the debris that the waters carried coated the face of the ice wall, so the sun's heat was absorbed and started melting it. Massive pieces broke off and exposed other trapped pieces of stone and dirt to the sunlight and melted more and more.

The melting ice allowed fresh water to flow, and even with growing hunger, the northerners were able to survive with fresh water. The plants on the riverbanks returned rapidly as the fresh water rinsed the poison out of the soil. The People lived on grasses and water and some flowers and what little else they could find with nutritional value. They continued to move northward with the ice away from the horrors of the Valley.

In the south the ice was gone. The long prairies that had been good farmlands and the deep quarries that once supplied the empire with currency were washed away. The grasslands were now bleached and barren. The gentle breeze carried the dead grasses and soil away. The waters had flooded the quarries and filled them with the soil and sediment torn from other places, leaving no trace of the production that once existed there.

Those on the frontier were used to the long supply chains and high cost of goods to get to their areas, so they were somewhat self-sufficient. They subsidized their diet with whatever milled flour was the cheapest from the nearest merchant. When the flood destroyed the civilization, they were devastated but not desperate. So they were a natural target for many survivors though a healthy, calm, and cautious frontier person tended to be more than a handful for a starving, tired, and desperate survivor, and few fell victim to the truly deranged. Often, the frontiersmen could spot survivors coming up the easiest path, so they left food and water and a message to keep on moving, keeping a cautious hand on a sharp blade and a shovel and having a pre-dug hole close by for anyone who got too cozy.

Villages still existed even after the flood. The same scrappy frontier people who'd banded together before the flood simply learned to do without luxuries afterward. These villages were a natural destination for those seeking refuge, and with nothing to offer but their skills and knowledge, they were given a free meal and then a job making shelters and gates and walls for the community to protect itself from others. These frontier villages, where civilizations re-emerged after the great flood, became the foundations of the great cities that followed.

35

"Unhindered calamity does interesting things to people," the Technician said, admiring the carnage of the Valley, now a salty sea. "Left with nothing, they must find everything they need to survive. Weapons for survival are made from whatever they find useful. Food is everything that moves, and sometimes anything that doesn't. Fuel is anything that will provide warmth for the cold nights high in the mountainous plateaus. The remnants of villages flooded but not washed away leave plenty to satisfy these needs."

No longer bitter over the Technician's actions, Joshua added, "So many civilizations come and go and are erased by this process. The walls are torn down for fuel, the metal is melted and reformed, and the knowledge of the past is slowly consumed and forgotten. Nothing remains but fragments."

"Now you understand. There is nothing permanent and nothing new," the Technician said somberly. "Metal rusts, wood rots, soil is swept away. Everything that can be made can be unmade by nature. Eventually, everything regresses to the mean, and in nature the average is always crowded and diverse, ignorant and brutish."

The Technician proved the quality of the system—if it was weak it would break. Joshua had learned long ago to resign the fate of this world to the Technician. These scenes were merely symbols of his own failure, failure that he could learn from. He could try again and make the system stronger the next time around.

The Technician was ever present throughout Joshua's experience. Where Joshua worked to design the perfect formulas, the Technician tested them. Joshua was often certain that he had created an unbreakable species, society, system, or whatever. The Technician always sought to prove him wrong. Where armor was created on a creature, the Technician, in his experience with running thousands of others through the Machine, knew exactly how to exploit that armor. Where a society created a perfect set of laws, the Technician ensured that an army of lawyers would pick at them, finding holes and technicalities that left gaps in the system that enabled predators to walk freely among the people. Where an individual proved perfectly loyal to Joshua in good times, the Technician proved that loyalty with suffering. This was not done to create the evil; this was evil that already existed in the recesses of Joshua's mind. This was done to prove to Joshua that there was no perfect system, that the only way to eliminate the evil was through elimination of the evil in each of his people. Some people were inherently evil, and no matter how large the cage or comprehensive the legal system, there was a way to let that evil escape. So, no matter how difficult it was for Joshua to bear destroying a part of himself, he had to destroy it.

This was the dynamic. Joshua recognized that the Technician was not his enemy. He was his adversary, but not maliciously so. It was critical that Joshua be tested in these ways, just as no product could leave a factory floor that hadn't received the quality assurance check that protected the factory from liability. This was the role the Technician played. And it was this role that strengthened

Joshua's abilities. He became smarter and craftier and could follow the logical series of events that ensured that a law or path was comprehensive enough to ensure there would not be any problems for a while. And so they went, Joshua building his perfect species, societies, and systems, and the Technician breaking them to prove their inherent weaknesses.

The warm Valley had been insulated by the exhaust from the people and fauna, making it very comfortable. But high in these hills, the wind took all the heat from a body and left people shivering. Where there was no standing wood, the thatch roofs and timbers that made the house frames were pillaged and burned for warmth. The stones that formed the walls were torn down and piled up to block the wind. Any metal tools were turned into weapons; any iron nails or bands were sharpened and prepared for hunting and murder. The homesteads that stood after the flood were reduced to rubble, the trash was burned or eaten, the finished goods were repurposed or taken, and the footprint of the homesite obliterated one stone at a time. Where once a family had thrived, nothing was left, not even the rubble for a historical record.

The Valley was not the first civilization to rise and fall, but it was the biggest and most advanced so far. As in every society, the quest to find out what came before assured each civilization that they were the first, that they were special. Their archaeologists found scarce evidence that anything before them even existed. The corpses found were deformed and provided evidence that religious ritual had preserved the corpses, even as the bones of those they themselves buried rotted away in the moist temperate soil.

The tools of the ancients were rudimentary and spoke to their ignorance, the layout of their homes suggestive of their profound ritualism and pagan religion. Yet they could not see the same in their own civilizations.

The lack of evidence became proof that they were the first true civilization—that they had reached the pinnacle, and that they had reached the golden age, and God, the gods, or a universal noncorporeal being would embrace them as the paragon of creation. Even as their homes were built from the bones of the cities that stood before them. Even as they carried the technology, knowledge, and stories left from those before them. Those histories, proved by artifacts and remains, became myth once those artifacts disappeared. The collection of those artifacts into single structures enabled singular destructive events to erase the evidence of the past. Whole civilizations that had lived and thrived, collapsed and died were erased from memory. And no one could prove otherwise.

The same was the case for the Valley. The greatest city that ever existed, created from catastrophe, born from population pressures and natural migration patterns of people, products, and ideas, now lay at the bottom of a great sea. The destroyed monuments to their greatness lay collapsed and covered in silt and salt, eroding under the great pressure of the water and the movement of the tides. Before long only the temples to government and religion would remain. The unpretentious parts would disappear without a trace.

Joshua had observed this at every scale. The corpse of the deer was not left behind as a monument to its life. The predator that killed it took the greatest share. The scavenger that found it later took its portion. The carrion birds picked clean whatever it could find, and the insects and bacteria consumed the remaining flesh and sinew. The bones were torn apart in the search for meat and the bones chewed and broken open to get at the marrow inside. Small chips and fragments remained but would decompose from the softening of the rain and trampling of hooves and the freezing of winter and the brittle dryness of the summer's heat. Eventually all that remained were grains of sand that nourished the plants all around. So, too, was the fate of even the greatest cities.

36

I applaud you." The Technician said this without the slightest hint of sarcasm. "There are few who take such violent action against such a cancer. Without regard to the potential damage to your being, you made the decision and followed through."

Joshua had forgotten the impact of these decisions. This one against a more advanced society surely would be catastrophic. "What does that mean for me? I can still think, so it didn't impact my cognition very much."

"No," the Technician replied, "you have many more societies hidden throughout the world untouched by this calamity. This represents only a part of your cerebral cortex. You have kept the critical parts of yourself alive, and as they survive and reproduce, you will find you have made your thought processes more efficient."

"What does that mean? That each of these people was useless?"

"In so many words, yes. They are the memory of the color of a napkin at a diner you visited once. They are the song that you vaguely heard when you saw the empress the first time. They are little more than bits of information that amount to nothing of consequence. They just take up neurons; they occupy space. They are the facts you studied that have no bearing on the real world. You are better off without them."

"But those who survived were more vital somehow?" Joshua wasn't sure whether this was meant to be an accusation or congratulation.

"Yes, they somehow understand the critical principles that allow you to assess those facts and see the archetypical idea they represent," the Technician stated matter-of-factly.

Cautiously, Joshua pressed on, "But I did not decide which individuals would live or die. I made very little effort to select them. I only observed their behaviors and helped or hindered them as I saw fit."

"True, but I did. And your parents and grandparents did. Many were chosen by conscious intent. Others were chosen by survival instincts. The conditions they survived were based on their understanding of those principles they represented. They were attuned to you in some way, and they survived because of it. Had you deliberately impeded them, you would have lobotomized yourself by killing them; however, you did not."

Joshua was quiet for a moment, then asked, "So you *helped* me?"

The Technician let out a surprisingly warm laugh, then replied, "In some ways, yes. In others, no. I am simply telling you, you have done well. You have learned to calculate, and the destruction was necessary. It was even well done. There was time enough to maneuver the good people from the danger area to safety, and it was long enough to create resentment toward the religion that was destroyed. My pure and genuine compliments."

Joshua suddenly felt at ease. Despite the destruction, the Technician's comments made him feel like the end was near. Though he still had no idea what that truly meant.

—∞∞∞—

The shambles of civilization made their way along the easiest paths, all seeking peace and serenity, food, shelter, and companionship. The great rivers that once flowed from high in the glaciers now percolated out of the rocks and collected rainwater and runoff in their constant descent to the sea. It was there at the mouth of the river—the estuaries—where the fertile lands and fresh water met the abundant oceans teeming with life. Joshua had learned that oppression was inevitable in a society without laws, and these people who had suffered found only that wherever they went. They sought to rebuild and leave behind the carnage, to establish a new civilization that would give them purpose after the aimless misery they had endured.

The hollow souls who endured the carnage followed the same paths, crossed the same obstacles, and as time wore on, found themselves at the same estuary. Newcomers were greeted warmly, their hardships known by all, and there they were able to begin rebuilding. Each carried with them a fragment of their old lives: skills that were useful and tools that would help them to rebuild.

Many had psychological scars not only from the flood but also from the choices they had to make to survive. Some knew what it was to cannibalize the dead. Most knew murder. All knew suffering. So they sought to start again and forget the shame of who they became when they were tested.

The scholars who escaped the dying society carried with them the knowledge of the old world. They could recreate it and accelerate the rebirth. Tomes of history, politics, and philosophy gave them a rudimentary idea of the structures of society that were best, and they organized the burgeoning city into a functioning society. It was in these cities that hope shone once more, and people started to remember what it was like to be happy.

The cities were governed by good leaders, and the people all worked for the sake of rebuilding the world washed away. It was virtue born from tragedy and guilt, but it was virtuous all the same, and the cities they built stood for thousands of years after.

—————∞∞∞—————

The sinful also found homes. Far from the abundance of the rivers, they built cities around choke points in the mountains and valleys. Highwaymen and bandits, they preyed on the weak. Serving only themselves and taking from others, the society they built had a foundation of sand, and the selfishness of the individuals ensured the villages stood only long enough to scour all life and wealth from the area. Marauders ambushed the helpless and consumed them. They tormented the innocent, and Joshua put a bounty on such Amalekites for all time.

A few of these bandits made their way into the cities of the survivors. They caused carnage and mayhem while they were there, and when they left, they spread the word of the city ripe for the picking.

For those unprepared for the evils on their doorstep, the cities fell and became cities for the damned. When the bandits took a stronghold, they killed and ate everything and everyone, the survivors fleeing again for the wasteland until they found other survivors to share their story with.

Joshua guided these people to the sanctuaries that lined the coasts and inspired them to take arms against these bandits and eradicate them. A great war ensued, and in the end the bandits were driven from the coastlines and forced to hide in the hills, a price on their heads for all time.

Trade networks were established. Alliances formed to ensure a mutual call to arms was heeded to fend off the raiders. The transmission of supplies, knowledge, and people ensured the rapid rise of these cities, and before long the populations far exceeded the raiders. It was a matter of time before they were extinguished.

Many of the highwaymen made their way into the cities to live in the shadows of the new society, and there they stayed, a constant nuisance to society.

The nomadic librarians who carried the knowledge of the old world with them were able to quickly form an ordered society. The strong men were the farmers and tradesmen displaced from the early floods. The city-states were supported from the frontier homesteads. The People were well established and able to recover quickly.

Though the preparation allowed these societies to rapidly rise, the missing pieces of the laws allowed many to rapidly fall again. The societies that emerged had to figure out the missing pieces on their own, and many went too far in their bureaucracy.

The cities of the survivors flourished. They tamed the wastelands and created abundant farmlands that nourished countless peoples. It was the lack of a complete guide that allowed the decay that led to the cycle of collapse and rebirth. Laws were written, and the people chafed under growing oppression. The alliances between cities broke down, and before long the same growing pains of civilization created the havoc that led Joshua to decide the fate of the People. They were, on the whole, more virtuous, but the allure of wealth and power and ease ensured that they were tested in their resolve. The Technician never gave respite from the corruption.

37

The swing from collapse to tyranny and rapidly back again was a natural order that could be sped or slowed in a number of ways, but the end result was always the same. It was a constant trial and error to figure out what combination led to the longest lasting empires, and it was always under the rule of a single figure that survival ultimately leaned toward.

Since no individual could be trusted to remain consistent throughout their lives, it became imperative that they be appointed on the condition that they respect the set of guidelines that protected the people from their swinging moods. The contract with the people gave them assurance that the single ruler would honor their rights and look out for their interests. Without enforcement, however, this always failed, and the dictator stole the rights of the many. So the people enforced it by remaining armed wherever they could.

The people alone had turned into nothing but a disorganized mob, so a strongman with an army could defeat a mob twenty times his forces because of the discipline and order an organized army was used to. It was vital that independent armies of varying loyalties be formed to ensure that a single rogue strongman could not usurp the throne and strip people of their rights. The threat of violence was necessary even in societies with the most virtuous foundations.

The society that was built on enabling the individual while punishing the sinful lasted. The simple rules that allowed a society to prosper ensured that individuals were allowed to succeed and fail at any endeavor that didn't harm others. Individual success was rewarded whereas selfishness was eradicated. The governments established the justice system that best served these purposes. Guarding society from within and from without was their sole purpose. But the nuances around this ideal led to the internal disagreements that led to societal collapse and civil war.

With armies needing to fight on any frontier, and supplies needing to feed and arm them, a system of roads was of the highest strategic importance. This employed the bulk of the unskilled labor to maintain, and the access to rugged terrain allowed the population to expand and stretch out, absorbing the resources of the whole territory because of the roads. Nations that failed to maintain these networks, using them once and then abandoning them once the war was over, invested more resources each time a war was waged. The population was then forced to remain concentrated and small. The more successful nations maintained extensive road networks continuously rather than as needed. This allowed them to absorb their neighbors and gain access to more resources, until they grew larger and larger and became dominant.

Even as society grew, the poorest were pushed to the fringes or crushed in the middle. The crime that sprang from these areas meant the state had a higher cost to maintain the peace, so social programs were instituted throughout the land to try and mitigate the impact of poverty on crime. Industries were kept artificially obsolete to employ more people. Farmland was subsidized to make it affordable to the poor. Military service was rewarded with benefits to encourage the poor to escape their lives of poverty while serving the nations they lived in. All government programs were designed to keep the population spread evenly and prevent the costly civil wars that left nations lobotomized and feeble.

The vanity of the powerful made them believe the poor couldn't survive without them. They were the brains of the society, better suited to guiding the people in the interests of the people. They manipulated votes, divided the commoners, and stepped in as objective middlemen, gathering power unto themselves. The people, fooled at first, were mistrustful of any who claimed to have their interests in mind and sought to seize more autonomy for themselves. The dynamic that had existed in previous civilizations thrived in each one after. The dominance of the elites ensured tyranny; the dominance of the masses ensured anarchy.

This balance within a society led to constant civil wars. Constant fighting prevented commerce from taking steady root, and people suffered. The nations as a whole suffered, and those who fought against themselves were open to attack. The most successful nations established ways of waging civil war without blood. A debate was as heated as a battle, but there were fewer scars and broken homes, and it left the strong military presence to destroy any invaders. Councils were divided by policies and philosophies, but they were united in the knowledge that the debate was moot if the nation was conquered and enslaved by these differences while killing one another.

Some societies deemed it necessary to maintain a constant foe—a threat always looming on the horizon, waiting for the moment of greatest division to pounce and destroy the nation. Many nations formed secret agreements with other nations to play this role. The small wars were useful for ensuring the poor never got too populous. They were able to face off in minor skirmishes rather than major conflicts, and the conflicts always remained on neutral ground where neither nation was truly impacted by the bloodshed.

Over time, the balance of all nations found the same equilibrium. Trial and error, collapse and reformation, led to the same conclusions. A single ruler commanded the forces that repelled the enemy from without. Independent councils maintained internal systems like infrastructure, education, and health. The economy was loosely governed, ensuring the highest economic output possible, without the barriers of bureaucracy to slow it down. Taxes prevented recessions from becoming catastrophic for the population. The people maintained their rights in the contract with the state. Foremost on that contract was the right to preserve their rights through violence if necessary.

The checks and balances of the system kept the society healthy and content. The law was given to the people to write, vote on, and enforce while the taxes were left to the council to apportion. The king retained the power to react to imminent threats. The series of rights that were developed over time in the society were protected by an impartial council of judges. It was up to the people to defend their rights, though the council and king sought to impose laws that would violate them.

Democracy was too fragile, so a republic eventually dominated. Yet the leaders were empowered to make decisions, and the people remained vigilant and armed to keep them in check. Clear laws were written so they could be understood by the youngest independent citizens. They applied to the meek and powerful alike and were enforced vigilantly.

The evolution of this ideal arrangement came from constant conflict. While every society remained swinging on the pendulum between the descent into anarchy and total monarchy, they slowed the process through these layers. Part of the system might collapse, but the diffusion of authority and powers ensured that while that part collapsed and reformed, the others remained strong, so society could persist.

At the reformation of the society, additional rules were added to slow the decay and bolster the inherent weak points. Joshua recognized that only those who slow the process long enough to prevent collapse endured long enough to reach mitosis. To divide and become its own competition ensured a nation's culture survived and spread. Those who clung too tightly to their empire found themselves succumbing to the rot within. Mitosis became the goal of every society. This, however, required the absorption of other societies.

It was this reformation that always brought about two opposing views. It was the necessity for absorbing other societies that made these opposing views necessary. Both were right half the time and wrong the rest.

This dynamic was not entirely wholesome or healthy though. Liberalism accepts all people without question, often allowing dangers to enter their society unabated. They seek not only to assimilate cultures but to homogenize identities as well, erasing both the good and the bad of where people come from. In seeking to correct errors of the past, they change whatever was associated with those injustices. The culture, the laws, the history all are subject to change, and all change is wholly embraced. The past is erased, and a new normal is embraced, often without recognizing the dangers ahead and the flaws inherent in the new and exciting identity. The individual who violates the society is simply broken, in need of repair. They will never give up on the individual who is destructive to their society, even when the individual denies that they are the one who is broken. They never see the sword as the answer and never stand against the forces of evil until it's too late.

Conservativism's natural distrust of all comers means that the innocent are lumped with the guilty until they can be cleared. Outsiders are isolated by the dangers they represent. The crimes they commit, from frustration of the conditions they are forced to live in, are held against their society, emblematic of the systemic problem. Change is met with resistance. Caution is the key. History serves as a reminder of the virtues of their founding, but never the failures. If flaws exist, it is in the decay of society rather than the logical progression of the gaps in the foundation. The mistakes of the individual are reflective of a rot in their culture, and the individual is too far gone to be reformed. The conservatives' first instinct is to destroy what is perceived to be dangerous, so their energy is expended in hypervigilance, and the society is left defenseless when true evil does finally come for them.

Fear and faith both conspire to create opportunities to sow discontent and cause harm. One side enables evil through acceptance, helping it sow the hate it represents, infecting the society it is introduced into. The other feeds it the innocent through isolation, the helpless forced to join the evil or perish. The conservative closes the gate ahead of the refugees; the liberal opens it ahead of the invasion.

Yet the virtues of both outweighed their inherent failures.

Liberals in all these societies were accepting of all comers. By being kind and helpful, they ingratiate themselves to the newcomers, who assimilate much quicker through the acceptance of their culture and their ways of life. The individual is given chances to reform and conform, and they find the will to change their ways and become part of the society where they aren't judged or rejected.

Conservatives isolate other cultures until they are assimilated, yet, without fail, identify both the positive and the negative qualities of them. Though the culture of the newcomers erodes as they homogenize, the most valuable and culturally characteristic parts remain to add flavor to their new society. They guard against evil behaviors and identify threats early to preserve the society at large. They protect the culture and preserve the history, and once injustice is identified and they accept the need for correction, they concisely and expertly amputate those issues from the society to prevent any further damage.

It takes both sides working in tandem, accepting, with caution, all comers, vetting and scrutinizing refugees but providing them opportunities and acceptance once they arrive. It takes the diplomacy of the liberal and the cold steel of the conservative. It takes the discriminating suspicion of the conservative to keep criminals and terrorists away, but it takes the indiscriminate love of the liberal to keep those immigrants from becoming criminals and terrorists. Both are vital to society, and both make it possible for societies to create cultures.

Joshua watched as the last guard wearily hung up his tunic and laid down his spear for the last time. The world had changed, and there was no one who valued what he did anymore. Most of his friends had left to find a quiet place in the countryside. "Let the peace-lovers have their city. They'll soon realize what we meant to them."

At the same time, the last wartime councilman sighed as he turned over the keys to his office to his successor. "I hope there will never be a need for my kind again," he said without a shred of disdain. He truly hoped that love and peace and happiness would conquer all and the world would be a better place where everyone lived in harmony. He knew it wouldn't, but it wasn't his fight anymore. The people had decided, and they decided his antiquated ideals of preparedness and caution did not fit in with the new world that came to fruition overnight.

Joshua saw the police force going through training to make them more understanding of those who created the mayhem in society they fought against. "You need to put yourself in their sandals. They don't steal because they *want* to; they steal because they *have* to. The murder they commit is a result of their life in poverty. Their anger is because of their fight against despair . . ." The reasoning was full of emotion, and the logic was based on empathy. A policeman needed to understand that the stones shot and arrows launched at them were cries for help, and they shouldn't retaliate in kind but should retaliate with kindness. Everyone left the session feeling like all their knowledge and training and field experience was worthless. It was a new world, and the healers of the down-trodden had a new way to cure the ills of society that was going to overcome the millennia of the tried and true. Half left the force within the year. Those who remained might as well have. They lost all heart and motivation for the job; the paychecks until retirement all that mattered.

Little by little, Joshua saw the tides of the blindly hopeful conquer the perceptive and cynical realists. In the end the society had no opposition to the creation of their utopian society. All people would receive bread every day. All people would be cared for until their deaths. All people would have access to the same education and the same opportunities. Discrimination was eradicated and so would be injustice.

It only took a day before the injustice of people receiving only bread, given their dietary restrictions, forced more discriminatory compromises. These people would receive bread, and those would receive cheese. It was impossible to satisfy everyone. Equality created injustices. There was inequality in the educations received, because the quality of teachers differed, and the best were hired by wealthier districts. There was inequality in health care—the medical staff were underpaid and overworked for the sudden volume of ailments caused by so much equality. Immigrants at the borders were welcomed freely, bringing with them illness and corruption from the societies they fled from. Unchecked by the tolerant police, they established themselves in enclaves where they displaced and harassed native citizens. Crime spread unabated because discrimination prevented witnesses from identifying characteristics of assailants and the police were not allowed to work from hunches that inevitably led them to the poor neighborhoods where minorities and immigrants resided. The decay spread faster than a love-based solution to resolve it could be developed, and the disease was finally eradicated when the army of the neighboring nation marched in unopposed and restored order under a new flag.

Joshua watched a nation with the opposite ideological bent close their borders with an iron wall. The last voices of tolerance were beaten and silenced and thrown out of the society. A priest begging for the well-being of the frightened and illiterate was mocked as the immigrants and impoverished were carted off to the holding facility where they would be made useful.

The artists ceased to capture the hope flourishing in the world and under threat of violence began to produce propaganda for the glory of the state. Capturing the essence of the ideal citizen, their hearts forced their hands to create caricatures. When they were deemed to be patronizing and disingenuous, the artist disappeared. Joshua led many to salvation and safety outside the walls, but many were not so lucky.

All people behind that wall were measured against the metric of loyalty. Their religious views, political leanings, hobbies, and associations all were cataloged and ranked against the ideal metric of what a citizen should be. They were not assimilated; they were not reformed; they were not told of their position in the society. Those who were trustworthy were given great benefits. Those whose identities disproved their loyalty to the nation were shunned. The state's inherent drive for discrimination and violence led to the cleansing of their society. Sterilization of the outliers created the same result as their liberal counterparts—homogenized society. Yet the homogenization weakened the society more than it improved it. While it kept the outside world away successfully, it created more enemies within. By isolating those parts of society that were not suitably conformed, they created enemies within. By eliminating those elements, they reduced their collective forces.

When the outliers no longer existed within the conquerors' borders, even greater scrutiny was put on their citizens' behavior and personalities. The oppression was total. Only those who fit the mold perfectly without conscious effort, who were living definitions of the model citizen, were able to thrive. As a society this created the stereotype of their culture. Yet the inherent weakness was a nation whose external enemies were only outnumbered by the internal ones they created, and at the first breach in that iron wall, the fuse of revolt was ignited, and that society collapsed from within.

Joshua observed the extremes in all forms. He found societies of all types—with all religions and all governing systems, with all degrees of homogenization—make the same mistakes. It was only by the tempering of his nature that he allowed them to exist. They would be destroyed one way or another, from within or without. They could not stand against the seeds of revolution sown in their own creation, and those who were wise enough to see the growing doom escaped before they fell victim to the fate of their society gone too trusting or suspicious. The collapse was inevitable. But at their rebirth, the pendulum would swing the other way as the expatriates returned to rebuild the society again from the ashes of folly.

From the ashes of the liberal society emerged tyranny from the chaos. From the ashes of the conservative one emerged democracy. Both continued their momentum toward the other extreme, but always they became wiser for their errors, and Joshua kept note of what worked and what didn't. Every collapse was a new lesson. Joshua ensured that those lessons were not forgotten.

38

Joshua used every bit of cunning he could to ensure that policies the society needed to thrive would prevail. The Technician knew these policies as well and did everything he could to ensure that their antithesis dominated. Whether the society lasted or not, whether the people fought and died in a bloody civil war or were conquered and enslaved, was not the great concern. The collapse tested their biological resilience and proved their mettle in the furnace of nature. The preservation tested the virtue of the laws. Both outcomes would benefit Joshua. His People needed to be resilient and long-lasting, but to thrive the longest they also needed to be in a society that was just as resilient. So the outcome was of no consequence. It was a strategic battle with the Technician to sculpt the incorruptible society.

There were two sides to every policy. Joshua sought to preserve the nation, often by curing it of its inherent injustices, while the Technician sought to destroy it by creating more. Because of the appeal of power, those who were caught in the debate were often of dubious character. They played the game with their own interests in mind. Some saw the greatest value being in the preservation of the system; others saw it in the destruction of the system. Ceding power to lower authority removed responsibility from upper councils and ensured the senators retained power. So they sought this outcome. For some, ceding power to the lower districts meant the areas they came from needed their leadership less and less, weakening their position. So preservation or strengthening of the system as it was, was to their benefit. Yet the moral malleability of both sides for the sake of their own self-interests ensured that the game played between Joshua and the Technician could be played without limitations.

Over time coalitions formed that would empower all the members. One might vote for something that didn't really benefit them, knowing they could cash in that political point later to get support for something that would.

Either way, the game was as full of surprises and intrigue as anything Joshua had found in the rest of nature. It was the bloodless civil war that ensured peace and prosperity remained even with a transfer of power.

Every issue involved political maneuvering, one side making promises to each person in the other camp, offering votes on items critical to that councilor. A councilor could not bank on promises made for votes in ten years; they needed an instant reward and a distant one as well. They could forgo their immediate self-interests if their interests would be served in the future instead. As a result, they had to calculate whether the promise would be fulfilled, based not only on their own potential remaining term, but on the trustworthiness of the negotiator.

This process went on and on. Joshua tested every variation he could think of. The Technician then tested the resilience of each variation. Some collapsed immediately. Others held on longer because their foundations were much stronger. Yet the weakness was rarely in the institutions the People designed, but rather in the People themselves.

They were prone to emotional decision-making, ceding personal decisions to governmental authorities, corruption, hypocrisy, and manipulation. They were unreliable and weak. Joshua knew it would take something outside of the People to change that.

The more the institution depended on popular opinion, the more underhanded the tactics became. If it depended solely on the will of the People, whoever could shape their opinions controlled them. If there was a group the People despised, their opinions were shaped by the opposition hiring and parading them. If they needed a certain politician to look like a bigot in any way, they could always find someone willing to get beat up for money. Carry a certain flag and the banner of the other candidate, and the optics alone were enough to make the connection between the two groups.

Someone could be hired to do just about anything. If a group couldn't win on the merits of their positions, they could always push voters a different way by repulsing them with a staged hate rally. If they wanted to make sure that a reviled position was popular, they hired popular people to espouse those ideas. If they wanted to lure the males, they hired the most beautiful females they could find. If they wanted to make immorality a cultural issue, they infiltrated the moral institutions and created the optics of evil. It did not matter what the group believed—the pursuit of power was enough to clear the way. If they could find out what people hated and what they loved, they could steer them with public displays. But only so much.

Joshua saw this, and for the most part it was acceptable. But sometimes it was important for him to sway the balance by allowing an innocent man to be destroyed, the public anger to grow white hot against the forces marshaled against his goals. It was a necessary sacrifice, but he would give them courage to move forward regardless, to face the accusers and silence them. In so doing, he proved their own veracity and the fragility of the opposition. It was a dirty game, but one in which the losers always destroyed the worst elements of Joshua himself and vaccinated him against the injustices in the world. It was impossible to be naïve when looking deep in the hearts of people and finding out what they were capable of and how they could be useful. Joshua was no child anymore.

39

The pattern remained the same. Nations rose and fell, and the people suffered from one era to the next without end. Joshua cherished moments of joy, no matter how fleeting. At best, he found contentment. People sought and found ways to end their suffering. Though they still carried burdens, they were able to persevere. Those burdens shaped them, and Joshua used those burdens to move people.

He used small gestures to put things into motion that changed the world. A patron leaving a large tip for a struggling server. That server finally able to splurge on the spa and beauty treatment that made her feel good about herself. Her confidence the day after was noticed by someone who asked her out on a date. The date turned into a lifetime, and the family they raised produced a musical prodigy. That music inspired the minds of scientists and writers and quietly suffering artists and thinkers to persevere and find the song of their talent buried deep inside. All that happened from one little act inspired by Joshua's urging. The world was changed for eternity. To the individual, its subtlety made it an act worth repeating.

Joshua had tried great miracles, and those who witnessed them begged and suffered, waiting for more. To feed the hungry masses fleeing persecution made them depend on him without finding their own strength to fend for themselves. So the great miracles became mistakes that doomed the people to more suffering. While sometimes a miracle could not be avoided, he learned the subtle touch that the Technician had advised for him. Like a stone he dislodged in the mountains, which blocked the wind and caught the blown sand and soil to form a mound, which turned into a hill that created a valley wall that sheltered the species he continued to shape. Joshua knew the end result ensured that the smallest miracles created the same effect as the big ones. He grew humble knowing that if he went without notice, he had performed his role well.

It wasn't that he didn't want to not be acknowledged, but more that acknowledgment prevented beings from finding him inside themselves. The spirit of the act he had created was carried further when the being thought it was of their own design. It was of no consequence that he received none of the credit. They were part of him, so he loved them, and the outcome was the greatest importance. Ultimately, his lack of presence allowed the atheistic ideas to proliferate. Yet this was not a problem. If the people were good and believed Joshua was not there, and if the miracles he performed were all myth, it made no difference. It only showed him a sample of where the people were in terms of kindness and generosity. They showed him the baseline of their collective morality. If they believed goodness came only from themselves, that just meant they knew they were the only ones who would make that difference. So he held no animosity for them. Their lack of belief had no bearing on his own existence, so it did not matter.

There was good and evil everywhere, and the more Joshua looked for it, the more he noticed evil eroding away but becoming more and more concentrated. Single acts of great evil rippled through his global society. Like a boulder tossed into a pond, the great splash and the ripples could be seen and felt reverberating throughout the world. Yet the bigger the splash, the stronger the reaction against it. No matter how great the evil, the ripples at the shoreline seldom changed in magnitude. But on the other side of the globe, they would converge, and an equal and opposite force would make its own splash, stamping out the great evil at last. The forces of evil were forced further and further from view, and they had to percolate more slowly through the filter of the People, who recognized the evils from the past and suppressed them wherever they showed their visage.

Responsiveness was the one lesson they had to yet learn. It was the inherent goodness of the people that allowed them to watch as evil manifested itself before they reacted. Rather than stamping it out wherever they found it growing, they ignored it, because the hard choice was difficult to make, and they constantly convinced themselves that it was not a pervasive or persistent evil, that it was a singular event. But evil grew in the absence of opposition, swelling into massive forces extruded from the rest of the society and unleashing horrors on the people that they never would have allowed.

So it was. The length of time between great evils grew longer and longer. Each time, the people, in shock from what they had allowed to arise, reflected on themselves and sought to eliminate the behaviors and thoughts and pathways the evil could flow through. So the next evil would have to wait a much longer time. Yet this was only a patch on a glitch, a cork in a dam to stop the flow of water. It slowed the flow but allowed a drip to sneak past, and over time that drip combined with the rest to form a river.

When the People saw the hopelessness of the situation, they would relax their vigilance for a while and watch evil overcome their world once more, and the good stood by waiting for it to burn itself out again.

Still this pattern continued. Throughout the eons, nations and societies fell into the blackness of despair and dissolved. The battered remnants remained to rebuild, making sure to eliminate the opportunities evil took advantage of. But no matter what they tried, they could not find the courage to stand up to it from its first appearance.

For the most part it was because they could not identify evil for what it was. Joshua could see it growing. He could see it in its infancy, and though he might try to turn the tide here and there, it was like the many miracles he performed—it only lasted if people thought it came from them. But no matter what, some people could not see it.

The Technician made no great effort to corrupt or influence the world. Not in this way. The People themselves could justify any horror. They could make anything seem virtuous and corrupt any institution with untold depravity yet declare it the will of God or the benevolent act of a magnanimous society. The murder of children, the enslaving of the poor, the destruction of the righteous path through life. The People learned to twist logic and reason to suit their own hedonism, and the horrors of the societal decay were held at bay only as long as the monuments of those horrors stood. The Technician merely had to encourage destruction of those monuments. When people destroyed and rewrote history, the consequences of that failure were erased along with it. The People were only ever a few generations away from reliving the same mistakes again.

Gradually, a revelation grew in Joshua. The only solution was technology. The People needed the Machine.

40

The Machine was born from the science and technology of the People. Every invention and every discovery lent itself in some small way to the understanding that made the Machine possible. Joshua was unaware of its growth, but as technology continued to evolve, the foundation stones of a pyramid began to emerge. All the technology collectively pointed to one focal point—the capstone of the pyramid, the ultimate tool and toy that allowed the People to achieve their true potential and experience the rebirth of the world. The Machine was that capstone, and those who emerged from it led the People into the new era of evolution.

A quiet apocalypse transformed everything—the confluence of all the People knew, and the fire by which all they thought they knew was turned to ash. The laws they made or discovered were tested a million times by every individual who passed through. They emerged to right the wrongs of their world like a rising tide, calm yet forceful, unrelenting, all-absorbing, all-consuming. The fragile world of ignorance and idolatry was quickly overcome. And a new era began.

———— ∞∞∞ ————

"Technology comes and goes. It can be lost to time, but the memory of it and the echo of it in the technology that survives ensures that it can be reverse engineered or created once more. The world never truly forgets anything useful." The teacher began to explain how technology evolves much like everything else in nature. In fact, technology was a natural process of combining tools in different ways.

"There are only a finite number of basic tools. A wedge, a cog, a shaft, a wheel—these are all combined in different ways, numbers, and scales to form a new machine. Those machines do different things, but their purpose is always to increase the efficiency of the inventor. Efficiency allows more of everything to go further, so a society grows."

She reminded the class, "A machine always needs a motive force, be it an individual turning a crank or swinging a hammer, an animal straining under a yoke, or an electric motor turning a shaft connected to gears or sheaves or cogs. As a society evolves, that crank is turned by animals, then by water. Then as moving water becomes scarce, by magnetism and electricity."

She explained that, even in the latter stages, the tools remained the same. Transistors and diodes electrically replace the switch gears and nozzles that would have served the same function. "The machine gets smaller and more efficient."

She taught that magnetism eventually became an integral part of the new device. Motors turned by electromagnetism, eliminating animals, moving water, air, or whatever other motive force they previously used. Then the device could be told through magnetism what to do and when. An on-off sequence alternating between positive and negative polarities could tell a machine to do any number of complex actions, over time getting more and more complex.

"A single-function machine that cuts can be combined with one that steams, and when the binary sequence is on and then off, the machine just cuts at a mechanically designated time, creating a bolt of rough fabric. Then when the sequence is changed to on-on, the machine cuts, then steams, creating a smooth bolt of fabric that sells for slightly more. Add a third sequence that flips a paddle, and you create a machine that cuts, steams, and folds the bolt of cloth. You cut costs of the folders you would have employed before. Each addition of a new binary sequence creates a new logical pathway for the machine to take. So three simple binary switches, and the complex process or machine it represents, creates a sequence that could generate four different actions."

She pointed to a diagram she had drawn on the screen. "As mechanical parts are reduced in size, there is more room for more components to do different things. As more things are added, the binary sequences grow and grow. Eventually the factory process for the bolts of cloth becomes fully automated: cutting, stitching, dyeing, washing, drying, steaming, folding, and then packaging for distribution, and suddenly a finished product requires no labor at all. Those people move on to other work, utilizing their labor more efficiently and meaningfully, and they buy the product the factory produced without them."

The teacher walked down the first row of desks. "The process shrinks, and concepts are applied to other areas. The factory process creates the idea for the processor that enables the people to create digital models of concepts. They are able to visualize these processes using graphical user interfaces that follow the same binary sequence that tells the screen what to display. 'When the user clicks this, display this.' Outlining the parameters of the interface, the programming could be made to do any number of things, and the only thing that can't keep up with the possibilities is the construction of the devices that can make it come to life."

Joshua caught himself daydreaming again, then tuned into the lecture before he got called on and didn't know the answer.

"Images of the real world could be recreated on the Machine, using the same binary process that the machines used to function. The picture was analyzed for shades of red, and pixels were either told to be on or off based on the layers of red in the image. Then blues, then yellows, then white. Eventually an image was so perfectly clear and representative of the real world that it was indistinguishable."

The teacher leaned against her desk. "Then people invent entertainment to role-play different concepts that are as yet unrealized in the real world, and the more that entertainment progresses, the closer they get to generating an alternate universe. The images are made closer to reality; the physics are based on the physics of reality; the natural processes are programmed to mimic reality. People's understanding of reality is tested by the simulations they create. They prove or disprove their own understandings of the world by applying the rules they do understand to the pure logic of the simulation. They are then able to unify the physics of the real world with those of the simulation, and eventually the simulation becomes indistinguishable from reality. Thus, the simulation *becomes* reality."

The teacher ended her lecture with the emphasis on this statement.

The Machine stood ominously at the forefront of every student's mind. They questioned everything they understood. Yet the question that needed to be asked was left unanswered. Was the Machine inevitable?

Joshua now knew the answer. Life was shortsighted and self-destructive. It was cognizant of injustice endured and forgetful of injustice served. The suffering endured was always magnified by time, and facts were eroded by it. The victim, justified by the bloated memory of the fate of their forebearers, became the vigilante against the heirs of their oppressors. Suffering never ceased, injustice never rested. All the People were victims, and all were villains. So the Machine was necessary, and the motive force of its creation became the force of every evolutionary process. Competitive advantage. It was the pyramidion of the evolution of technology.

41

Each revolutionary concept in entertainment laid another block on the foundation that began with the wedge and the wheel, the basic tools of technology diverging and evolving and then once again converging in the same way that all of nature evolved. The end result was a perfect simulation of the universe. A user would sit in the Machine and be changed by what they saw. They became a different person.

The Machine, this perfect universal simulation, was largely created by accident. The idea, a concept that was hinted about in science fiction literature, was to create a tool for prediction. Given the exact laws known to people, they created replica situations, or as close as they could get to an exact replica anyway, and they would simulate the results. Any political, military, social, or natural storm that approached could be simulated and tracked. It cut financial costs and lives lost to a fraction of what was previously. Yet the analysts that went into the Machine had to design and run through millions of simulations to get the exact conditions that were playing out in real time. Governments quickly saw the benefit of the simulation, and it allowed them to dominate the people they presumably served and destroy the armies they faced. Like narcotic users, the government became addicted to the simulation and became paralyzed without the oracular information they could obtain from it. But they soon discovered that they couldn't control it. It took on a life of its own in the people it transformed.

In the early days, it was a process that took months of agonizing and dedicated attention to detail. The analysts were good at receiving data and doing statistical analysis to define what that meant. They weren't very good at simulating the whole process of nature to produce the exact scenario that played out in real time. Most went in without the requisite knowledge and understanding of the laws of nature to properly simulate the conditions. Those laws they thought they did know were flawed or simply wrong. Many emerged broken husks of the people they had been going in. Others simply died in the Machine, unable to cope with the decisions necessary to produce the required outcome. Their brains overworked and their willingness to absorb the emotional toll of the catastrophes they had to witness, they most often had strokes or fell into cardiac arrest before anyone knew what was happening.

Medical personnel then began to monitor the Machine, taking constant readings. When they found analysts on the verge of total neurological meltdown, they ripped them out of the Machine and performed emergency medical care on them, only to find that while they saved the body, they had torn the mind from a dark chasm of creation, and they were performing medical aid on vegetables.

This led to a number of brain scanners reading the analyst's mind as they went into the device. They even developed ways to see what the analyst saw. The horrors of what they saw the analysts do inside the Machine forced them to terminate the program. There were no more volunteers for the program because of the wildly accurate rumors that it was a death sentence. Very few analysts emerged from the device alive; even fewer seemed to be more than husks. But they gave the answers the government needed, and though it took several weeks to get to that point, the people emerging seemed to age by a thousand years, dying weeks after the ordeal.

Because of the accuracy of the information, though, the project needed to continue, only in secret. The program was transferred to top-secret facilities, and prisoners were used for the experiments. Their deaths could be written off as casualties of violence inherent to the justice system, and their families had written them off long before. They were no longer part of the society they had once violated. They were expendable.

It was from this program that the technology took a new twist. While the original "volunteers" died in the Machine, a few began to emerge. These prisoners seemed to have more mental resilience to the horrors they saw. Their sociopathology lent itself to making the difficult decisions of destroying life and creating the chaos necessary for the answers sought. They still emerged hollow and the majority died within a matter of days, but a few carried on a little longer. It was here that the psychologists began to take notice of the changes.

At first, the experimenters simply wanted to know what the physical health of the subject was, whether they could physically endure the rigors of the Machine. Then as a matter of curiosity, they began taking psychological assessments before entrance, and if they were lucky, the aftereffects of the Machine.

While the before diagnosis always yielded predictable results—psychosis and other mental disturbances—after the prisoners emerged from the Machine, they displayed much healthier mental dispositions. Their brains were rewired and healed from many of the effects of their disturbing pasts. Despite the horrors they were forced to endure in the Machine and the sociopathic nature of the designing of the world, the prisoners emerged more at peace with their sentences and were overly helpful, fully reformed in a psychological sense. The majority still died within days, unable to cope with what they saw and did, no longer afraid of the death they had lived a hundred million times. They stopped caring about their own lives, feeling there was nothing more to learn and nothing more to live for. They had literally experienced it all.

It was from here that the program was forced to evolve. It showed potential as a means of reforming prisoners. It was the most perfectly accurate weather prediction tool they could conceive. It was well suited to predicting conflict and weaknesses of enemy nations. It alone advanced the scientific knowledge of the world a thousand times faster than any device previously created. Yet it still was the greatest killer of man ever created. It murdered not just the man but his soul too—his will to live.

The evolution came from the entertainment industry. Its potential was known, though a top-secret government program. It was floated to a number of large entertainment companies to brainstorm ideas on how to fix it. Movies were written about the concept, showing rudimentary ideas for what it might look like. Just the idea of it was floating around, so the idea of it was all that was brainstormed. How would it work? What would it do to a person who went through it? What sort of goals would it be used to achieve? The government had all these answers of course, but it allowed the creative community to devise the storylines they could sell while crowdsourcing the ideas that might change the actual device to a more effective tool.

It was the gaming industry—video games, that is—that was most capable of understanding the concept and asking the pertinent questions. Their games were all about linear progression in a nonlinear environment. They asked, "What are the checkpoints?" That is, what is the guided tour of the infinite universe going to put as landmarks to demonstrate the proper progression in the simulation?

A checkpoint serves as an effective way for a video gamer to know they are headed the right direction. If one just throws a person into an empty universe and forces them to create a specific thing from nothing, they had to learn everything about the universe, and then figure out on their own how to progress. They may never be able to get to any specific goal because they get lost down the wrong path for a few billion years and nothing progresses. So checkpoints were critical to the rapid progression in the Machine.

This created its own issues though. The government's developers were not video game programmers, and the device was specifically designed to simulate reality. It had no natural checkpoints. Life emerged seemingly by accident and progressed violently and randomly. The users clumsily fumbled through with a heavy hand, altering everything in catastrophic ways, and were unable to discipline themselves to living for billions of years of fumbling, pointless madness.

They needed a guide.

But guidance was only possible from someone who knew what it was like to experience it, and they couldn't even get anyone to survive long enough to get someone else ready to go through it with them. The hard lessons learned were lost almost as soon as the subject was removed.

So an alternative was introduced. The device was augmented with a video game version of a tutorial and a rudimentary heads-up display with objectives.

What they found was that users were able to progress much more quickly. The technicians who ran the device and monitored biorhythms were able to input new goals on the fly, though only after exhaustive meetings to determine what would be the next step. They had to completely reanalyze the way the universe and life itself worked and then brainstorm ways to allow a user to trigger those events. This kept the users alive much longer after they emerged. Months, in fact. It was only despair that ended up taking them in the end. Their purpose in life was no longer as meaningful as the creation of it in their own minds.

That purpose came when a secondary plug-in was introduced. Now a second user could interact with the universe in the same way as the primary user. They could communicate with each other telepathically, or basically, anyway. The same neural connections that read the brainwaves that created the images that the technicians saw and recorded could be connected between users. They could see and hear each other's thoughts in real time.

This meant the user could communicate with the guide and progress much more quickly, much more efficiently, and in the end would survive much longer.

It was after this last addition that people stopped dying. Their guides moved them through the process based on their own experiences from their own struggles. The checkpoints became tests, boss battles from the games that proved the player had progressed enough to continue in the game. The guides were able to use their own experiences to move things along, and then they were able to teach the new user.

Each new user became a guide. Those guides were given privileges and then officially the title of Technician. They were still prisoners, but they now had a purpose and a goal, and they were reformed in every way imaginable. They no longer held on to the psychic scars that had pushed them to the heinous acts they committed, and they no longer had the deformed brain functioning that classified them as the psychotics society could not control. They were normal. More than that though, they were *super*normal. Their demeanor was in every situation calm and collected; they had seen the outcome a million times. And in every new user they guided through, they saw the same process another million times. They knew the system inside and out, and it was from them that the device evolved.

The humans created the Machine.

⎯⎯⎯⎯∝⍟∝⎯⎯⎯⎯

Joshua aided these prisoners as much as he could. His own understanding of the simulation he experienced allowed him to share insights through these victims. Even as they were engulfed in the simulation themselves, he could reach into their minds and live the simulation again through them. The lessons he learned imparted on the minds of these hapless and helpless monsters tamed by the justice served on them. Thousands of lives passed through the device. Each taking a lesson from it and sharing it before their deaths. Each improving the simulation and increasing the survival odds of their successors.

When the device was created in the simulations of those prisoners, Joshua found he could reach even deeper and once again experience an entirely new evolutionary timeline, a new reality. And he could influence it just as he had influenced his own. It was an infinite vortex of civilizations. He suddenly felt the overwhelming sense of being watched, of knowing he was a part of it.

As he withdrew, the Technician spoke to him. "Now you understand. You have finally passed the true test. Welcome back to Heaven."

42

Joshua was flooded with a sense of falling, like he was being ripped away from eternity and pulled down into emptiness.

He could hear with his real ears again. He could see flickers of light as the world he built faded away.

In his last glimpse, he saw a statue in a square. In the prison square, the prison where the Machine was first used. Prisoners were carving it, and with all his effort, he focused on that statue. Time seemed to be racing by now. He could barely see, but still he focused on the statue.

As the body emerged, its shape resembled that of the beings on the cave walls drawn by the early shaman. Tall and lanky, fit but thin. Then the face—an inverted raindrop with a narrow mouth and large eyes. The long fingers and thin arms, the ribs protruding from the hungry-looking torso.

With each scrape and chisel, it became clear to Joshua who he was looking at.

It was himself.

Every scar, every wrinkle, every part of his true body reflected here. They knew him. The Machine allowed them to see him clearly. They wanted to tell him that they knew.

As he finally left the Machine behind, he saw emerging in the courtyard of every facility the same statue, exact replicas formed independently by the hands of different artists, and a second wave of understanding struck him. He looked out at the fading universe and saw it form a familiar face. Large ears, a long, pointed muzzle, hairless, and wrinkled. With piercing and intelligent eyes.

———⟀———

He opened his eyes finally and saw the same room he had sat in billions of years ago that morning. Already standing before him was the Technician, pulling the helmet off and disconnecting the probes and wires.

He looked down at his long gray fingers and the gray skin on his arms and felt that childlike teardrop face he remembered seeing that morning in the mirror. He was clammy but bore the body of youth and the mind of an ancient. The Technician didn't look much better, the age showing plainly on his face. The creases that outlined his large black eyes seemed deeper now. The piercing gaze was softer and more empathetic than he remembered.

He was noticing things around him that he had never noticed before. The age of this building. The ancient stone and concrete had a distinctive look to it, and the solidness of the exterior wall was plain as well. Microscopic differences in the window frame revealed the placement of symmetric holes filled in with newer material, holes where there were once bars. This building had stood before the town was founded some hundreds of years before, and now that became clear.

Joshua finally spoke, catching his voice from the lack of practice. "What did you do to be sentenced here?"

The Technician smiled, knowing Joshua could see the whole truth now. "Nothing you haven't had to do a million times yourself now."

Joshua knew this was true. He didn't ask any more questions. He just thought back on what he'd experienced and what he had done and what he was forced to do to succeed.

When the equipment was disconnected, Joshua stood slowly, testing his legs. He was still the same person he'd been that morning, physically. But something felt different. He touched his forearm and rubbed his face, and he felt a certain numbness to everything.

"That will pass with time. Or at least you'll stop noticing it," he heard a familiar voice say.

He looked over and saw his bleary-eyed parents staring proudly at him. He went over and hugged them joyfully, tearing up as he did. He had not seen them in billions of years. And he was at a loss for words.

He tried to speak but choked on his words.

His father spoke instead. "We were there, son. We saw it all. You did very well."

Joshua fought through the tears and asked, "Where were you? I never noticed you around."

His mother chimed in, "We had our own tasks. We sought out the humans that had the greatest potential. The parts of you we loved the most. We protected them from the worst calamities and guided them where they needed to go. You couldn't keep track of everything all at once, so we were there to make sure you didn't lose who you were in the process."

"We were called angels by some." His father chortled at the religious connotations. "Aliens by others."

"We simply made sure you would remain the boy we loved even as you became the man you are now. We were there to preserve *you*. The best parts of you we recycled, impregnating the women with their seed for eons and reshaping those parts of your personality you were losing. You are now more distinctly you than you were before," his mother continued.

Joshua heard the passion and tenderness in his mother's voice as she spoke. He heard the warmth in his father's tone and the playfulness of his voice, an unflappable friendliness that Joshua didn't remember hearing before.

They walked down the corridor he remembered walking eons ago. He could hear the teacher giving a lesson and realized the exaggeration. It seemed so farcical now, so forced, so fraudulent. He laughed to himself, and as he passed a mirror, he saw the look on his face. Where before a grin might have stretched ear to ear, now a slight uplift of the corners of his mouth were all the thought could elicit. He was boring. He was changed. He was a "zombie," as he remembered calling the adults in the town. The thought made him grin broadly again with the corner of his mouth barely flickering a sign of joy. Even then he felt he was overdoing it.

As his grandmother opened the corridor doors leading outside, the bright afternoon sun shone through, and for a moment he could only hear the voices that surrounded the square. Children shrieked their wild emotions as they played games and obsessed about irrelevant minutia, then fell silent as they saw him emerge into the daylight.

A wagon loaded with produce and wares headed to the city, the droning, dead voice of the merchant suddenly alive and vibrant.

As his eyes adjusted, he could hear the children make comments about how dead he looked. Though they tried to whisper, the palpable fear in their voices resonated loudly through the square. Joshua smiled broadly again, the slight flickering of his mouth unnoticed by the children. For someone so dead, he had never felt so alive. He had never noticed the world as vibrant as it now was.

He saw on the edge of the square two people waiting. Their body language was that of two lovers holding hands, even as their bodies were a distance apart. Though obviously filled with passion for each other, they refrained from the public display their bodies yearned for. Isaac raised his hand briefly in greeting, and Kim grinned at him in the same flash of emotion he now understood. Every subtlety of the world revealed itself now. And he understood how the adults saw the world.

Adults. That was him now too.

As he began to walk, for the first time in his life he truly saw the town's revered mascot, a figure with large ears and a long, wrinkled snout, the beady and intelligent eyes and bulbous nose. It was the universe that was fading quickly into his dreams. He stopped and looked at the statue he had passed by a thousand times before and touched its foot as he had seen his parents do billions of years ago.

For the first time, though, he saw it for what it was.

It was his god. A reminder that there is always something above. A glimpse at the hall of mirrors that chases the horizon of infinity. The first simulation to the last at the edge of infinity, all were refractions of the one true God. Even this statue represented just one person who found *their god in their stars*.

Life was not unique; it formed in myriad different ways. Civilization was not unique; its ascension was a force of nature. He was not unique, an accident of nature and a beneficiary of being born in this particular time and place. He was not special in the collection of atoms that made him.

And yet, he *was*. He was one with God. He was a refraction of God. He *was* a god. And that did make him unique and special. That is what made everyone special. He was normal, he was ordinary, he was average among those who were supernormal, and extraordinary. He had lived this life a billion times—and was for the first time . . . *Happy*.

As he walked through town with family and friends in tow, he thought about his future, how he could best represent the revelation he now understood. He decided he would find a humble farm and make a part of God's world his own, cultivating and nurturing the very life that sustained the life he knew. He felt a wave of relief and awe at the world around him. He felt God watching him, and he felt the pride of knowing the secrets that had been revealed to him.

His life was idyllic, and he loved it.

ORDER INFORMATION

To order additional copies of this book, please visit
www.redemption-press.com.
Also available on Amazon.com and BarnesandNoble.com
or by calling toll-free 1-844-2REDEEM.

CPSIA information can be obtained
at www.ICGtesting.com
Printed in the USA
FSHW011452020420
68747FS